THE LONG DROP

THE LONG DROP

BRIAN D. KHARPRAN DALY

PARTRIDGE
A Penguin Random House Company

ISBN:	Hardcover	978-1-4828-3431-4
	Softcover	978-1-4828-3430-7
	eBook	978-1-4828-3429-1

This is a work of fiction though some of the events in the book are based on true facts. The characters however are all fictitious, and any resemblance to actual persons, living or dead, is purely coincidental.

To order additional copies of this book, contact
Partridge India
000 800 10062 62
orders.india@partridgepublishing.com

www.partridgepublishing.com/india

CONTENTS

To J'ratt
(Late Anthony R. Jarratt)
A Master and dedicated 'digger'
who dreamed of a vast subteranean world
beneath the Shnongrim Ridge

ACKNOWLEDGEMENT

I would like to express my gratitude to Jennifer Brooks for her valuable suggestions and to Bryan Khongwar for the cover design of the book.

GLOSSARY

Bah	: An elder brother; a term of respect; sir (in Khasi)
Chapatti	: A flat cake of wholemeal bread
Dal	: Pigeon-pea (pulses) made into a gravy or sauce with water, turmeric, salt, onions, etc.
Daloi	: Chief of the elaka or group of villages
Dkhar	: Anyone from the plains; not a local tribal
Dohkhlieh	: Pig's head, boiled and cut into very small pieces and mixed with the pig's brain, salt, onions, ginger, chillies etc. It is a delicacy of the Khasis
Jainsem	: An outer garment of Khasi women worn across the shoulders
Karst	: A landscape created on soluble rock with efficient underground drainage. The term derives from the German form of kras, the classical karst straddling the border between Slovenia (Krst) and Italy (Carso)
Kong	: an elder sister; a term of respect; madam
Krem	: Cave
Kwai	: Areca nut eaten with betel leaf and some lime (slaked)
Ma	: A term of respect, sir (in Jaintia)
Mei	: Khasi word for mother/mummy/mum
Momos	: Steamed dumplings made with flour and suffed with meat
Paneer	: Indian cottage cheese
Sambar	: Dal as cooked in South India. Pigeon-pea made into a gravy with vegetables and flavoured with tamarind juice.
Shaktiman	: Trucks manufactured only for the Indian Military
Stalagmite	: A formation that grows upward from the cave floor

Thlen	:	A devil in the shape of a serpent supposed to be kept by certain clans in the Khasi Hills. He is propitiated with human blood and is believed to bring wealth and prosperity to the owner
Tungrymbai	:	A chutney of mashed and fermented soya-bean usually cooked with black sesame seed

PART ONE

Man has been endowed with reason, with the power to create, so that he can add to what he's been given. But up to now he hasn't been a creator, only a destroyer. Forests keep disappearing, rivers dry up, wild life's become extinct, the climate's ruined and the land grows poorer and uglier every day.

Anton Chekhov

PROLOGUE

The story of limestone is the story of romance – a romance with nature; a romance that has seen the test of time. Limestone is a sedimentary rock most admired for its usefulness; it is a rock most loved by Nature for it forms the perfect canvas for Nature's work of intricate and infinite art. It allows nature to carve underground rivers through the hills – short cuts in the dark, circumventing the long and circuitous surface route. It allows nature to nurture life forms that are constantly evolving in its deep fragile and unique eco-systems. It forms a treasure trove of the past, hiding secret chambers untouched by man. It connects man to the times when he himself had not even evolved. It tells the history of our evolving planet. And the karst surface features of weather-beaten outcrops or giant exposed pinnacles are indeed a very pleasing landscape, adding a greater and richer dimension to the varied contours of the earth. And it's been a long romance which started as long ago as the Precambrian Period more than 550 million years ago, during periods when areas now land were under the sea. Limestone like many sedimentary rocks was formed in the sea, by the precipitation of calcium carbonate from lime-bearing waters or by organic processes involving lime-secreting animals.

When the lime-laden water from rivers reach the sea, calcium carbonate can be precipitated due to the heating and evaporation of the sea water; this deposit can accumulate on the sea floor as a limey mud. Further, in these primeval warm, shallow seas, life like plankton, algae, shellfish, corals and snails thrived. Those creatures used the calcium carbonate from the water to build their shells, and when they died, these shells or skeletal remains were deposited on the sea bed. The shells decayed and combined with the limey mud and other sediments to form a thick deposit rich in calcium carbonate. During many periods of earth history, such as during the Devonian and Carboniferous Periods, certain marine life forms predominated which favoured the formation of reef or platform limestones, while at other times these organisms became extinct and limestones less likely to accumulate. Some limestones also formed by the direct precipitation of calcium carbonate around tiny nuclei such as grains of sand. These grains, being agitated by the waves and currents, become coated by thin layers of calcium carbonate to form tiny round pellets called ooliths. Millions of these ooliths then get cemented together in the limey mud to form oolitic limestone.

These sediments build up in layers, and as they pile up, the lower layers get compressed by the massive weight of the younger sediments, and they therefore become dense and hard. Other sediments like mud, sand and gravel are commonly brought down by the rivers to the seas, and they can also be deposited along with the limestones. In this way, the deposits keep accumulating and a sequence can build up consisting of different bedded layers, representing several episodes of sedimentation.

Over millions of years these sedimentary rocks can be gradually raised above the original sea floor by lowering of the sea-level or by earth movements. Initially, when laid down, the bedded sedimentary rocks typically were horizontal. However, in many places the global tectonics of the earth have pushed, uplifted, and contorted these rocks to form high mountain ranges like the Himalayas and the Alps. In these zones the original horizontal bedded layers become intensely folded and faulted.

The mega-continent Gondwanaland broke up around the end of Jurassic times, 145 million years ago, with the Indian sub-continent separating from Antarctica, Australia, Madagascar and other land masses, to drift away for an epic scale continental collision with the Asian continental masses in the late Eocene. Prior to the Gondwanaland break-up, Meghalaya likely abutted onto Western Australia and Antarctica and it comprised a relatively stable high structural block, cored by Precambrian aged igneous and metamorphic rocks, including granites, gneisses and quarzites. This high block formed a promontory of land which, after continental separation became surrounded by oceans, teaming with shelly marine life. The birth of Meghalaya was not a smooth and easy process, but rather a succession of dramatic events, where parts of the land were uplifted only to sink, before rising above the sea again. For example during the Paleocene and Eocene Periods limestone was deposited on whatever part was under water, while rivers from the island brought sand to the coast, building up sandstones and burying mangrove forests doomed to become coal.

Some sections of Meghalaya experienced uplifting and subsidence several times, over time accumulating up to five cycles of shelly nummulitic limestones, which alternate with sandstones or laterally pass into each other. More recently most parts of Meghalaya were uplifted to considerable height, forming the Shillong Plateau. Here, and until today, survive the sedimentary rocks either as remnant erosional outliers, such as those found at Lum Iawpaw Plateau or as an extensive flanking rim which forms a two hundred km long belt along the southern border of Meghalaya.

The west-east trending Meghalaya limestone belt turns north at Khaddum and spans the area between the Lukha valley in the south-west and the Kopili Valley in the north-east. Above the west (left) bank of the Litein River, the Shnongrim ridge rises some 150 to 200 vertical metres above the valley floor. The ridge is partly covered by a katatectic layer (capping rock) of shales above a more than 120 m thick succession of clean limestones. The romance, far from being over, picked up in intensity after the Eocene Period, when the wondrous power of water found its way through the dark depths of the ridge, which is today captured beneath the surface. With the skill of a master craftsman and the patience of infinite time, Nature carved a delightful world of subterranean passages and chambers resplendent with all the glories that only Nature can bestow. The location and form of the caves have been strongly influenced by faulting and other geological controls.

The caves on the Shnongrim ridge exhibit the typical Meghalayan characteristics of large river passages, but a significant proportion show a noteworthy degree of vertical development. The entrances to these pothole caves are typically situated below the edge of the caprock – water flowing from the grass-covered shales drains into wide open pots and narrow vertical rifts. The streams sinking in the potholes resurge at the foot of the ridge. At these low elevations, the second type of caves occurs, which are represented by stream caves. These 'low level caves' have several entrances in between fallen boulders and are often segmented by collapse areas. The third type of caves in the Shnongrim ridge is found at relatively high elevations. They are represented by often meandering (sub-) horizontal stream cave passages which are occasionally pierced by shafts. This third type of cave seems to have developed as stream caves when the base level of erosion was at a considerable higher elevation and the Litein River was in a premature stage. Inside these 'old generation caves' relics of coarse, fist size fluvial deposits indicate a stage of infilling followed by a period of sediment removal. The penetrating shafts clearly represent a later stage of cave development when the old passages were partially rejuvenated.

The Shnongrim ridge with its thick and pure limestone is no wonder a caver's paradise, offering a new dimension to caving in Meghalaya; also being an area with the highest density of caves in the entire sub-continent. The ridge is literally riddled with subterranean passages which harbor rare forms of cave fauna not found elsewhere in the world. In the same breath it is also a dream-of-an-area for the miners and industrialists – the easily mined and excellent limestone for the cement plants and the coal seams fifty metres below the valley floor for the coal barons. The ridge born of an ancient and dramatic romance has disappointingly and inadvertently become a hotbed of warfare and deceit by the beginning of the twenty first century, when large chunks of land were grabbed, illegally staked, or 'bought' by threats and intimidation at give-away prices by unscrupulous elements. The local community could no longer live a safe and secure life; their ideal rustic life of agriculture and horticulture has been severed and broken. Their green and pristine lands have been scarred and polluted; the clean fresh air now smoggy with tiny dust particles of coal, dirt and limedust; the springs and rivulets choked to death while the toxic rivers harbor no more life; the lush green paddy fields now rendered acidic, barren and dusty; the women folk driven to breaking stones in the lime quarries; the rich fauna and flora disappearing as it had never been. As greed took over, the peaceful co-existence among the villages took a severe beating, as killings and murders occurred at the slightest whim; the social and moral character degenerated, exposing the dark and ugly nature of a society suddenly corrupted. The rich resources of the Shnongrim ridge, formed and deposited hundreds of millions of years ago have inadvertently triggered the dormant and hidden savagery of a simple and peaceful rural people into a cruel awakening of greed, lust and power. The pristine virgin green hills have begun to be traumatized by the brutal onslaught of unrelenting rape. The innocence of the ridge has been vandalized and nothing will ever be the same anymore.

Or is it resilient enough to survive the holocaust?

1

"Matted with a thick undergrowth
she lay
exposed and gaping
to the clear open sky
her dark and rugged entrance
weathered by the elements
invitingly beckoned
and thrilled with anticipation
long sought for
I entered."
--Krem Lymput (Imaginary-1993)

(From "Jagged Lines – Poems" by B. D. Kharpran Daly)

It was the time of day when the sun had spent its force and was slowly sinking down over the horizon beyond the distant dark hills. A man who had been sitting unobserved atop a slope overlooking the village of Shnongrim looked at his posh and brand new Citizen watch and realized he wouldn't have to wait much longer. Children playing in small groups across the village had stopped their playful activities of the day; he could hear mothers calling out to them to come home for a wash and supper. Somewhere he heard a child bawl out on being thrashed by his mother. Chickens having had their last meal of the day with a few handfuls of paddy scattered by the housewives were glad to retire after a long day foraging. Slowly lights appeared in the houses one by one; the village roads were dark as there was no street lights which was not helped either by the low voltage the village had been experiencing for many years. The village began to settle in as the noises and shouts died down. His eyes were trained on a particular house in the centre of the village. Soon it would be too dark for him to see anything.

He lit himself a cigarette to ward off the flies and to break the monotony of waiting. Hardly had he taken a couple of puffs when he saw the door open and a man emerged. He snuffed out his cigarette immediately and watched as the man switched on his torch and walk away. He took out his mobile and dialed a number.

"Abhi aao!" He said, in Hindi to the person at the other end of the line.

He knew where the man was heading for; he had found that out earlier that day. He waited for a while before he followed the man from a safe distance, walking in the dark. He had to be careful walking without a light for the many potholes and rocks lying scattered about. There was no one along the dark silent way. On one occasion he heard a truck and saw its headlights coming up from the Litein valley; he quickly got off the road and into the bushes where he hid himself. He wouldn't want to be recognized. When the truck had passed he got back on to the road again. The lights of the truck had blinded him; he stopped, closed his eyes and slowly opened them. When his eyes had adjusted to the darkness he saw that the man was far ahead of him. He was not unduly alarmed for he knew where the man was going to, as he continued following him into the village of Khaidong. There he stood in the shadows watching the man enter the village headman's house. He stood in silence waiting, longing for a smoke but decided against it; no point in attracting attention. Besides the village dogs were barking showing overly excitement; at what he knew not. He just hoped it was not his presence lurking in the shadows. Soon he heard a vehicle arrive and could see the lights through the trees. He could tell that it was a Sumo and that it was his.

The Sumo stopped in front of him and put out its lights. There were two men inside.

"Yaha se turn karo aur chup chap baitho. Lights bhi bund. Turn from here and sit quietly. Put off the lights also." He told the one driving the Sumo.

The Sumo managed a tight turn on the narrow dirt track road and stopped a little way ahead out of sight and in darkness, while he kept vigilance on the headman's house. He was a bit worried at the obnoxious barking of the dogs, for some curious villager might just come out to investigate. The mosquitoes were bothering him and he wanted to take refuge in the Sumo and take a puff; but he couldn't do that for fear that it will wreck his mission. Then the door opened and he tensed. The man and the headman came out and both started walking in the opposite direction. He was alarmed! Where were they going? Probably to the next village, Nongthymme, he thought. He would just have to wait. But for how long? Maybe at least forty five minutes – fifteen minutes to Nongthymme, if it was Nongthymme they were going to, and fifteen minutes back plus another fifteen minutes for their business. Better relax in the vehicle he thought and get my smoke.

Forty minutes later he was out and on the watch again. He was more alert now after having drunk some water and smoked a cigarette. He waited for another twenty five minutes before he saw torch lights coming up the road. It must be them he thought.

When the two separated at the headman's house, he left his post and got into the vehicle.

"Ai gaya," he told the two occupants.

The two occupants got out of the vehicle and walked down to meet the man. He did not even bother to watch even as he heard a muffled cry of pain and alarm. He sat waiting for the men to return for he knew they had done their job perfectly. A few minutes later the back door of the Sumo was jerked opened and they dumped the dead and limp body inside. The three of them squeezed in the front seat and drove off.

They drove with a single purpose of mind and that was to get rid off the body; and he knew of just the right place where to bury their crime – an ancient and silent tomb carved by the limitless bounties of nature. At the junction to Lelad he bade them to stop and ordered them to rub some dirt on the number plates; just in case anyone should recognize his vehicle. They drove without a hitch and were not stopped on the way for a lift; it would have been awkward and embarassing not stopping and giving the villagers a lift. It was almost eight thirty when they passed the silent and dimly lit village of Lelad. The road began to deteriorate with deep potholes and slush. Before reaching the village of Tangnub he indicated to the driver to stop and side the vehicle.

He got out of the vehicle and looked up and down the road; satisfied that all was quiet and no one would be coming along, he told the two men to hurry. They got out, opened the back door and pulled out the body. Between the two of them they half carried, half pulled the body up the hillside following him. It was exhausting work through the jungle; up the hillside then down the other side and up again before another small downhill rocky slope. The thorny bushes pricked at them but they were too intent on accomplishing their task. His face stung as the sweat got into the cuts he had acquired rummaging through the thick bush.

"Etna dur kyu humlok atta?" The stout muscular man asked, panting from the exertion.

"Yaha toh admi ne atta. Sab dorta he – bhoot ka gufa bolta he. Nobody comes to this place. Everyone is scared – believing it to be the cave of the devil." He answered. He had come to investigate this place a number to times and had therefore noted the way; otherwise it would have been impossible to find especially in the dark. The two were really struggling and mouthing expletives when they suddenly arrived at the entrance of the cave. They stared at the enormous deep black gaping hole in front of them and shivered at the eeriness of the surroundings; still panting from their horrendous ordeal.

"Joldi, joldi" he told them, wanting the thing over and done with.

They took hold of the body from both ends and after two gentle swings hurled the body into the dark emptiness. Seconds later they heard or so they thought, the unmistaken sound of dead meat smashing the bottom of the shaft. They stood awed and silent at what they had done; then one of them unfolded a bloodied and dirty piece of cloth, probably his handkerchief, took out the knife and threw it also into the depths. Pocketing the rag, he rubbed his two hands together as if to cleanse himself from his nefarious act.

"Aao wapas chalejayen. Ab lash ko koi nahi dhund payega. Come, let us go back. Now no one will ever find the body."

As they scrambled up through the bushes the skies opened up and it poured, making their progress difficult and slow. It was good though he thought, as all traces of blood would be washed off; even dogs would not be able to sniff the scent. They had done a good job and he was pleased; even nature had been on his side.

By the time they reached the vehicle they were totally drenched and drove off in the heavy downpour, carefully manouvering through the slippery patches and muddied hidden pot holes. After Lelad, somewhere along the road going downhill from the junction he made the vehicle stop at a limestone quarry. He took out his wallet and counted ten thousand rupees which he gave to the muscular man and another ten thousand rupees to the other man.

"Bahud shukriya," they said thanking him which he acknowledged with a nod.

"Abh jao khudka nehlake ajana aur Sumo ko bhi pani se saaf karlena. Main yahin utarjata hoon. Now go and wash yourselves and clean the Sumo too. I am going to get off here."

"Abh ham nadi ke taraf nikalte hai. We will go now to the river." The muscular man said.

He got down and watched them drive away. He shuddered to think that they were going to bathe in the river. He wouldn't; not even dip his feet in the water. For the river had turned highly acidic from the leaching of the coal being mined all along the base of the ridge. It was now a dead river. Worse its colour too had turned yellow. He pitied them not knowing that they could suffer skin rashes or skin ailments or worse. Soaked to the skin he slowly made his way to his little Maruti car, hidden from the road and drove off home.

The next morning at 9 AM he was knocking at the door of an otherwise splendid modern mansion in Khliehriat. The spectacular mansion, sporting a unique colour mix of pink, purple, parrot green and yellow looked garishingly out of place in the dusty little town, made more obsene by the obnoxious coal piles in front of the house. The door opened to reveal a maid servant.

"I ma i don?" He asked the girl.

"Ho'iod. Ale rung, shong hapoh; aap jynjang mo? Ngan leit khot ia i. Yes. Please come in and sit down. I will call him."

He relaxed on the big cushioned red armchair which was glaringly highlighted by the bright yellow colour of the room and the parrot green windows. The room was overly decorated with pictures and a large collection of little bric-a-brac bought as souvenirs from the metro cities the owner had visited. The big glass windows were shut – permanently he presumed so as to keep away the dust; dust which has been polluting and coating the foliage of whatever trees that still remained. All these coal barons are building huge expensive mansions in the middle of dusty and godforsaken rundown and corrupted countryside littered with huge dumps of coal; besides buying collosal properties in and around Shillong. He was told that the cost of property in Shillong has skyrocketed, making it almost impossible for the middle income group to be able to afford to buy even a small plot. He will milk these fat cows he decided – subtly and cleverly. He was admiring the huge photograph of the owner of the house hanging at one end of the room, when the person in question appeared.

"Kumno ma?" He said getting up from his seat and shaking the other's outstretched hand.

"Oh ma Wilis, take your seat. All is well with you?" The coal baron smiled, his teeth stained scarlet with the juices of kwai as he took the opposite chair.

"Everything is well with me, ma; including the job you had entrusted to me. It was accomplished last night."

"Are you sure the job has been properly dealt with?"

"Absolutely! As dead as that stuffed tiger over there."

"And what if they link the murder to you and then my name eventually surfaces in the process. I can't have that, you understand?

"Ma, you need not worry. There is no evidence at all. After snuffing him out we took the effort to go to that evil place in the dense jungle beyond the village of Tangnub where we dumped the dead body into the huge abyss. No one would ever go near the place much less be able to access the cave. The individual is now non-existent; he has vanished from the face of the earth and no one will ever discover the dead body. We couldn't have done a better job." He replied, pride shining on his face at his professionalism.

"Good. You have done a thorough job and I appreciate it. Now do you want your money in cash or by cheque."

"Ten lakh rupees in cash," he demanded, deciding to start milking him when he was on such an advantageous position.

"Ten lakhs? But we had decided on five?"

"Yes we did decide on five. But that was for exterminating him. Not for totally erasing him from the face of the earth. The man has now disappeared into thin air. No one will ever know that there was even a murder. It is absolutely foolproof and I could have asked you for more you know. No one could have done a better job you can be sure of that. And it is because of our friendship that I have not raised the price substantially. Moreover I had to use extra help also, the services of which I had to pay handsomely."

The coal baron sat, thinking; the man could have asked for much more and I would still have to pay. I think the price is reasonable enough. He himself could not have dreamt of such ingenuity.

"Very well, I will give you what you want. Just ensure that my name will never be dragged into this murky business." He said, leaving the room.

He returned a few minutes later with a heavy plastic bag which he handed to the man.

"Check it" he said.

The man poured the contents of the bag on the table. There were ten packets of one thousand rupees denomination. He leafed through each bundle just to make sure that they were genuine notes. Satisfied, he put them back into the bag.

"Thank you, ma. I know I have done a very good job and I'm proud of it myself. It was a real professional job, so you can relax. There will never be a case at all for no one will ever find the body. It will be a mysterious disappearance for all

concerned. No doubt there will be a lot of theories and conjectures about the sudden disappearance, but that would soon die when all efforts to trace him prove futile."

The coal baron suddenly grimaced and shook his head. "What about those cavers who have been coming to these areas for the last five years? They are back again this year; I saw them arrive yesterday and they are camping at the same spot as last year. They could get to the cave and find the body and then report to the village or the police."

The man grinned, expecting the question.

"Those cavers have heard about the cave for some years now, but they could never find anyone willing to show them the cave; for the villagers are very scared of even going near the area. I'm sure it will be no different this year. And if they stumble upon the cave next year it will be too late, for what they will find will be only the skeletal remains. It wouldn't matter then; for the bones could belong to any of the many people missing every year in these parts. I wouldn't worry too much."

"That may be so, but still one never knows."

"Ma? Even if they come upon the cave and find the body, there is no way it could ever be connected to me. I have made sure of that. It will end up as an unsolved crime as so many others. And I think they are used to finding dead bodies or skeletal remains in the caves by now."

He got up, shook the coal baron's hand and thanked him once again, holding the bag close to his chest.

"I hope so! Anyway, when I need you again I will contact you. Just don't barge your way into my house, okay? It will not be good for my reputation. You do know that I am going to contest for the Assembly Elections next year don't you?" The coal baron said grinning at him.

"No I don't. But it will be good for you. You are rich and powerful but getting electing to the state Assembly will definitely give you more power especially if you become a Minister – you will have great political clout and respect. You would then have fulfilled even your wildest dreams, I imagine." And to himself he thought, a minister? a law maker who could not even write his name?. Pooh! What will this state of ours come to?

The coal baron stood expansively, a wry grin on his fat cheeks, thinking of that prospect of himself adorning the Civil Secretariat in the very near future – reading prepared speeches and ordering senior bureaucrats to do his bidding. He could afford to be generous to the man. Who knows when he would need him again; and by the look of things the man would be more than useful to him in the days to come.

The man went straight to the State Bank of India and deposited the money to his account. You could never tell what will happen with so much cash on your body; for the coal belt of the Jaintia Hills with all types of criminals working in the mines, is not a safe place nowadays. He chuckled, having made a neat little sum without really getting his hands soiled in the process. A real pleasure to work for these overnight rich and greedy cutthroats and there were quite a few of them around. Pompous bastards who think the world revolves around them. However they were good for him – he could bleed them, a bit from each one of them. They were the geese laying golden eggs for him. There would be plenty of golden opportunities for him in the coming years. Life was definitely looking good. And the elections next year he said? He smiled to himself thinking of the big kill that lay before him.

At last, they were upon that great big black hole. The white pinnacled limestone outcrops rising from the rocky floor encircled the pothole as if hiding it from unwanted intrusion; and all along the edge of the perimeter the thick and luxuriant undergrowth and pine trees completely obscured the rocky karsts clearing. Located in a very inconspicuous place, they would have to be very lucky to find it on their own. Even the local guide who led them there had some difficulty finding it. But there they were at the massive shaft entrance of the legendary Krem Khung - the cave that had occupied his mind since he first heard of it; the cave that had become almost a myth; the cave that he had woven his dreams around those last few years; the cave that had become his obsession. Now that it was suddenly thrust upon him, he felt awed and humbled at the prospect of exploring his dream. Thrang heaved a sigh of relief! The five long years of wait and dream was over – now his dream was to be lived.

Thrang had heard stories of Krem Khung over the last five years or more. Some say that if a stone is dropped into the hole it would take more than five minutes to reach the bottom. Thrang gave a wry smile at that, but would goad them to tell him more of that fabulous cave. A great mist would rise from the cave in the early mornings which could be seen from a distance, another would add. And when the sun sets and the sky is getting dark, thousands and thousands of bats would fly out of the cave like a big black cloud, an old man had proudly proclaimed. A wizened old man had then stepped forward and in a hoarse and trembling voice had added, "An evil place indeed it is… a forbidden place, a place to be avoided," he had said, "and cursed would be the man who had inadvertently strayed too near the evil hole, especially when the air is thick with the devil's breath."

The village boys who had gathered would absorb all those stories with awe and fear. Thrang, however, would be engulfed with a sense of excitement and couldn't wait to see that enchanted cave.

For five years he couldn't find a guide to show him the cave and it was impossible to find it on his own. He had to be content with the fact that it was there and that one day he would see it. On a few occasions, some villagers would appear at the Camp and would promise to take him and his friends to the cave the next day, but invariably they would never turn up; that is, until yesterday.

It was the first week of February, as in every year, when the Meghalaya Speleological Group would kick-start their month long International Cave Expedition. For the last eight years the expedition had been having their Base Camp on the Shnongrim Ridge and had been exploring and mapping the caves in the area. The Shnongrim Ridge had proved to be one of the richest areas in terms of cave density in the whole country and was the location of the longest cave system in the Indian sub-continent, with Krem Liat Prah-Um Im-Labit system at 31 kilometres in length. Much remained to be done in the region.

It was around nine in the evening, when most of the thirty odd cavers had returned back from their day's caving. A few were huddled over their laptops to feed in the day's data, some busy updating their dairies, while the rest, all in a circle enjoyed the warmth of the bonfire with the inevitable bottle of Asia 72 tightly in their possession. As hot and steaming food was brought in and dinner announced, a dark middle-aged and wiry man with a single barrel old flint gun slung across his shoulder entered. He looked around hesitatingly, saw Thrang, and came forward.

"Bah" he said "If you want to go to Krem Khung I will take you there tomorrow."

Thrang couldn't believe his ears. This man is going to show him the cave he had been dreaming of all these years; a cave that had grown in his fantasy to become almost a legend.

"Great," he replied. "This is fantastic."

He beamed at the man. "If you come by eight in the morning you can join us for breakfast, and then we can leave by nine, if that's okay by you."

The man looked at him and said, "The last few years I have seen you all going down some of these deep holes on ropes, exploring the caves, coming out dirty and exhausted but enjoying yourselves and ready again the next morning. You have made our villages and our region known the world over. You are totally dedicated to what you are doing although I do not understand what you get out of it." He grinned showing a row of reddened teeth from chewing a concoction of areca nut, betel leaf with some slaked lime. "I will be here tomorrow morning at eight. Now I will take your leave."

"Come, have some dinner with us," Thrang invited him.

"Thank you Bah, but I am late and have already had my food. When you have explored Krem Khung I would be happy to share an evening of beer and dinner with you." With that he bade goodnight and left.

"What is your name?" Thrang shouted after him.

"Rodik," he shouted back.

Thrang turned around and looked at his fellow cavers. Most of them were oblivious of the good news he had and were busy with their own work and distractions.

Joe however was inquisitively eyeing him, having heard him talking of Krem Khung.

"Is that chap showing us Krem Khung?" he asked.

"Yes," Thrang replied, a big smile on his face, "Tomorrow we go to Krem Khung."

This caught the attention of everyone and they crowded in. "Are we finally going to Krem Khung?" they cried in unison.

"Well, some of us are surely going," he replied, as he faced them.

During the next half hour, the next day's programme was finalized and settled. The honour to be the first to tackle Krem Khung would go to Joe the Englishman, Jorge the German and Thrang, a member of the Meghalaya Speleological Group.

"Cheers to Krem Khung!" shouted Pete from the circle around the bonfire and everyone drank to that.

After a while of merrymaking Thrang took his leave to retire to his tent, after having first discussed the morrow's plans with Joe and Jorge.

Thrang stood out in the open dark night, savouring the cool damp breeze and looked up at the vast expanse of bright and twinkling stars. *I have never seen so many bright and happy stars,* he mused; *maybe a good omen for me in the days to come.* He could see the dim lights of Shnongrim village a kilometer away as the crow flies. He has often wondered why the voltage in the villages were so low; sometimes there are no lights even for weeks on end. Maybe the concerned authorities believe that the villages don't require as much energy as their more illustrious urban brethrens? What a glaring disparity of services being meted out to different sections of the people – exposing our hypocritical traits.

Far away into the distant horizon, to the north and north-east from where he stood, he could vaguely make out the thinning landscape; all that range until very recent times was once a thick forested area, where elephants and tigers freely roamed. To the east some remnants of the forest still stood, as the Narpuh Forest Reserve; but for how long will it remain so? Rapid encroachments of human population, claiming vast tracks of faunal land; and the keen smell and hungry appetite of investors of every hue, crowding out the age-old trees; all these have deprived the wild denizens of their hearth and homes, some of which have been doomed to extinction like the *khung. The khung? Who knows what this animal is – except that it looked like a bear with a much narrower snout and known for its ferociousness; for more often than not it would never hesitate to attack humans if cornered or shot at,* so explained the elders of the villages. No khungs have ever been sighted during the last three decades or so, they opined. The younger generation has no knowledge of this mysterious animal except through the stories of their fathers and grandfathers. Thrang had tried all he could to find out more about that beast but information was scant and vague. He had even met an old man who had shown him a small cave with an open karst narrow canyon entrance.

"A long time ago,' he had said, 'I and my friend, armed with shot guns, had waited up there on the top; when the khungs came out they were easy prey for us. We shot three of them," he had proudly boasted.

"Must have been the last of the species, that you killed," Thrang joked.

The old man appeared lost in thought for some considerable time, before he finally replied.

"No; we were still shooting khungs for a few more years after that. Then the khungs just disappeared and we have never seen another one again."

"A great pity, indeed!" Thrang lamented.

The old man had looked at him incredulously, wondering what he meant.

Today, the khung had become a myth, a legend - an animal of the past, an animal hunted to extinction. Maybe one day he hoped, he would come across the skull or the skin of the animal in some one's hut in some remote village. Then he would be able to identify what animal it was and set his inquisitive mind at rest.

As he made his way to his tent he sadly reflected, that he has to bear the tragedy of wanton destruction all his life - a deep, ugly scar to live with. He cringed inwardly. He was looking forward to the next day when the explorations would start in full swing. He relaxed in his sleeping bag, knowing that for the next three weeks he would have nothing to worry about except the success of the expedition.

As he was about to doze off, he faintly heard some voices somewhere near the kitchen tent. A voice, probably someone from the near village, enquired if Romen Bamon, the Daloi of the elaka, was there with them and he heard Ban, the Camp manager cum driver say: "No; the Daloi had not been to the Camp."

Faintly he heard the other voice saying: "My father had not come home for the last two nights and no one had seen him. This is odd...I fear something terrible must have happened...this behaviour is totally unbecoming of him."

Again Ban's voice: "Sorry, but we have not seen him."

"It is late ... tomorrow we will organize a search party." The boy's voice floated drowsily to him: "Goodnight, and sorry for troubling you."

Thrang heard Ban's reassuring voice: "We hope nothing serious has happened ...please call on us should you need any help."

Thrang wondered what it was all about as he drifted off to sleep.

2

The next morning, while most of them were still asleep in their sleeping bags, the Krem Khung team with the guide Rodik was having a big and hearty breakfast of fried rice, fried eggs and baked beans with cups and cups of hot tea, served by the camp cook.

By 9 AM the team was ready to leave. They loaded their tackle bags packed with their personal gear plus the team equipment of ropes, drilling machine, flexible ladders etc. into the back seat of the yellow sumo. Rodik got in next to the driver while the three of them got in the back seat and they were off.

The road had improved over the last few years with most of it having been black-topped, so the drive was quite smooth till they came to the outskirts of Lelad village. From there the drive became very slow and bumpy with deep ruts created by shaktimans. Rodik asked the driver to stop not too far away from the small village of Tangnub. They got down, heaved their heavy tackle bags on their backs and were ready to be led by Rodik.

"Joe, what time would we want to be picked up?" Thrang asked.

"7 PM should be fine," he told the driver.

The guide led the way up the steep jungle clad slope. With their heavy back packs they strove to keep up with his brisk pace. He used his machete to try to pave a way for them through the thorny bushes. Up, down and up, they scrambled for half an hour through the thorns and were running out of breath with the exertion. A couple of times the guide couldn't find the way on.

Suddenly they were upon her. A big, gaping black hole lay just in front of them. The famous or rather infamous Krem Khung docilely awaited them. Thrang looked at the big opening, his heart pumping with excitement and thought, "This is where the beginning of my dreams will start." He smiled, in anticipation of what lay ahead of him. All caves have a story to tell and this one would have a great one; it was for him to understand the cave and to unravel its secrets.

The rugged, sharp pinnacled limestones were clean and white, encircling the clean-washed fluted vertical passage to the bowels of the earth. They gazed into the dark bottomless depth where the devil was supposed to reside. "Oh Subterranean Spirit! Let us probe into the secrets of your domain," they prayed silently in their own hearts.

"Bah!" the guide Rodik addressed Thrang "I will leave you now for I have to attend to my own duties."

Thrang woke up from his reverie. "Thank you so much for guiding us to this cave, Bah Rodik. I am personally ecstatic with this find." He put his hand in his pocket, took out two five hundred rupee notes and handed them to the guide saying, "Here, take this for your time and help."

The guide accepted the notes with a smile, revealing his betel chewing red teeth and said, "Thank you Bah."

With that, he bade farewell and disappeared into the thicket.

The three of them sat for a while, soaking in the serenity and grandeur of the place. Gradually, they got down to the business at hand.

"Give me a hand will you?" Joe said.

Jorge and Thrang got up and helped Joe in anchoring the 50 metre long rope around a couple of strong limestone outcrops, fixed some rope-protectors around the rope on the edge of the shaft and dropped the other end of the rope into the yawning hole. With the top of the shaft rigged, they quickly got themselves into their caving gear, fixed their SRT climbing equipment around them and were ready to descend.

Joe picked up the extra 30 metre long Marlon rope, shoved it into his tackle bag, clipped his cow's tails into a loop on the anchored rope and fixed his chest descender on the rope dropping into the dark abyss. He stepped to the edge of the shaft, tested his descender and satisfied, unclipped his long and short cow's tail from the loop.

"Thrang, you come after me when I'm down and Jorge will follow you. Well chaps, I will be waiting for you down there." With that he was off, slowly descending into the devil's yawning throat.

Jorge and Thrang waited, seeing the tension on the rope as Joe worked his way down. Minutes passed. When 20 minutes passed and the rope still taunt, Jorge looked at Thrang. "I think we have ourselves a really deep one here," he said.

They waited, getting restless and almost to the hour, they heard Joe labouring up the rope. Both of them went over to the edge and looked down. They could see the warm and steady glow of Joe's carbide light flickering in the dark. "Shortage of rope," was what both of them thought.

Twenty minutes later, Joe was over the edge exhausted. He freed himself from the rope and sat down next to them.

"I did not reach the bottom. We need more rope," he said. "Another 50 metre length would do."

"I fixed a re-belay at about 30 metres from the top with the 30 m rope I took with me and was surprised to still find myself hanging in dark space. I could barely see the bottom of the pit with my light but I distinctly heard the sound of a stream," he continued.

"I think we have a hundred metre shaft," he smiled at the excited faces of Jorge and Thrang.

They sat for a while, shared a small packet of coconut biscuits and washed it all down their throats with some mineral water.

"So, what do we do now?" asked Jorge.

"Go back to camp," Thrang said. "There is no point sitting here, for the driver will come to pick us up at 7, which is another five and a half hour from now. We can therefore slowly walk back to camp. Maybe recce along the way; we could be lucky and find an unexplored cave."

"Yes, I suppose we could do that," agreed Jorge.

They got out off their heavy caving apparel into their outdoor clothes, slung their tackle bags unto their backs and slowly made their way back, leaving the ropes already rigged to the cave intact.

On their way to camp they investigated likely places where caves could be found; pushing themselves through dense and spiky undergrowth. After two hours of thrashing around the dense jungle and almost giving up hope, they suddenly and surprisingly emerged upon the edge of a shaft, startling a humming bird by their over enthusiastic scramble.

"Look, now what we have found," Joe burst out, his face all writ in smiles.

"Do you think this cave has been found earlier and already explored and mapped?" Jorge asked, hoping in his heart that it was not so; it would be a terrible shame if it was.

Thrang smiled at him. "Definitely not; we have found ourselves a new cave, of that I'm absolutely certain."

All three stood round the shaft peering into its depths and marveling at the clean washed fluted walls. Joe picked up a stone and dropped it into the shaft counting the seconds before it bottomed.

"About forty metres," he said. "But at the height we're on, I'm sure there will be a series of more pitches before the cave bottoms to become horizontal."

"This is fantastic. This is what I love most; to discover caves on your own," Thrang said, exulting in their great discovery.

"We have to give it a name," Joe said, while Jorge had already switched on his GPS to get the co-ordinates of the cave entrance.

"Yes, we have to name it; at least for the moment. Later on, we can find out if the locals have a name for the cave." Thrang said his mind already at work thinking of a suitable name.

"Humming Bird Cave, that's what we'll call it," he pronounced with satisfaction.

"That's a good name," agreed Jorge and Joe.

They lingered for the next hour or so making notes and taking photographs.

"It's a pity we don't have any ropes with us. I'm just dying to go down and start exploring the cave," Joe uttered dejectedly.

"I know,' Thrang sympathized with him, 'so you are coming here tomorrow?"

Joe was silent for a few seconds, contemplating on what Thrang had just said.

"No! I think all three of us have to concentrate on Krem Khung. Another team can take up this cave. A great pity though! I would have loved to explore this cave myself."

"I would too; but that's how the die is cast. One cannot be the first to explore all the caves that are discovered. I'm sure we will have a chance to explore some sections of this cave; that is if it turns out to be big and cannot be explored in a few days time." Thrang consoled Joe.

"It's only three o'clock,' Jorge said looking at his watch, 'should we search around some more; at least for an hour or so?"

"Why not?" Joe said, to which Thrang readily consented.

They braved the spikes and dense bush, up and down the hillside; at times, practically crawling through the thick thorny lantana, for they did not have a machete with them. They found a little stream of water and traced its source, to find the resurgence gushing from a little opening too small to be a cave. Every little depression or doline was thoroughly investigated. Time was catching up on them and they were slowly working their way towards camp, when Joe who had gone ahead, suddenly yelled.

"Hey, come over here, you two."

In less than sixty seconds they were with him, looking down into another shaft. Joe was already taking the GPS location and making notes in his notebook. Jorge took out his camera and took a number of photographs from every angle he could.

"What do we call this cave now?" Thrang asked.

"Keeping the bird theme, why don't we call it Song Bird Cave?" Joe suggested.

"Good enough for me," Thrang said, with Jorge also nodding his assent.

Contented and happy at their two new discoveries, and as it was getting dark, they called it a day and made their way straight back to camp. On the way they met herds of cattle being herded back to their sheds for the night by small boys, whose duty it was to mind the cattle.

They got back to camp just as the Sumo was leaving camp for their pick-up. Seeing them coming down the hill the driver stopped his vehicle, somewhat surprised at their early return.

"What happened, Bah?" He asked Thrang.

"It just happened that we didn't have enough rope and therefore couldn't explore the cave. So rather than wait for you we walked back all the way."

None of the other cavers had returned yet from their trips, except Danny who had stayed in Camp with a cold.

Seeing the three of them come in, Aseem, the camp cook rushed in with a pot of fresh tea and cream crackers with a jar of jam and a small bowl of butter.

"Water, hot for a bath?" Thrang inquired of Aseem.

"Oh yes. The water had actually been boiling for the last half an hour and I have pulled out the logs from the fire, Bah."

"Good. I am ready for a bath; get rid of the grime and the sweat of the day."

3

The next day the Krem Khung team left camp half an hour later than the previous day. They had with them another precious 50 metre long Marlon rope. The sumo stopped at the same designated spot and they got out.

"Come for us by 8," Joe told the driver, "I think we will need the extra time."

They made their way to the cave in no time at all and lost no time in getting into their caving gear.

The more I look at this dream-like cave entrance and its rugged and sculptured surroundings the more I am enchanted with it, thumped Thrang's pulsating heart with sheer joy. Without even seeing the insides of it, he felt deep inside his heart, that Krem Khung would top the list of all the beautiful and great caves that he had ever explored....

His reverie was rudely broken by the sound of Joe's voice, "I am ready to descend. Thrang, you are next," and he soon disappeared into the dark depths, carrying with him the extra rope.

After about twenty minutes the rope slackened which meant that Joe had crossed the re-belay and was on the next stretch of rope. Thrang quietly and nervously jammed the rope through his chest descender and stood poised over the edge. Soon he too began his descent. By the time he reached the first re-belay he realized that Joe had already crossed the second re-belay. He carefully switched his descender to the second stretch of rope and continued to go down marveling at the clean-washed fluted walls of the cave. He was hanging in mid air; a lonely soul in the dark – entering an unknown subterranean world. The rope stretched and he felt like he was hanging on a thin string which could snap at any moment. He felt exhilarated at the thought of defying death, though he knew the rope was strong enough for more than ten times his weight. Everytime he abseils down a shaft, he would experience a thrilling sensation of exhilaration and awe at the great wonders of nature; many of these herculean works of nature offer man an avenue and an opportunity to challenge and overcome his adventurous spirit, where he polishes and hones on his skills to perfecting his achievements. Abseiling down that moment was no different, as his whole being thoroughly absorbed the pleasure of his actions in an atmosphere hidden and unseen, and all his own.

When he had crossed over the second re-belay and was on the third stretch of rope, he looked down and saw that Joe was already at the bottom. Joe's carbide light was flickering off to one side of the cave, probably having a quick investigation of the cave before he and Jorge were down Thrang thought. Suddenly the desire to reach the bottom faster tickled his imagination. What is it that awaits him down there – big underground highways going off in all directions? Beautiful and giant sized formations, the likes of which he had never encountered before? Or will the devil await him down there; the subterranean spirits of Krem Khung? Thrang mused, a feeling of excitement flowing through his soul. Or maybe if he was lucky, the preserved skeletal remains of the mysterious khung.

He thought he heard Joe's voice when he was suddenly aware that he had reached the end of the shaft. He pressed on his descender till he was sitting on the floor so as to slacken the rope when he stood up. He then easily unfastened himself from the rope and joined Joe.

Joe was silent and appeared to be shaken.

"Thrang," he croaked. "There is a dead body here."

"What?" Thrang said in bewilderment.

"There, beside that stream on the sand bank." Joe pointed a wavering finger.

Thrang turned in the direction of Joe's finger and could make out a sprawled figure on the soft sand.

"Now what is all this?" muttered Thrang under his breath "...an anti-climax to end an otherwise beautiful day."

He turned to Joe and hesitatingly enquired, "Should we go near and investigate?"

Joe nodded and they both slowly and cautiously approached the still and apparently dead body. By the aid of Joe's carbide light and Thrang's LED they saw that the body was of a middle aged man, although they could not see his face as it was buried in the fine white sand. The body was lying in an awkward position, twisted and mangled for the fall had been endless; it was a long, dark and fatal drop. The sweet smell of death was wafting up their nostrils and they shivered nauseatingly.

"Hey! What are you looking at?" shouted Jorge, as he too reached the end of his descent.

They waited till he was free off the rope and called him over.

Jorge was aghast at the gory sight before his eyes and was absolutely silent.

"When I got off the rope and walked to one side I almost stepped on the body. I was so horrified and shocked that I ran to the other corner...and I have been trembling ever since," whispered Joe.

"Now what do we do?" nervously enquired Jorge.

Summoning up enough courage Thrang ventured, "First, I think the day's caving is over for we must report the matter to the police. Second, we should leave everything untouched. Third, we should take as many photographs of the body as we can from different angles...so as to assist the police in their investigation."

"Let us get it over with," replied Jorge, taking out his digital SLR camera.

The next few minutes were spent busily clicking photos after photos of the mangled body of flesh and broken bones. The three worked silently, as if any talk would disturb the corpse from its eternal sleep.

When their work was all done, they all wanted to be the first to climb out and not be left alone with the corpse. Finally, it was decided that the order of ascent be in reverse order of the descent. "Lucky me," Thrang thought to himself.

Jorge lost no time in starting his ascent on the rope. Thrang soon followed him and thereafter Joe.

Thrang tried to quicken his pace but only to tire himself out. The climb out was endless and exhausting and he was soaked with perspiration. On and on he exerted himself but the faint light of the outside world was so far up. It was a nightmare of a tortuous climb, and he felt as if he was not making any progress at all; as if something was holding him back. He rested on the rope for a few minutes, taking long and easy breaths; when he felt he was calm enough, he slowly and carefully prusiked his way up, controlling the urge to quicken his ascent. While descending he had not really realized the massive depth of the cave.

Eventually, totally exhausted, unnerved and shaken, and much to his relief he was out of the cave, to be joined a few minutes later by Joe.

"You were trying to race up the rope?" Joe grinned at Thrang.

Thrang smiled sheepishly.

"Just trying to get out of the smell of death, and I thought I couldn't get out sooner enough. What a shaft this is, I dare say!"

"Yes, it is, isn't it? It is really a very long drop. This shaft would surely be the deepest in India."

The long, dark and fatal drop was later measured to be 113 metres deep.

4

There was gloom that night at the camp. Although a four team member of the expedition had discovered a new cave that day with a lot of potential, the atmosphere at the camp was depressing to say the least after the events encountered by the Krem Khung team were made known. After discussing the matter with Tim, the Chief Co-coordinator of the European and American cavers, Thrang immediately informed the Superintendent of Police, Jaintia Hills District, who was stationed at Jowai town. Thrang in turn, was advised by the Superintendent of Police, a Mr. Snowell Pala, to wait for a police team to arrive the next morning and to lead them to the site for retrieval of the body. The Superintendent also enquired of Thrang the exact location of the camp site.

News spread like wildfire especially in remote villages. Soon the camp was crowded with inquisitive visitors wanting to know more of what had happened.

"Bah," a soft voice accosted Thrang, "Did you see the body? Was it the body of my husband the Daloi?"

Thrang was astounded and rooted to the spot with such a query. He remembered the night before last when he was drifting off to sleep he heard the Daloi's son enquiring from the expedition camp manager if his father had visited the camp, as he was missing from home for the last two nights. Thrang had forgotten about that incident, though the next morning he had discussed about it with Ban. He had not taken it as something serious, presuming that the Daloi was held up somewhere, especially with the coming state Assembly elections and somehow or other had failed to inform his family members of his whereabouts. Such things do happen, especially with the Daloi being a very busy person.

Was the body that of the Daloi? He did not know for he did not see the face.... but on second thought it very well could be, he reflected. Panic gripped his heart as he realized the catastrophe that would befall the village and also his own expedition programme in the area.

He looked at the stricken face of the lady and said, "I don't know for I did not see the face," he replied apologetically.

"Are you going to bring the body out?" she pleaded.

"Yes, I suppose so. The police are coming tomorrow and we have to lead them to the site," he made himself to utter.

"I am coming too!" she said with a resolute finality in her voice.

The night wore on with the last of the visitors finally leaving by 11 PM.

It had been a hectic day and every one was tired especially with the sad events of the day. Most of them were ready to hit the sack.

Thrang sat down with Tim and they agreed that the original three- member Krem Khung team will be accompanied by Dr. Spencer Ward, the expedition doctor; Phil a paramedic and a member of his club's rescue team; Andre; Bruce; and Tim himself. The rest of the expedition members would go about their business as usual.

In the meanwhile Joe, Jorge and Phil had collected, in a neat pile, all the necessary equipment like ropes, pulleys, cave-rescue stretcher, etc. for hauling the body out of the cave.

"Tim, do you remember the first time we found dead bodies inside a cave? Well, not bodies anymore, but skeletons."

"Sure, that was in 1998 wasn't it? I remember that one of the skeletons was still intact with its clothes still covering most of its skeletal remains."

"It was a rude shock, though we already knew what we were going to find in the cave, as the villagers had told us beforehand," Thrang reminiscence.

Tim nodded, remembering the incident of many years ago.

"Yes, it was still a shock; and later to learn that the partly clothed skeleton was of a notorious thief with his two partners in crime from across the border, lying by its side."

"Today's gruesome find makes it the third of such happenings. Aren't you now used to finding corpses in our caves?" Thrang asked Tim, looking intently at him.

Tim shook his head vigourously.

"Not on your life! It gives me the spooks. I don't like dead bodies, more so in dark confined spaces; it is as if the spirits of the dead are still trapped in the dark subterranean world."

"I know,' Thrang conceded, 'no one would relish finding a corpse in the deep underground."

"Thrang, do you remember that corpse we saw that was stuck halfway down a shaft? Probably pierced by a sharp stalagmite? I was so aghast and horrified seeing the terrible evil looking expression on the face of that still putrefying cadaver."

Thrang closed his eyes and tightened his muscles as if to ward off that terrifying sight from his mind.

"You know I was overcome with the stench; it was so nauseating I was almost sick. I averted my eyes and tried to avoid looking at it, but in spite of myself I could not help glancing furtively at it. I don't know what I would have done had I been alone. That is something I would never want to experience again; absolutely terrifying."

"Gruesome!' Tim commented, 'I remembered that we both got drunk that night."

"Do you think we will go to that cave again? We have not surveyed it, if you remember."

"Very likely, in the near future; when we are done with the ridge, maybe. Do you think we can leave a known cave unexplored? For all you know it could be a very big system. Anyway I suppose by now the bones must have come apart and fallen to the bottom of the shaft, probably carried away by the river during the monsoon or calcified on some rock; to be discovered and unearthed hundreds of years later and examined by some anthropologist."

"I think I really need a drink now," Thrang said getting up from his seat.

"And I could do with another bottle of beer myself," joined in Tim.

Tim helped himself to a bottle of the Asia 72 and joined the small group around the bon-fire. Thrang poured a little scotch into a glass, sipped it neat and immediately felt the smooth, yet fiery liquid burn his throat and warm his cheeks. He felt much better and relaxed as he walked over to the fire with the glass in hand, to join the high-spirited and jolly hard-drinking caving friends.

5

As if on cue everyone got up early and at the same time. The morning was already beginning to warm up. The air around camp was abuzz with excitement at the gruesome incident, though tinged with the sadness of such death and the gravity of the situation they now had to face.

"Good morning Helen," Thrang smiled at her, as she was applying a sun screen lotion on the exposed parts of her body and rubbing it in. This was Helen's sixth expedition to Meghalaya and she was thoroughly enjoying it as she always does. She would have loved to be able to come every year but the exigencies and responsibilities of her job coupled with the extra responsibility of taking care of her ailing widowed mother would not permit her to do so. She had to be content with coming only on alternate years when her elder sister, who was married and living in Scotland, would reprieve her by coming over to care for their mother.

"Morning Thrang," she gave the sweetest of smiles. "You look cheerful this morning."

"Do I?" Thrang smilingly replied.

"Thrang, a moment please,"

Thrang turned and saw Alex, ".....is anyone going to Lad Rymbai for marketing? If so,' he said, 'I need a carton of cigarettes ....Wills Classic."

"Okay," Thrang assured him.

Thrang looked around and saw that everybody was busy with something or other. Joe and Oliver were at the carbide dump cleaning their generators while Sean and Teibor were breaking the big pieces of carbide rocks into smaller pieces with a hammer. Ken, Josh and Gretel were putting out their wet-suits and caving suits out in the sun to dry and June was brushing her teeth. The four latrines were closed and in use. Franz, Andre and Katrin lazing in the sun with their mugs of tea and Reggie engrossed in a book *Pig Island*. The good doctor was seen sorting out his SRT kit. All the while, Bruce was busy clicking away with his digital SLR camera.

It was an everyday morning scene that Thrang remembered so well.

His observations and thoughts were suddenly interrupted by the announcement of breakfast. Breakfast was noodles, baked beans and boiled eggs with pots of hot tea and coffee.

By the time breakfast was over, the villagers had started drifting over to the camp excited at the prospect of what lay ahead that day. There was a festive air about them. Many had taken the day off from their daily chores. The Daloi's wife, son and other relatives were also there. Thrang invited them to the camp kitchen and told the cook to give them tea and some food which they gratefully accepted. In order not to miss out on any of the action, in the recovery of the dead body from the depths of the dreaded Krem Khung, some of the village men who did not have the luxury of a vehicle had already started walking towards the site.

All were ready and waiting for the police to arrive. The morning wore on and everyone was getting fidgety and impatient.

The four caving teams not going to Krem Khung had all left to explore and map the three new caves discovered just a few days ago.

The police finally arrived at eleven fifteen in a white Maruti Gypsy with a white ambulance following them. A police officer got out of the Gypsy and walked towards the camp. Thrang went to meet him halfway.

"Good morning sir," Thrang offered his hand.

"Good morning. I am Inspector Harlin Passi, from Khliehriat sub-division," as he took Thrang's hand in a handshake.

"And I am Thrang Mawlong from Shillong and a member of the Meghalaya Speleological Group." Thrang introduced himself and added, "This is our annual international caving expedition so you can see a lot of foreign cavers here."

The inspector was short, stout and dark complexioned. He had been trying to cultivate a mustache which he was proud of, not realizing that he would look far better off without one. He exuded an air of confidence and authority about him.

"Inspector, may I introduce you to Tim Warren," Thrang said as Tim sided up to him. "He is a professor, teaching geology in the University of Bristol, UK. He has been the mainstay of these expeditions."

Tim accepted the proffered hand and shook it warmly, "My pleasure to meet you sir, even though under such trying circumstances."

"My pleasure too, Professor" the Inspector replied nonchalantly.

During those introductions the other team members had joined in and were all introduced in turn.

"Would you like to have some tea, Inspector?" Thrang asked, "Before we attend to the business on hand."

"I would love a cup of tea if it would not take too much time," he answered.

"It wouldn't take more than 5 minutes," Thrang assured him.

A huge kettle of hot and steaming tea was brought up from the camp kitchen in less than 2 minutes. Plates of cream crackers and butter and jam were all laid out on the dinner cum work make-shift table. The police team helped themselves to the refreshments.

Over tea, Thrang narrated the incidents leading to the discovery of the body and answered to the best of his ability all the questions posed by the inspector.

"I suppose you did not move the body?" enquired the inspector.

"Definitely not!" assured Thrang, "We were too scared to do anything of the sort. All we did was take a lot of photos."

"Can I see them?" The inspector asked.

"Sure," said Thrang and led him to Jon who had already opened the photo file on the laptop.

The inspector was attentive and examined the photos slowly one by one.

"I would like a set of these photos please," he said to Jon.

Jon smiled and handed him a CD, "I have already burned them for you."

"Thank you" smiled the inspector and handed over the CD to one of his police men who carefully put it in his briefcase.

"Do you think it is murder?" The inspector looked enquiringly at Thrang.

"Good heavens!" exclaimed Thrang, "We never thought of it. But as we didn't touch the body, we had no way of knowing whether he was murdered or accidentally fell in, or for that matter committed suicide."

"I will rule out the possibility of his falling in accidentally, for why should he go to the edge of the cave entrance, when in all probability he would have feared the place as all the villagers do,' the inspector spoke his thoughts, …. 'And, it would be a long shot indeed for him to go and commit suicide in a place he would dread to be even close to its vicinity."

The inspector smiled more to himself than to anyone at his brilliant deduction.

"It must be murder!" he deduced with a firm conviction in his voice.

Tim was aghast at the thought of such a possibility. His worried look conveyed to Thrang .... *Now, what do we have on our hands.... as if we haven't had enough troubles already.*

Thrang nodded silently, *yes, we do have enough problems on our laps, and remembered with dismay the events of last week.*

A cavalcade of vehicles; jeeps, sumos, and marutis had suddenly appeared on the ridge, bearing down angrily, or so it seemed, towards the Camp. You could almost feel the ominous threat of the eleven angry vehicles. They came to a screeching halt just above the camp site and out spewed angry miners led by a few equally ferocious leaders. They came down the slope towards camp, agitated and roaring for a fight.

At that time of the afternoon there would normally be no one at the camp except for the cook, his helpers, the camp manager, drivers etc., but on that particular afternoon there were eight cavers in camp who had just arrived for the expedition.

The angry mob spilled into the camp, behind the two obvious leaders. One of them, grave and sombre, plucked at his unruly moustache and addressed them.

"You better pack up this very night and be gone by tomorrow. We don't want you here."

"Why?" Thrang had asked.

"Because,' and he looked directly at Thrang with a wicked scowl on his face, 'You fellows are trying to stop these people from mining their coal. They are earning their own livelihood and you want to deprive them of that? What business is it of yours to meddle into our affairs?"

"That is not so!" Thrang had retorted.

"Then what is this Public Interest Litigation you have filed in the Supreme Court? Is it not to stop us from mining our coal? Huh?" The second man had hissed lividly.

"You come here to explore our caves and we are happy for you. Yet, you now bite our hand," he had continued.

"Leave this area by tomorrow or face the consequences," the unruly moustache threatened. "If you do not heed to this advice and any mishap befalls any of you, we shall not be responsible. Moreover, mishaps could also happen to the people of Shnongrim village that is if you still hang around these parts. I promise you, these villagers would not dare leave their homes and you would be solely responsible for their fears, sufferings and safety."

"You have got it all wrong," Thrang had interrupted. "We were never against the mining of coal or limestone. Our interest is in the conservation of caves. The mining of limestone poses a real physical threat to the existence of caves for they simply remove the roof of the cave. No doubt quarrying of limestone anywhere would destroy caves, for the limestone belt of Meghalaya is like a Swiss cheese full of holes. All we are asking for," he went on, "is that areas with master cave systems or areas with a high density of caves like this ridge, should be protected and conserved at all cost. They should be considered as our heritage assets."

Thrang had looked at the two of them in the eye, unflinching and unnerved, and had said, "We never had any problem with coal mining, that is, until you started mining in this area." He had let it sink in, before continuing, "You see, this ridge is such a unique place in the whole of the country. There are literally hundreds and hundreds of pot-holes on this ridge which would match any place in the world with the same area. It is indeed a very special place, having some very ancient caves which would be of great scientific interest to scientists, especially as these caves harbour some very rare forms of cave-life."

Thrang had looked at the mob all around him. He had sensed the bewilderment creeping into their faces and therefore had pressed home his point: "You are boring into the hill and into the earth at the base of this ridge for extracting coal. Don't you see water rushing out of those pits? Do you know what is happening? You are lowering the water table. The effect of your actions will deprive the villages on the ridge of water. Is it fair to them? Your own people? You are also depriving them of their livelihood for you are destroying their paddy fields by the sulphur leached from your coal mines. Is this not true? And what about the rivers and streams around the coal mining areas? Do you find any life in them?"

Even the deep dark holes of the earth have great usefulness to mankind, which I'm sure you could not ever comprehend. Thrang had voiced the thought in his own heart, looking directly at the unruly moustache.

The silence was so profound it could be heard; and Thrang had felt a sense of triumph. "All we want is the conservation of these natural heritage assets that we have, without depriving the people of their livelihood and without any destruction or degradation of the environment. Further, whatever mining there is, has to be regulated and for which the Government has to formulate a Mining Policy for the state," he had finished.

The vociferous and murderous mob had become docile and a sense of shame had crept into their hearts. The wind had been taken out of their sails and they felt deflated. Their body language said it all.

"Will you give us in writing that you are not against mining as such?" the unruly moustache had asked.

"Sure, I will get the written statement ready for you by tomorrow," Thrang had assured him.

The unruly moustache had looked piercingly at Thrang and with an air of bravado and had said, "Okay, you can go about your cave exploration, so long as you don't bother us. If the Government brings out a mining policy, I assure you we will abide by it."

There had been handshakes all around and then they had left.

Thrang was suddenly brought down to earth by the urgency in the voice of the inspector.

"I think we should leave now and get our work done. It is going to take most of the day."

With that they all piled into their vehicles. The cavers in their sumo led the way, followed by the police in their white Maruti Gypsy and ambulance. The Daloi's wife, son and relatives followed in their old Mahindra jeep at the rear.

6

There were quite a crowd of men and women waiting beside the road where all the vehicles came to a standstill; eager to go along with them to Krem Khung, the cave of 'fear and evil' as they were told by their own parents when young. They timidly followed the cavers and policemen up the slope and through the thorns each making sure that he or she was not left too far behind.

When they were upon her, they stopped, fear lurking in their hearts. What they saw was a small clearing dotted with sculptured and beautiful limestone outcrops much like a fairy-place, though none had ever seen one. The rocks were clean and white. There in the centre was the ravenous black mouth of Khung, the source of many a nightmare for them as kids.

They all stared in awe and astonishment. Soon they found their voices and began to sit around in a semi-circle to watch the proceedings in the retrieval of a dead body from the depths of that deep shaft. This would be a story to tell their children, grand children and great grand children in the years to come, they mused.

The eight cavers quickly got into their caving suits and strapped on their harnesses and climbing gear, ready for the messy job at hand. Ropes were taken out of the tackle bags and one end of a rope was securely anchored to another solid rock close to the earlier anchor, pulleys were fixed and positioned over the edge for smooth and easy hauling of the dead weight.

"Joe, Doc, Phil and you Jorge go down; the four of us will stay up here to do the hauling," Tim directed.

"Tim," Thrang said, "I think I should go down also, to identify the body. Should it belong to the Daloi, then I can come out first to prepare the Daloi's wife of the bad news. I only hope it is not so."

"Sounds good to me," and Tim nodded.

They descended the hole with Joe in the lead, followed by Doc fifteen minutes later when the first stretch of rope to the re-belay had become slack, then after every slackness of the rope followed by Thrang, Phil and Jorge in that order. All the while the activity was carefully absorbed in minute detail by the excited crowd. The inspector had gathered his men to help Tim and the other cavers in whatever help they would need.

To assert his authority the inspector had ordered the crowd, "Sit quietly where you are. I don't want any of you to shout, move around and disturb any rocks. Least of all do not come near the edge," he commanded.

Time passed and waiting can be very boring and taxing. The crowd was getting restive but no one was willing to leave even for a moment lest he or she miss something. Some of the ladies were peeling the skins of areca nuts and cutting the nut into four or five pieces and distributing the piece of nut together with half a betel leaf smeared with slaked lime to all around. Suddenly, a strong wind stirred and rain clouds appeared; rain splattered angrily yet no one moved. It rained for just five minutes or so before the wind drove it away.

Down in Krem Khung all the five cavers were safely on ground floor.

Joe put down the rescue stretcher close to the body, while Phil helped the Doc to move the dead body, so that they could assess the state of its condition. The nauseating, sweet smell of death clung to their clothes and found its way into their systems through their nostrils. Thrang was appalled. He looked at the upturned face of the body and shook. *It is the body of the Daloi*, he realized with horror and shock.

"Look here, this is a wound," observed the Doc pointing to the scarlet blotch on the chest. "We have a murder on our hands," he said.

"Doc!" shouted Jorge. "I have found the weapon."

"Don't touch it,' shouted the Doc in reply, 'I'm coming over."

He got up from his kneeling position and walked the few metres to where Jorge was. There on the ground, just beside the huge stalagmite was the bloodied knife. The Doc took it up very carefully from its tip and put it in a plastic bag. They went back to the mangled corpse. Carefully the Doc, Phil and Joe lifted the dead body and put it on the stretcher and began securing it.

"We didn't see any bloodstains up there did we?" The Doc asked, as an afterthought.

"No" Phil replied.

"I don't think so too either,' Thrang said, 'otherwise we would have noticed it yesterday for we did spend a lot of time at the entrance."

"I think Thrang is right; there were no blood spots at the entance area, at least I never noticed any," Joe offered.

"I think this poor chap was murdered elsewhere and his murderers must have carried the body and dumped it into this pothole - most probably to hide the crime." The Doc murmured, more to satisfy his own thoughts.

There was an air of serious contemplation for a few moments at the thought of such a hedious crime. Suddenly everyone wanted to get out into the open sunshine.

"Doc, I am going up to the surface," Thrang said and he started on his ascent up the rope.

Halfway up the shaft he sensed that the body was being hauled up. He quickened his pace; it would not be good if the corpse passed him by – he should be out first. It would be bad luck for him should it happen, or so the Khasis believed.

Twenty minutes later Thrang was out of the cave. As he topped the edge there was a shout and a clapping of hands from the crowd. He unfastened himself, nodded to Tim that it was really the body of the Daloi and walked over to the Daloi's wife.

"Kong,' he began hesitatingly and apologetically, 'I am sorry but it is the body of your husband, the Daloi."

At that she screamed and beat her body about the chest, "Oh father of my children! Why leave me so, all alone to fend for our children and this yet unborn child of eight months?"

She wept inconsolably, joined in by her son and relatives.

Soon the cavers were all out in the open sunshine as also the body strapped on the stretcher. The villagers rushed in to have a look at the body of the Daloi, but were restrained by the police. The Daloi's wife stepped up to the stretcher, looked down, and kneeling over, hugged the body, weeping inconsolably, "Why, my husband?" she cried. "Who did this to you? You were such a good man …a good husband and a good father …how can I live without you? Oh God!" she wept.

Thrang stood by her, not knowing what to do, until her mother picked her up and led her away to the jeep.

This galvanized everyone into action. The policemen smartly picked up the stretcher with the corpse in it and deposited it in the ambulance. Leaving the ropes, rigged to the cave the day earlier, for continuation of the exploration, the cavers de-rigged the other ropes and pulleys used that day. The crowd was milling around the Daloi's wife, offering their condolences and showing their sympathy.

'The Daloi was a good man, always ready to listen to their grievances and had always offered sound advice.'

'We have lost a good Daloi and a wonderful friend,' ....they lamented.

The long slow retreat of the vehicles presented an ambience of tragedy and sorrow. It was a silent procession winding down the narrow and dusty bumpy road. Engrossed in the sad events of the tragic murder of the chief of their elaka they remained silent and lost in their own thoughts.

When the vehicles reached the junction after the village of Lelad they stopped. The inspector got down, walked over to the sumo and smiled at Thrang and Tim and all inside.

"Thank you, all of you, for your co-operation. You have been most helpful; without your expertise we would not have been able to recover the body. We go back to Jowai now and send the body for post-mortem and I have to file my report also."

"In the next few days," he continued, "we will have to bother you again with our investigation of the case."

"You are welcomed Inspector, but to find any of us at the camp, please be here before nine in the morning or after six in the afternoon," advised Thrang.

"We will get the post-mortem done by tonight,' the inspector said gravely, '.....and the family will receive the body by tomorrow morning for the last rites." With that he gave a smart salute, turned briskly and got into his vehicle and drove off.

The rest wound their way up the hill into camp while the Daloi's wife and relatives continued on to the late Daloi's house in the village.

That night the atmosphere in camp had brightened and picked up on its normal jovial mood, though the tragic murder of the Daloi was never far from their minds. They knew that their daily routine would be interrupted by frequent visits of the police, poking their noses in camp, asking questions and prodding for answers. They would only be doing their duty of course, but even so, this gruesome murder would be telling on all at the camp.

Thrang had had a good scrubbing in one of the four bathing cabins constructed out of the local bamboo with plastic sheets covered from the outside. He had used two buckets of hot water to rid himself of the smell of death. Clean and feeling good, he put on a warm jacket and joined the others at the bon-fire, finding a seat next to the professor. The night was cold with a damp breeze blowing across, though the sky was bright with millions of stars.

"A good day's work, eh Tim?" Thrang said.

"Excellent I would say, under the circumstances," Tim replied.

"Well, I suppose we should pay our last respects to the Daloi by attending the funeral tomorrow?" Thrang continued, "The family would expect us to be there as also the entire village. We cannot disappoint them, can we?"

Tim looked around to get the attention of all and said, "No, we cannot disappoint the family. The Daloi had been very good and co-operative to us all these years; giving us this place to camp and permission to cave anywhere within the jurisdiction of his elaka" Tim took a large sip from his Asia 72 and went on: "In fact, the Daloi had been on our side in not granting permission for any coal mining on the Ridge. He had always been on our side and ready to extend any help we needed." Tim raised his bottle and said, "Cheers!" and everyone drank to that.

"Yes," as Tim warmed up to the idea. "We will do the family and the village proud. We will all take a day off from our heavy caving schedule and attend the funeral of our friend, the Daloi; our last farewell to a man of principles. And may his soul rest in eternal peace," he ended.

Once again, bottles and glasses were raised to their lips, in honour of their friend, the Daloi.

7

It rained that night, but not so much as to worry them in their sleep about any water seeping into the sleeping quarters. It was a rain in mourning, shedding tears of sorrow. They all slept soundly after the fatigue of that day and overslept the next morning.

When they woke up, the last remnants of the clouds had disappeared and the sun was shining bright and clear.

After breakfast they lazed around. Wet and muddy caving things were taken out to dry in the sun; the sound of a guitar strumming emanated from somewhere inside the camp…

Tim and Andre were busy feeding expedition data into the laptop; Alex, Helen and Maya updating their personal dairies; Allan in total concentration doing his yoga exercises; the rest were reading, drinking coffee, washing and generally offering as much of their exposed parts to the sun. It was a peaceful and relaxed morning – a leisure day.

Thrang had slept well that night. The excitement, sorrow, shock, disbelief, exhaustion, rain and rum had induced such a wonderful sense of oblivion that he just drifted off into a slumber that would have put Rip Van Winkle to shame. When he awoke the sun was trying to penetrate the thin fabric of his tent. He relaxed a few more minutes in his sleeping bag recollecting the events of the previous day. Suddenly he felt a deep sense of loss. He had known the Daloi for the last five years and they had become good friends. *Who had murdered him*? He wondered. *I hope the new Daloi when elected, will also be co-operative and helpful to us; we have so much to do in these areas.*

After a rather light breakfast Thrang sought out Ban the camp manager.

"Ban,' he said, 'we should make a wreath to take to the funeral. Do you think we can get some wild flowers?"

"Let me see what we can do. Just leave it to me," he said.

Thrang walked over to Tim, still busy at the laptop, "Tim,' he interrupted, 'I think it would be nice if we can collect some contribution from the expedition team and hand it to the bereaved family as a way of help."

"Sure! That will be good. I will get a plea for contribution circulated to everyone," he promised.

The day wore on, lazily.

Ban and Lung, the second camp manager, had somehow managed to collect some wild flowers from the nearby forest scrub land and some soft, willowy bush stalk; a plain and simple but elegant wreath was fashioned with a note pinned with the words:

> "In loving memory of a man,
> plain, simple and brave,
> who lived,
> to uphold his belief and principles.
> May his soul rest in eternal peace.
>
> From: The Caving in the Abode of the Clouds Expedition
> Team."

In the meanwhile the donation circular had done its bit of traveling and had arrived back and placed in front of Tim with a sum of Rupees Twenty two thousand five hundred.

Suddenly there was a loud honking. Lung peered into the dining-cum-workroom of the main camp, saw Thrang and said, "Bah, the police are up there on the road. I think they want you."

Half expecting this, Thrang lost no time in coming out. He looked up and saw the white Maruti gypsy and the ambulance beside the road just above the camp-site. He half ran up the slope to where the vehicles stood.

"Ah! Inspector,' Thrang waved in greeting, 'Good to see you again."

The inspector still inside the gypsy smiled in return.

"Is the post-mortem done?" Thrang enquired.

"Yes,' beamed the inspector. 'The post-mortem was done this morning and I had to wait till it was over. I have brought the body back to deliver it to the bereaved family for the funeral."

He looked at Thrang and implored, "Can you send someone to show me the house in the village?"

"Sure!" Thrang turned towards Lung who had joined him "Lung, why don't you accompany the inspector," he asked him.

Lung obediently got into the back of the gypsy.

"Thanks, Bah Thrang" the inspector smiled in appreciation. "I will be returning back to Khliehriat, as soon as the body is handed over. I have so much to attend to,' he apologized, 'but I will be seeing you again in a couple of days with regard to the investigation."

With that they left for the village, a kilometre away.

It was 1 P.M. and the family would not have much time to get ready for the funeral. Under normal circumstances the body of the Daloi would have been kept for at least two nights, so that all people within the elaka would be able to come and pay their last respects. But this was no normal circumstance; the Daloi had been murdered at least five days ago and nature had taken its cruel destroying effect on the body. It had to be put under the earth as early as possible.

By 3.30 P.M. all the members of the International Caving Expedition had reached the Late Daloi's house. As they filed in into the compound, all eyes were upon them. Never before had the people coming from all over the elaka, seen so many foreigners. The Late Daloi wherever his spirit was, would have been astonished and extremely happy at the huge assemblage of so many people from so many nationalities honouring his funeral. In the midst of such a sad calamity the Daloi's family was also aware of the great honour brought on them.

Ban carried the wreath and handed it over to someone minding the pile of wreaths which had already arrived. Tim and Thrang were escorted to the late Daloi's wife, mourning by the body of her husband. She rose from where she was sitting and accepted their outstretched hands. Through her wrought stricken face she acknowledged their presence and gratefully accepted the sealed envelope enclosing the camp's contribution.

Tea and biscuits were served by young girls, to all. Plates of betel nuts and betel leaves were placed on small tables all around the compound for people to partake of.

As was the custom, the dead body of anyone who had died an unnatural death either from suicide, accident or murder, was never taken indoors but kept outside in a temporary make-shift shed; so also was the body of the Daloi placed. From inside this shed emanated the anguished and desolate cries of the late Daloi's immediate relatives, as the lid was finally screwed on the coffin.

Ten minutes later the coffin was carried out and laid on two benches placed side by side and covered by a white cloth. The wife, children and near and dear ones gathered on one side of the coffin, sobbing uncontrollably.

The Presbyterian Pastor stood up, cleared his throat and began the proceedings.

"Before the Church take over the actual religious rites, I would request all those men and women, other personalities and NGOs to give their messages in as short a time as possible as the night is about to descend."

Headmen of various localities within the elaka, the Daloi of Sutnga, the representative of the constituency to the State Legislative Assembly and representatives of some NGOs spoke and read their messages, all eulogizing the goodness, honesty, integrity and upright character of the Late Daloi. The Daloi during his tenure as a Daloi of his elaka had appeared to have endured himself to all. The Daloi had been a simple and God-fearing man but why does a man's goodness and unblemished record become more pronounced when dead? Thrang wondered.

His reverie was suddenly broken when he heard his name.

"... Bah Thrang, please would you like to say a few words on behalf of the people from overseas? .... the late Daloi was always so proud and spoke so highly of all of you ...... it will indeed be a great honour for the bereaved family," clearly rang the words from an elder of the family.

Thrang was rooted to the spot. His face flushed as he felt himself trapped. "Serves me right not to have thought of this earlier," he rebuked himself. Summoning up his courage, he unsteadily walked the few steps to where he was supposed to face the mournful congregation.

"On behalf of the project 'Caving in the abode of the Clouds', the Meghalaya Speleological Group and all the cavers present here today, I stand here before all of you to weep and mourn at the sad demise of our great friend the Daloi. I personally, have known him for the last five years since we first came to this Ridge. He welcomed us with an open heart, gave permission to explore caves within his jurisdiction and allowed us to make our camp near his village."

"His was a simple and rustic life, but a man true to his belief of protecting and conserving the environment he lived in. It is only a brave man like him who would die at the hands of greedy and coward men."

Thrang felt a lump in his throat but steeled his heart on, "I am deeply grieved because the Daloi was very proud of his land and his people; a down-to-earth man of the people and a God fearing one."

"He had a vision, this simple and unsophisticated man; a deep desire to lead and give his people, without compromising, the basic amenities of life," Thrang paused, took a deep breath and continued, "I offer my and all our expedition team member's condolences to the wife he has left behind, his children and his relatives."

With tear-filled eyes, Thrang scanned the hundreds of mournful faces before him and choked, "The village has indeed lost a brave son of the soil; in fact, the Nongkhlieh elaka will be very much the poorer at the loss of this well loved stalwart. On a personal level I have lost a friend. May his soul rest in peace."

Thrang somehow made it into the midst of his caver friends, his heart still beating furiously. The sense of a deep loss…a vacuum created, filled his heart with trepidation.

The Pastor took over the proceedings and began by reading a few verses from the Bible …a hymn was sung ……

Thrang was lost in his own thoughts and oblivious of his surroundings.

Just about ten days back Thrang had gone to meet the Daloi to pay his respects and to thank him for his kind permission for them to cave. The Daloi had been very pleased to see him and had welcomed him and Tim into his house. They had had red tea and biscuits; then kwai was offered which Tim politely declined. Thrang took the kwai offered, popped the nut into his mouth, took off most of the lime from the betel leaf and deposited it in the ashtray and folding the leaf put it into his mouth and began chewing as is the culture of his tribe. They had chatted away …… about the great ancient caves on the Ridge, the unique forms of cave-life found inside some of those caves, the potential of the Ridge itself which if developed into an eco-park would attract adventure tourists for caving, camping, trekking and para-gliding. The Daloi had expressed keen interest in the idea of tourism and had smiled with hope in his heart at the benefits his people would then receive.

Thrang remembered that the Daloi had suddenly frowned and a scowl had appeared in his face. The Daloi had gravely told them about the frenzied mining of coal being carried out all along the base of the Ridge ... this, in spite of his not giving any permission for such mining. He was powerless he informed them, as those coal barons were powerful men ... rich and with a lot of political backing. They had appeared one morning and had staked their claims over land all along the base of the Ridge ... some had coerced a few landowners into selling their land off cheaply.

Thrang could still see the sadness and bitterness in those eyes ... those eyes that had pleaded for help ... help to prevent the madness that was going on ... raping the lush green virgin forest slopes and littering the countryside with huge dumps of coal. Their paddy-fields have been rendered fallow and their streams and rivers have been polluted by the sulphur leached from the coal, he lamented.

"I have even been threatened," he had said and had put up a brave smile, "but I am not scared ..... I will stand for what I believe in."

They had chatted on ....

Thrang was rudely brought back to earth when everyone started singing. He had missed the Pastor's talk and condolence message.

Soon they were wending their way to the graveyard not too far away.

The coffin was lowered into the pit and a short service was again conducted.

By the time everything was over and the last wreath was placed over the filled-in grave, the sun had set and the sky had darkened.

That night Thrang slept fitfully. His mind wandered to Ri, not that he never thought of her everyday. He lived in and out of his heart for her. She was to him, the embodiment of all that love stood for. She was the meaning and soul of his life.

At 39 years of age, Thrang was supposed to be a confirmed bachelor. His parents had been pestering him to get married. His mother had even told him that there were a couple of girls who were very much interested in him. Thrang kept his peace and his mind for he had not yet met his heart-throb.

That was until Ri stepped into his Photographic Studio looking for a digital camera. She came in tall, slim and erect with very sharp features. Her complexion was light brown and she wore her hair to just below shoulder length. She came forward and beamed a smiled at Thrang.

"I would like to buy a camera. A digital," she explained.

"What mega-pixels would you want?" he asked her.

His knees swayed and shook uncontrollably. He had to know her; her name and where she lived.

He politely asked her what her range was, and when she said, "Anything, between twenty to twenty-five thousand rupees," he showed her a Canon digital camera with 10 mega pixels.

"This beautiful camera takes very good pictures at low light intensity and cost twenty-six thousand eight hundred and seventy-five rupees only, but you can have it for twenty-five thousand only," he quickly added, foregoing his own profit on the deal.

He quickly demonstrated to her how the camera works and explained if she was not satisfied with it she can return it within the month.

Not taking much time to decide, she accepted Thrang's offer. She paid in cash and Thrang was writing out the receipt.

"What is your name?" he enquired.

"Riakor Kharwan," she replied in a deep husky voice, as he wrote it down.

"Your address, please?"

"Upland Road, Laitumkhrah," she said.

"Can I have your telephone number please? ...... in case I need to contact you," he elicited quite innocently, his heart pumping furiously in case she should see through his motive.

She gave him her mobile number and he carefully noted it down.

He repacked the camera back in the box and handed it to her with the receipt.

"In case you have any problem please feel free to ring me up or, better still, come over to the shop," he smiled, as he looked at her full in the face.

"Okay!" she smiled and he was totally captivated, "I would most probably come to trouble you as I am not very conversant with digitals."

"It would be my pleasure to have you grace my shop," he uttered, excitement coursing through his throbbing veins.

She left, leaving him transfixed, starry eyed and happy.

Since that day, Thrang's total concentration, centered only on her. She had appeared as an "angel from heaven" he reflected.

Two days later, she came back to the shop and on seeing her, Thang's heart leapt to his mouth. It was evident in his eyes as he welcomed her.

That was three years ago.

During that time they had become the greatest of friends. He had learnt that she was a teacher, teaching in one of the more prestigious missionary schools in Shillong and that she loved her work. They had enjoyed each other's company, meeting everyday in his shop over a cup of tea or coffee. All his friends knew that he was soon heading for the marriage altar. *Love was the most important experience in life*, thought Thrang. *Without it, life would have no meaning. Love is the beginning and the end; nothing, nothing, comes in between. After all, isn't it a universal language that everyone, man, woman and child understands?*

Tonight he was tossing in his sleep. His world had collapse, as he brooded over the events that had lead to the catastrophe just a few days before his expedition, when she had told him that her mother was against her marrying him, for his family was believed to worship *U Thlen*. She herself does not believe in such things; but she had expressed that she cannot defy her mother. There was this man she had said, who was interested in her and whom her mother approved.... she had to give it a chance. With tears flowing down her eyes, she had told him that they will still be great friends and that she will meet him at his shop, as often as she could.

Thrang's head had spun in a dizzy of emptiness; he did not hear anything more. *Why oh God, why*? He had cried.

It was at the break of dawn when he finally fell asleep, faintly hearing through the dim obscure tortured corridors of his mind, the lonely howl of a solitary jackal.

His pillow was partially soaked with the bitterness of his heart.

8

The week passed off with a lot of activity. Many new caves were discovered, explored and mapped; old caves were extended and linked to new finds making them jump up the rung in terms of length.

The exploration of Krem Khung was taken up three days after the funeral. Thrang was one of the members of the two teams assigned to explore the cave. After four days of exploration by the two teams with a change of cavers in between, the cave had yielded over three kilometers in length with much more to be mapped. Krem Khung was revealing its secrets, hidden from the eyes of man, in its eternal darkness..... the beautiful crystal-clear stream, pools and waterfalls, huge streaked curtains hanging from the cave roof, fragile calcite straws and helictites, sparkling flowstone along the walls and floors of the cave, intricately carved columns, smooth great gours, yellow crystal flowers, and literally thousands of cave pearls. These formations came in colours of red, black, grey, green, brown, yellow and of course white. Thrang had never seen anything like this; a treasure unparallel. Above all, the cave is rich in cave fauna; Thrang had personally seen white cave fish, which appeared to have no eyes at all, as also enormous spiders. Another great discovery is the sighting of a tarantula, which they had never come across in their last fifteen years of exploration. The healthy abundance of cave fauna could be attributed to the tens of thousands of bats that roost in the cave, thereby contributing their guano as a source of food. Though he could not differentiate one species of bat from the other, he was certain that there would be some species that were still unknown to the scientific world. This cave harbours a unique eco-system of its own, he thought. How he wished he could have brought Ri there, to share with her the marvels and magnificence of Nature; to appreciate the evolution of life in a closed and confined unique eco-system that is unlike any other cave environment. If this is not God's temple then what is? He mused.

The end of the week saw the inspector arriving at camp at about six-thirty in the afternoon, as the first of the cavers started reaching camp after their day's caving. He had got it timed to perfection. He had spent the earlier part of the day asking questions in the village.

Most of the questions were now directed at Thrang and Tim.

"Do you think the Daloi had any enemies?" he enquired.

You know he does, murmured Thrang under his breath.

"I suppose so,' Thrang replied, 'because of his staunch opposition to the mining of coal in the Ridge area."

"Do you think anyone of them could have murdered him?"

"I really wouldn't know," Thrang stoically answered.

"And we shouldn't be making any guesses," intervened Tim.

"Rightly said!" heaved the inspector with a sigh.

"Anyway,' the inspector apologetically continued, 'my men would now want to take fingerprints of all of you present in the camp."

A sub-inspector came forward and took out all his paraphernalia from a bag and began the process of fingerprinting each one of them.

"As we have a clear set of fingerprints on the murder weapon, we would want to eliminate you all of any suspicion, so that we can narrow it down to the real culprit," he rejoined.

'Fat chance you have, what with the thousands of immigrant miners down there,' thought Thrang to himself '....... the murderer whoever he is would have long disappeared by now.'

Soon the fingerprinting was done, more questions were asked around and noted meticulously and they were off, finished for the day.

The moon was up in the night sky, round and bright.... its soft seductive light, bathing the hillside with a warm embrace. The air was fresh and crisp and Thrang felt a sense of nostalgia. He could clearly see the village in the distance and wondered. *When will the election for the next Daloi be held? Will the new Daloi be as supportive of our work? Will he stand up to the mighty temptation of wealth? And will he uphold the principles of the last Daloi?*

Thrang shivered at the thought of what lay ahead.

"Thrang?"

He jumped up inwardly, turned around and saw Maya coming up towards him.

"Thinking of someone?" she said.

"As a matter of fact I was,' he replied giving her a shy smile, 'someone as possibly dear to me as I could ever imagine."

"Could you share it with me?" she appealed.

"All I can say is that I love her with all that I have in me; heaven means nothing to me without her. I know that she loves me, yet...... does she love me?"

"What do you mean!" she was concerned.

"What I do not understand is why she would go out with someone she hardly knows? Has she fallen in love with him just like that?" Thrang croaked.

Maya was silent not knowing what to say.

"I feel that I have known her all my life; that I have waited all these years for her. Oh God, why?" he cried.

Thrang choked on his sobs.

"Maya? Please excuse me. I am not myself tonight. I don't know what I'm saying; but I truly love her."

Maya was moved by the deep emotions that were expressed on Thrang's face.

"Thrang?' she tried to console him, 'take a stiff drink and go to bed. The moon has bewitched you; when you wake up tomorrow morning everything will be alright."

Thrang forced a smile on her, "Yes, I suppose you are right,' he said. 'Goodnight Maya," as he slowly made his way to his tent.

Bewitched by the moon? Oh yes! I definitely, am, cried out his heart. *But Ri is engraved in my heart as she will always be.*

He stumbled into his tent, sick and empty at heart.

9

Three days later all the fish in the Lukha River died. Thousands upon thousands of them died.....big and small, some as big as thirty kilogrammes. The river stank with dead fish, floating and washing up to the banks.

The newspapers screamed in their front pages with big headlines and pictures of the dead fishes. The fishermen and the anglers living by the river gave vent to their anger and frustrations as their source of livelihood had been destroyed. They pointed their accusing fingers at the cement plants not too far away. It is the effluents and chemicals washed from the cement factories that have found their way to the river and killed the fish, they shouted. They demanded an immediate enquiry from the state government on the cause of the pollution.

They had never seen or heard of a river turning blue as the Lukha had become.

The cement plants immediately issued statements refuting such allegations. They pointed out that theirs' is a state of the art pollution free technology and no chemicals are ever discharged as it is a dry process. They also welcomed any investigative agency to probe into the matter.

Thrang, as do all at the camp, knew who the real culprit was. It was the damned coal, being mined recently at the water-shed areas of the Lukha River. At the start of their expedition it had rained quite heavily for three days; the sulphur had leached and the rainwater becoming a weak sulphuric acid had, taking some time, found its way into the Lukha River. Thrang had seen it all too often; all the streams and rivers in the coal mining region becoming highly polluted and dead. The beautiful rivers loved by anglers for their sporting mahseers are now, all as lifeless as tepid water in a tub.

Everyone knew this but none dared raise their voices.

The fear and dread of the powerful coal barons held sway. The poor villagers just simply turn their heads the other way and shrug their shoulders as if nothing is amiss. Theirs is to bear the brunt of the spoils when all is done with; for when an area is mined out it is just abandoned. No development or beautifying of the mined area to restore it to its original state is ever attempted.

While the coal barons became richer by the hour the villagers became poorer, for even their rich and fertile lands were being poisoned by the acid, their water sources disappearing and the whole country-side being invaded by cheap labour from Nepal, Bihar and Bangladesh. Their once green and forested hills and dales are now all barren with the crisscrossing of Shaktiman tracks all over the countryside; ugly scars of dusty tracks when dry and slushy and slippery when wet - the total scene pockmarked with huge dumps of coal and slums of miner's tin shacks. *If this is what development is all about then I will have nothing of it,* thundered Thrang in his heart.....*for I see only destruction and filth all around.*

The Meghalaya State Pollution Control Board immediately made their presence felt. They collected samples of the blue water from the river for analyses and made public their preliminary findings as those identical to what was believed by the cavers; that the rainwater had turned into a sulphuric acid after reacting with the sulphur content of the coal and the blue colour being attributed to the reaction of the sulphuric acid with limestone.

The days followed with many a non-governmental organization voicing their concerns at the river pollution by the cement plants or so they claimed.

The return of the eight member team who had spent six days at the village of Sielkan, to push and extend one of the passages in Krem Chympe was an occasion for all to celebrate, more so as the team camping at Semmasi to continue exploration of Krem Tyngheng had also returned that same evening. The Camp was brimming with excitement.

Everyone was back at base camp and a party was beginning to take off, not that it was lacking every evening.

The happy and buoyant mood of the cavers drifted into the kitchen, where the chef was preparing a big feast for them of roast beef, mashed potatoes, rice Palau, mixed vegetable curry, *sambar*, and a huge dish of Russian salad.

The evening started off with plates of hot fried aubergine being served. These were gobbled up in no time. Extra crates of beer were brought up from the store room. A bottle of scotch appeared from somewhere adding variety to the Indian whisky and rum on the table.

Franz, a bottle of beer in his hand which on other evenings would have been a bottle of coke, flushed with excitement of the Krem Chympe exploration and the bubbly beer, spoke with the stirrings of a slur.

"It has been an exciting week for us at Sielkan. The trek down to the village from near the village of Moolian was a beautiful and invigourating experience. On the way down we discovered a deep pot-hole just off the track."

"Goddamned this place!' he exclaimed with a grin, 'It is literally riddled with holes."

"The village headman welcomed us into his spacious hut and ordered his wife to make tea for us. He then led us to a hut, which we took on rent for the week. The one roomed hut belonged to his brother who had temporarily vacated it for our use. It was just off the main cluster of huts in the village and it suited our sojourn very well."

Franz took a swipe of his bottle and enjoying the attention continued.

"For one whole week our breakfast and dinner consisted of rice and some boiled green leafy vegetable, served with the soup. We kind of liked it though."

He looked around, smiled and with a flourish said, "On the last night we were treated to eagle meat, shot by the headman's brother earlier that day."

"Not bad really!" smiled Maya.

"And for one whole week we had to nurse the two bottles of whisky we had with us," grimaced Jon, opening another bottle of Asia 72 for himself.

"What about Sielkan Pouk?" interrupted Thrang, impatient with himself.

"Well, what do you know?" Franz took over, luxuriating in the role of a self proclaimed story-teller.

"Sielkan Pouk is going; after a few swims the passage was all walking, along sand banks and wading at times. We came to this stretch; beautifully decorated with formations of various sizes and colours and practically glittering in the dark .... *The Perfect Passage,* we have named it."

His gaze fell on Thrang, "Yes Thrang, this cave system first explored by you ten years ago is not yet finished ....even today."

"This great and magnificent cave, Krem Chympe or as the local Hmar villagers call, Sielkan – Pielkhlieng Pouk, is today India's sixth longest cave at 12,434 metres in length."

"It is my dream cave," he murmured, deeply lost in his own thoughts.

There were animated voices all around, as beer bottles were being popped open.

The narration of the exploration of Krem Tyngheng near the village of Semmasi had very few takers, though according to Tim .... Krem Tyngheng had more unexplored side-passages as they went deeper and deeper into the cave......would be another great cave system, he proclaimed.....when fully explored.

Dinner was attacked with great gusto especially by the Sielkan party. There was an air of explosive merriment in the camp. The night vibrated with the boisterous and restive cavers.

"Thrang," a voice broke through the din of spirited festivity.

Thrang turned around to face an exuberant Josh, with the once in a blue moon glass of whisky in his hand.

"Thrang," he repeated, "tomorrow we will try to make the connection of Krem Labit (Moolasngi) to Krem Rubong. Would you like to join us on the Krem Rubong team?"

"Brilliant!' Thrang cried out, 'I will not be left out."

He raised his glass of rum to Josh, "Cheers!" he said with a faint slur in his voice. "Tomorrow, we make history."

How do you say 'Cheers' in Khasi? Josh asked.

"*Shakiya*." Thrang replied.

Josh raised his glass of beer, looked at Thrang and in an even and controlled voice, said: "*Shakiya*!"

"*Shakiya*!" Thrang returned his salute.

Beer, whisky and rum flowed that night. The air around the camp was intoxicated with its fumes.

It was one o'clock in the morning when Thrang managed to escape the ribald songs that seemed to pierce the dark and silent night. The cool damp air hit his hot and flushed face as he unsteadily found his way to urinate under the open sky, luxuriating in the simple act of relieving his bursting bladder. He had never ever been so high, he ruefully grimaced to himself as he groped his way to his tent. The warmth and security of his sleepy bag claimed him immediately.

The party gradually died down after half an hour leaving only the die-hards behind, drinking, singing and muttering away into the night.

They too finally staggered to their tents and into their sleeping bags, with the first hint of dawn breaking across the far distant horizon and the stillness of the night being broken by the chirping and chattering of the birds as they flustered about at the events the new day would bring.

10

The next few days were quiet and peaceful with everyone trying to get in as much caving as possible. The end of the year's cave expedition was just four days away and then all of them would be back home to their own work and daily routine.

Teams were coming back to camp late in the evenings, tying up loose ends and trying to push as hard as ever. In life, activities of any kind normally attain a frenzied state on its last legs, so too the activities of the cavers during the last few days. A team of eight decided to finish off Krem Synrang Ngap by spending the whole night in it, only to emerge knackered the next morning, with the cave still offering possibilities of more knee-wrecking passages.

"We have to find a new way in from its southern side," grudgingly muttered Ken, "…. this cave is becoming a bloody hell of a nuisance."

Inwardly he smiled in satisfaction at himself. His theory that all the caves on the ridge were all connected into one great system of over a hundred kilometres was slowly unfolding itself. Over the years back home in England, he had been pondering over these possibilities over and over again. This year's expedition had brought about a distinct pattern at such a possibility.

"---------* Ridge!" he gleefully exclaimed, "I could spend the rest of my life on this ridge connecting all these bloody holes."

Krem Khung had been de-rigged and the ropes washed and cleaned. True to its legend, the cave was still yet a mystery ….winding down and descending through a number of pitches, the cave could probably lead to a sump. In some of its deep crystal clear pools were the greatest collections of blind cave fish that Thrang had ever seen. This would truly be a paradise for the biologist, mused Thrang.

With no second entrance at the lower reaches, Krem Khung had also become a major dilemma for them. Unless another entrance is found soon, further exploration of the cave would be hampered for it would take four hours to descend the shaft and reach the last point of survey and another four hours or more to get out, leaving no time for any forward exploration. Future teams would have to bivouac inside and test their muscles and mental capability to the limit.

With a vertical range of 307 metres and a mapped passage of 9.1 kilometres Krem Khung still held out on its secrets. I am sure, thought Thrang inwardly smiling to himself, Krem Khung will beat Synrang Pamiang as India's deepest cave … there is no doubt about that. As all cavers have their own favourite cave, so too did Thrang have in Krem Khung….a sojourn of hope, trust and down to earth reality…. an elixir to his childhood secret of fantasy.

The connection of Krem Labit (Moolesngi) to Krem Rubong went like clock-work precision. While Jon, Maya, Patrick and Clive abseiled down the Krem Labit entrance shaft, working their way downstream the second team of Josh, Andre, Grethel and Thrang worked their way up from the horizontal entrance of Krem Rubong.

Krem Rubong was one of the first caves on the Ridge to have been explored eight years ago; a beautiful cave with red glittering flowstone not seen anywhere, it ended abruptly at a huge boulder collapse. Attempts to pass through that boulder collapse had proved futile; *it was too dangerous.*

The recent discovery of Krem Labit (Moolesngi) and the direction it was heading to, gave a fresh impetus to the expedition to try another attempt through the collapse. That was where the two teams were heading for from the two ends.

The Rubong team soon reached the red glittering flowstone and the virgin gours or dry fairy pools above.

"This is really very pretty. I have never seen anything like it!" exclaimed Grethel excitedly.

Thrang smiled broadly, "It is, isn't it?"

"This is where we take off our boots," he said as he began taking off his.

They negotiated the beautiful stretch of formations on their stocking feet.

They got back into their boots only when they reached the cliff, where they squeezed through a very small opening and climbed down the cliff using a flexible wire ladder. They traversed a canyon passage, a duck and they were at the far end of the cave facing the mountain of boulders blocking their way, which was why they were there that day….*to find a way through.*

They could not have timed it more perfectly.

As they stood facing the impregnable wall, more like Ali Baba waiting for a door to open, they heard voices from the other side of the rocks. They looked at each other and smiled.

"Did you hear that?" Josh looked enquiringly at Thrang.

"Sure did. It must be them!" Thrang replied triumphantly.

Josh cupped his mouth and hollered, "Helloooo......helloooo!"

Immediately the rocks answered, "Hello there!"

It was un-mistakingly Jon's voice.

"Hi Jon!' shouted Josh, 'How's the weather on your side?"

"It is hot, suffocating and claustrophobic!" was the laboured reply from somewhere deep in the rocks.

"Okay Jon! Just work your way towards my voice," said Josh, as he began guiding Jon out of the rocks.

All eyes were trained somewhere on the rocks above where they thought the voice was emanating, when suddenly out popped Jon from the boulders beneath their feet.

"What are you all gazing at?...... the stars?" grinned Jon with his face all smeared with slime, not unlike a camouflaged soldier in combat, as he slid through the crack in the rocks and stood up.

There were handshakes and congratulations all around as Maya, Patrick and Clive also emerged from the rocks one after the other, all disheveled and dirty faced.

"This is a great occasion," asserted Patrick, shaking his head in amazement.

"It sure damn is," replied Thrang, looking at him.

"A celebration is called for tonight!" he ended, nodding his head in agreement.

"Well? We have to survey this section through the boulder collapse" said Jon as he got himself ready for the purpose.

"Joining us Thrang?"

"Sure," Thrang said.

They crawled back in through the boulders, working their way up and down and sideways, always careful not to dislodge any rock. Once in the section of Krem Labit they began surveying from its last survey point and retraced their way back through the mass of rocks to the other last survey point of Krem Rubong. It was a very tricky maneuver which required quite a bit of effort. Taking readings in such tight and cramped spaces proved to be quite a nightmare for Thrang.

Their job done and with a lot of time on their hands, they busied themselves with taking lots of photographs of Krem Rubong.

Not to be outdone, another team which had been poking around the shaft of Krem Wah Lukor also hit jackpot that same day.

Crawling on knees and hands through grubby passage they soon encountered a big walking size passage. Their hearts rose at the new discovery… it is always such a thrill when passages open up to lead on and on to its deep dark and unknown secrets. As they were mapping, Ken noticed a small round red mark on the wall.

"Fred!' he said, 'I think we are into known passage."

"See here," as he pointed to the survey mark.

Fred's spirit which was so high a few moments ago sagged and said, "Oh!" in a very disappointed voice.

"And which cave is this?" as he looked crestfallen at Ken.

Ken scratched his bristly graying stubble of a beard, screwed his eyes and with a broad smile on his face said, "We are in Krem Umthloo, I'm sure of it."

Having made the connection they then thoroughly searched the vicinity for any holes worth investigating. And who would find that hole worth investigating but Ken himself…..*the mole-man*; as he scrambled up into a claustrophobic rat-hole and belly-crawled in.

Fred and Katrin stood and watched dumbfounded. Belly-crawling was not much fun to Fred; his weak knees could not withstand the ordeal of them scraping and pressing against the rocks and hard floor, more so that day when he had forgotten to wear his knee-pads. Serves me right to forget when I do really need them, he muttered disgustingly to himself.

They stood, listening to the grunts and curses of the labouring Ken.

Bloody skinny bastard, thought Fred of Ken; *he can slid in where no one else can*, as he looked at his own barrel chest and felt his big fat head; *I can't get in there*, he swore at himself.

"Fred…..Katrin!" the muffled shout of Ken came floating out from deep inside the rat-hole, "Come in … follow me."

Braving the ordeal, Fred scrambled up the ledge and trying to press his whole body flat and close to the ground he inched his tortuous way in, followed by Katrin a few paces behind. *A mad man in front of him racing away and a lovely slim brunette calmly and easily belly-crawling behind him, Fred cursed himself at being caught in such a situation for with his huge bulk, he had to keep up with the pull of the mad man and the push of the beauty.*

The low meandering crawl was agony. Fred felt as if his sore knees were torn and bleeding and his neck stiff and aching from bending.

"Oh God! Will this -------- crawl ever end?"* he cried in misery. *And to think that I joined the expedition because of the big river caves so typical to Meghalaya.*

The crawl did end fifty-five metres away. Ken was waiting for him, coolly sitting on a rock writing his notes in a notebook.

Ken looked up at his arrival and Katrin immediately behind him and casually proclaimed, "We are now inside Krem Synrang Labit."

"So chaps, this means that we have today, connected Krem Umthloo to Krem Wah Lukor and to Krem Synrang Labit," he proudly ended.

"What?" they cried in unison, for both of them had never been in Krem Synrang Labit before. Incredibility was writ large on their faces.

"Yes, we now have a system that is eighteen kilometres long; and by my reckoning India's third longest cave."

"But the hell of it all is this: *Why wasn't, these passages pushed earlier?*" Ken gravely lamented, "It is another classic case of CHECKED ALL PASSAGES."

The evenings in the camp had become more animated, more frenzied and more boisterous with the end of the expedition close at hand; everyone working overtime; updating notes, drawing up plans, feeding data to their laptops and, of course, overtime partying.

The linking of Krem Labit (Moolesngi) to Krem Rubong had proved to be very significant as it had been established hydrologically that it is part of the larger system of Krem Liat Prah. What would be needed would be diving equipment to attempt the sump and physically connect the two systems. Meghalaya would then have a thirty kilometre cave system.

"Yes!" Ken proudly pointed his finger at the caves plotted on the wall map of the Ridge, "This Liat Prah system should be connected to Synrang Ngap and to Synrang Labit-Umthloo and some of these smaller caves around here…." as he traced his finger along the cave plans.

"As I said, we have, a huge cave system under our feet; potentially more than a hundred kilometres …" as his eyes flashed daringly, with conviction and belief, at some of the skeptics smiling knowingly at him.

If I had my way...... a crowbar, chisel and hammer...... a few sticks of dynamite ......I'd bore my___ way ......yeah, oh, oh, yeah ...... These___* holes would open up...... yeah, oh, oh, yeah......I'd travel the length......along subterranean streams...... and come out ___* in China ......yeah, oh, oh, yeah...... I'd come out ___* in China...,* he sang in that rich baritone voice of his; a bit dragged and slurred, as he popped open another beer and settled himself on his haunches beside the brightly glowing fire.

Thrang was savouring the cool open air under the star spangled sky. Shooting stars whizzed past his head far away in the horizon. He had never seen so many of them in the space of a few minutes. He must wish something for himself he thought and looked up at the sky ready to wish at the sight of another streak.

It was long in coming, but when it did Thrang was ready. "God, I love Ri! Let her love me back," he prayed, with the intensity of one totally lost in love, as the blaze of star-light burnt through the dark expanse in a couple of seconds.

Fancy me thinking and behaving like a teenager, he smiled ruefully to himself. *But Ri has really got into me. I feel as if I have known her all my life and my heart aches to imagine that she is going out with some nitwit this very moment. God, but it does hurt! Can I ever forget her? I don't believe I ever will.*

He looked up into the night with the sky speckled with millions of twinkling stars. His eyes searched and found the constellation of Orion, brilliant and watchful as ever like the great hunter he was. *Yes,* he thought to himself, *I will be like the legendary hunter Orion ...... I will always keep my sights on Ri.*

He breathed long and deep the cold fresh air, pungent with the whiff of the pine trees. When he felt he had somewhat controlled his emotions, he rubbed his eyes and taking a last look at Orion, he turned back to join the others at the fire dancing merrily in the night.

Am I the hunter? He mused, closing his eyes and creasing his forehead. *No! I have been willingly and blissfully captured, heart and soul......and I would have it no other way.*

11

"Bah Thrang? Hey, Bah Thrang?"

The faraway voice broke into the sleep-wearied, head-throbbing brain of Thrang.

He fought the sleep off his eyes, cursed the voice calling his name and tried to clear his mind as the bright sunlight pierced through the fabric of his tent. He groggily looked at his watch, saw that it was nine o'clock and shook himself up. He had overslept; he had had a bit too much that night.

He must keep himself in check and not drift away into a drugged state; it is so easy to succumb and let go, he visualized, still reluctant to get out of bed.

"Bah Thrang?" the voice was persistent.

Thrang shook his head, stretched his body and tensed his muscles. He unzipped his sleeping bag, slipped out and unzipped the tent.

The headman of Shnongrim village, Kendro Dkhar, stood there smiling at him. Accompanying him was another man, Thrang did not recognize.

"Hello, Bah!" Thrang greeted him, "I slept very late last night. In fact, it was early this morning," Thrang apologized, smiling sheepishly at him.

"I am so sorry to have disturbed your sleep, Bah," the headman said, feeling a bit awkward at the early intrusion. He took off his woolen cap and scratched his head furiously, "As you are leaving tomorrow, I just came to wish you all the very best….. I won't be here tomorrow as I'm leaving for Shillong today to attend to some business and I'm probably staying overnight."

"Come, have a cup of tea,' Thrang said as he led the headman and his friend to the kitchen-shed. "Just give me a few minutes to wash up."

Having done his toiletry, Thrang found the headman and his friend chatting with Ban, drinking tea.

Thrang sat on an oil-tin turned upside down and was offered a steaming cup of tea by the beaming cook, "Morning Bah," he wished.

"Good morning," he wished in reply.

The headman looked at Thrang, "Bah,'....he hesitated.... 'Could you give me one of your calendars?"

"Sure will,' Thrang said, 'I have one kept aside for you."

Thrang returned a minute later with the calendar and presented it to the headman who was all smiles. The twelve beautiful pictures appearing on the different calendar months were all of the caves of the Shnongrim region. These are the pictures sought after by the villagers to proudly adorn their homes.

"This is my friend from Jalaphet, Bah Linus Dkhar," he said introducing his friend to Thrang. The two shook hands acknowledging each other.

The headman put his cup of tea down, cleared his throat and said, "Bah, there will be an election for the new Daloi sometime next month. We hope to get Welborn Sukhlain from our village, elected."

"That will be good, for all of us,' expressed Thrang. 'Bah Welborn is a good and very helpful person. He had told us of many caves and even led us to some of them, including Krem Liat Prah which is now turning out to be the longest cave system in India," he added.

The headman and Bah Linus accepted the *kwai* offered by Lung as they both rose to their feet.

"Bah Linus, a long time ago sometime in the early eighties I think, I remember reading in the local newspaper about your village; where two anti-socials or criminals were apprehended by the village, beaten up and killed and their bodies thrown into a cave. The police from Jowai went to investigate, but could not retrieve the bodies for the shaft was very deep. With no evidence no case could be filed and the matter ended to be soon forgotten. Do you know anything about it? Is the cave really deep?" Thrang asked him.

Linus appeared surprised at the question but nevertheless proud to respond.

"Yes, what you read was true. It happened many years ago; and the cave is very deep. But if you were to enter that cave you will not find only two skeletons; you would probably find hundreds, if the underground river has not washed them away."

"Hundreds?"

"Yes, hundreds; for any criminals caught in the village, are summarily disposed off and dumped into the shaft."

Thrang wasn't sure to believe him or not, but smiling at him said, "We would like to come to your village one day to explore this cave."

"Bah, let me know when you plan to come. I will sort out the permission with the headman, okay?"

"Yes, I will contact you first."

"Bah,' the Shnongrim village headman interrupted, "We must be off, otherwise we would not get our work done in Shillong."

He pumped Thrang's hand in a furious and emotional sort of way, "Bah, you have brought honour to our village and elaka and the world now know of us. We are very grateful to you and your team; we are just simple folks and we need you to help and protect us from the imminent disaster that we feel we will have to face."

"Our leaders are with the rich and powerful; we cannot raise our voices against them and we are slowly being squeezed out of our own lands," he softly uttered, looking furtively left and right, as if the trees would hear him.

Thrang looked into his eyes and felt a great warmth for this rustic soul before him. "Bah Kendro,' he said, 'You are a good man. A man of God and of the people; I am proud to know you and to be of any service to you. You have my address so whenever you are in Shillong please come over.'

'I shall certainly do my best to try to stop the destruction that is being done on this Ridge by the mining activities," he assured him as he felt the hard and callous hand on his two own urban smooth and soft ones.

"Thank you Bah, for this calendar,' he said, reluctant to move, 'I hope to see you all again next year."

He turned to leave, walked a few steps, stopped and turned around again, "Bah? Pease take care of yourself; the world is full of evil and there are so many murders taking place every day, especially in these areas. These once innocent hills are today a hotbed of deceit and lawlessness," he said, turning back and walking off resolutely with Linus by his side.

Thrang felt a sense of premonition and a shiver went up his spine. But he was a man with steel in his heart and a pugnacious soul under the cool and calm exterior of his demeanour. His face was a picture of unruffled calmness, which belied the volatile anger he felt.

He felt the arteries in his body flow with the heat of outraged environmental abuse and deprivation of the poor villager's subsistence, the intrusive invasion of the so-called development shattering the quiet and peaceful village solitude, the complete reversal of the perfect harmony the villagers had lived for generations with nature ... all brought about by the greed of a few unscrupulous and money-hungry individuals who would not think twice in robbing their own toothless grandmother.

Thrang resolved to go his way and never be cowed down by any intimidation or threat. There had been times when his bulldog attitude would get him into trouble but that was his character ...... *the explosive aggressiveness always hidden beneath his cool exterior, ready to erupt at the slightest provocation of any danger to the environment he lived in.*

The day was very warm; just the perfect day for getting the equipment washed and dried. All the ongoing vertical caves had been de-rigged the day earlier and the ropes hauled and brought back to camp. It was a busy day for the cavers who had stayed back in camp. Some of them had taken the ropes to the camp's spring water a hundred metres away, where they were scrubbed clean of all the dirt and grime. Personal equipment and other personal effects were washed and soon dried under the hot sun.

The rest had gone caving, trying to get as many more metres as possible in that their last day of the expedition; and it was a fruitful day indeed for them for they harvested 700 and odd metres of new cave passage, with the added discovery of another promising pot-hole. That had always been the trend; to discover more caves than they could explore.

That afternoon, there was a visit from the inspector. The case was far from being anywhere near solved. The inspector was glum faced and not happy at all.

"Thrang? I hear that you are all leaving tomorrow?" he said.

"Yes!' Thrang replied, 'Our expedition has come to an end and we will be winding up tomorrow."

The inspector produced a notebook from his pocket and handed it to Thrang,

"Please write down your address and mobile number, in case I do need to contact you," he said.

Thrang complied and handed back the notebook to the inspector.

"Inspector,' he slowly voiced his thoughts, 'How can you ever solve any crime with thousands and thousands of migrant labourers all over the country side?"

The inspector shook his head, "It is a real nightmare," he declared, "...with none of them registered; how could you identify anyone? He is here today and gone tomorrow." He took the cup of tea he had been nursing and drowned the remains in one gulp.

"Yes, the life of a policeman in this sub-division is so frustrating and dangerous too," he quietly added.

They chatted on for the next half an hour before the inspector left with his assistants following behind him.

The last of the cavers had returned back to camp by 8 PM. Thrang had seen their lights a kilometre away as they came into view from the bend on the slopes; Tim, Jon, Maya and Jorge. He knew it was them as all the others had been accounted for. He waited out for them in the dark night, his eyes following the flickering and bobbing up and down of their LEDS. Soon he lost sight of the lights as the fog appearing from nowhere began to envelope the hillside.

Lately, he had developed a habit of coming out and standing all alone in the silent night; whether it is a moonlit night, a starry night or an absolute pitch dark night. The peace and tranquility of the night brings about a passionate solitude to his troubled soul. *Here in the open, dark night, no one could see the innermost feelings of loneliness reflected on his calm and inscrutable face,* he imagined. Ri filled his mind, his heart and his soul. His eyes see her everywhere.....the trees swaying to the breeze breathes out her name, as his senses swooned to the fragrance carried by the gentle breeze.

He was suddenly brought back to earth from his reverie.

"Jolly good day, Thrang!" Tim bore down the slope to camp with his long and easy stride, "This cave is still going; plenty more to do on this Ridge next year."

"And the next year, and the next year," joined in Jorge, his suit wet and covered in mud

"Wonderful!" replied Thrang, "that means we can still have our base camp on this Ridge, at this same site."

"Yes! This Ridge would still be excellent for next year," said Tim, as he strained to pull his feet out of his slippery and muddied boots.

Activity inside the bon-fire enclosure had started to spill over into the misty night. It was eerie, thought Thrang, as he entered the noisy din. The enclosure was thick with smoke from the not too happy fire. His eyes smarting, he retreated out into the open air and shouted for the cook's assistants to bring in dry and smaller logs for the fire.

Gopal and Vishnu soon appeared carrying smaller pieces of dried chopped logs. In a few minutes they had the fire roaring brightly. It was the cue for the party to begin.

It was another evening of fried aubergines for snacks. Straight from the kitchen, the aubergines were hot and delicious with the outer gram-flour layer crisp and golden. It did not take long for the aubergines to disappear.

A last minute rush of writing reports, feeding data and drawing up cave plans filled the work room to capacity.

"Seventeen point eight, twenty seven degree, minus one, one point five, three, two point five, one point two; ...nine point three, thirty six degree, minus one point five, zero, three point five, two, one point five; ...five point seven, thirty two degree, zero, three point five, zero, two, one point five;" the monotone voice of Andre could be heard over the confusion of noises, as Jon was feeding the laptop.

"Hey Thrang!" yelled Katrin over the pandemonium, "What does Krem Mih Tdem mean?"

"Literally, Krem Mih Tdem means cave with smoke coming out; in this case it would mean vapour or air belching cave," he replied coming towards her.

"I think it would be appropriate to call this cave as Vapour Cave, don't you think?" he suggested hesitatingly.

"Sounds good to me,' she said, 'so Vapour Cave it shall be!"

The sound of a strumming guitar wafted through the din, trying desperately to drown the hullabaloo.....soon to be joined by someone attacking the drums. It was a cacophony of sounds and getting madder by the minute.

The last night camp-party finally got underway after dinner when all expedition work was over or shelved for the night. Some of the local villagers had also joined in as had become the custom every year, bringing their own musical instruments with them --- the mandolin and the harmonica. It was a gala evening of music.....a perfect blend of assorted cultures. Music was the language they communicated and during the whole night session the motley group was one soul.....understanding and acknowledging each other. It was a night the local musicians always look forward to.....with pride that one day, they would be able to tell their grand children of their musical tryst with the mad foreign cavers from far away lands.

The mist had lifted and the silent sky was star-lit, except that the calm night was not silent. It was reverberating with the excited sounds of happy people.....happy with the expedition, the hospitality of the locals and the friendship they have made and cemented.

This is what life is all about, Tim mused thoughtfully to himself, ... *it was fifteen years ago when I first came to Meghalaya and I've not missed a single year since then. I have made so many friends and my life has been so enriched with each expedition.*

He looked deep into his heart and the years that have gone by and realized that this country was his second home with its green hills, great caves and friendly people and he smiled with a feeling of belonging, when he remembered the first time he had come to Meghalaya, he had slept in a mustard seed godown and eaten nothing but plain boiled rice, in a wild and far obscure place in South Garo Hills. He did not mind the hardships; just the hope to find caves to explore was all that really mattered.

"Thrang,' he said, slurring a bit, 'A great expedition! One of my best; I think it is destiny that brought us together; and we have come a long way indeed."

Thrang looked at him and smiled, "Yes, I believe so. Do you remember when you first came we didn't even have a proper helmet? Yes, our association has been wonderful; this is something I shall always cherish and be proud of." *And in the process I have discovered myself,* acknowledged Thrang, a feeling of emotion overtaking him.

Dawn was silently breaking over the horizon and the party had fizzled to a couple of diehards still nursing their bottles, when Thrang stumbled sleepily to his tent. The last thing he remembered was taking off his boots and socks before the silvery dawn claimed his groggy-mind.

12

Thrang felt as if he had been roused from his sleep a few minutes later. Through his muddled mind he could hear people moving about and a lot of talking going on. He could not comprehend what was all the activity about. He thought he was dreaming, when he suddenly heard Ban's voice giving directions, "Ma Korin, unloosen that rope holding the roof first .... I need to put it away....then get some help to fold the tarpaulins."

Then, it dawned on him; the expedition was over and the camp was being dismantled. They were leaving for Shillong that day. Sleepy as he was, he had to get up. He forced his eyes open and the brightness of the sun even through the tent blinded him for a moment. He could feel the day warming up; he relaxed for another few minutes, looked at the time on his watch and was amazed that it was already ten o'clock. He felt guilty that he had slept so late and hastily pushed himself up.

Outside, everyone seemed to be up and busy. The tarpaulins and plastic sheets from the camp roof were being taken off, individual tents were dismantled and neatly folded in their bags, equipment packed into steel trunks, the camp site was cleaned of all rubbish which was all put in a heap and burnt.

Thrang brushed his teeth, shaved and had a quick wash. He felt so thirsty; his throat was parched and he had difficulty in swallowing...... *too much spirit.*

He made his way straight to the kitchen where the cook had a steaming cup of tea ready for him. He sat on the grass under the bright hot sun sipping the scalding liquid. He was perspiring profusely as he got the liquid past the arid zone of his throat into the welcome embrace of his belly. Soon he felt like a human being again. He got himself another cup of tea and refused the breakfast offered him......*he would not be able to hold any solid food for the next hour or so*, he felt.

Within the next hour all the steel trunks containing caving equipment, tarpaulin and plastic sheets, haversacks heavy with personal effects, plastic chairs and other knickknacks were loaded into the back of the big bus, which had arrived that morning, to take them back to Shillong. Thrang realized he had yet to load his personal stuff into the bus. He popped back into his tent and looked round his little cosy space that had served as his private sleeping quarters during the last three weeks. He had packed most of his stuff late last night, leaving just the sleeping bag, a few clothes and his toiletry. As he was folding the sleeping bag he heard his name being called out.

"I'm here, Ban" he shouted.

"Can you come out for a minute?" Ban asked.

Thrang stopped his work and crawled out of his tent.

"This small boy wants to talk to you," Ban said, indicating the boy with him.

He was one of the boys who regularly frequented the camp, oftentimes guiding and showing them new caves.

"Hello Morningstar?" Thrang smiled.

"Phin liet noh mynta ka sngi? Are you going back today?" The boy asked in Khasi.

"Ho'iod, kumne sa shi kynta ei ei. Yes, in the next hour or so."

"Bah, nga kwah ban pynih krem ia phi. Bah, I want to show you a cave," the boy stammered.

"Ymdon por shuh ban liet piet krem mynta. Ngin sa ia liet ha uwei u snem. There is no more time to go look at this cave. We will go see next year."

Morningstar fidgeted, shuffling from one foot to the other.

"Ka bha ba phi liet piet mynta. Kam jyngai nang ne. It will be good for you to see the cave today. It is not far from here."

"Ymdon por shuh mynta. Hynrei, lada phi kwah bai ialam ngan ai san spah ia phi mynta; ngin sa ialiet piet patde la shimsnem ynda ngi wan biang. There is no more time now. However, if you want your guide fees I will give five hundred now; we can see the cave next year when we come back." Thrang said taking out his wallet.

Morningstar shook his head.

"Em, ngam kwah pisa. Nga kwah tang ban pynih kane ka krem ia phi. Sngewbha she Bah, ia liet piet. Ngin ym slem; tang shiteng kynta ngi la wan phai. No, I don't want any money. I just want to show you the cave. Please Bah, let us go. We will not be late; just half an hour and we'll be back."

Thrang was perplexed. Why is Morningstar so insistent. He was normally a quiet and silent boy.

"Where is the cave?" He asked in Khasi.

"On the other side of that road up there," was the reply.

"And the name?"

"It has no name."

"Are you sure I can get back within half an hour?"

"Absolutely! It is close by."

"Okay then. Let us hurry; I don't want to disappoint you. Let me just get my headlight."

"Here take mine,' Ban offered, 'you must have packed away yours."

"Thanks Ban."

"Let's go." He said, turning to the boy.

They hurried up the slope to the road on top of the ridge, walked along it for some distance; then down the other side of the ridge till they came upon a forest path which led them along parallel to the road above and further away from camp. We are going in the direction of Krem Risang, Thrang thought. Twenty minutes had already elapsed and Thrang was getting worried.

"How far?" Thrang ventured to ask.

"Not far now."

After a few more minutes of walking, Thrang could not contain himself anymore.

"Are we going to Krem Risang?"

"No, very close to it."

"Then it must be Krem Skei?"

"About a hundred metres away from Krem Skei."

Thrang was ready to turn back, but after having come so far he may as well get it over with. He decided that he would just look at the entrance to confirm whether or not the cave had been recorded earlier; then rush back to camp. In the same breath he couldn't understand how they had missed the cave if it was that close to Krem Risang or Krem Skei, for the area had been well explored.

When they reached Krem Risang, they turned downhill, walking parallel to the gully. As they neared Krem Skei Morningstar decided not to go any further.

"If you keep going down you won't miss it," Morningstar said, sitting down on the grassy hillside.

"But that is Krem Skei," Thrang complained.

"Yes, but this cave is just less than a hundred metres below Krem Skei."

"But why are you not coming with me? You were insistent on showing me the cave."

Morningstar grimaced.

"I just hurt my foot. I have to rest awhile. I thought you should go on so as not to be late."

Thrang was stumped. What is happening? This is totally weird and strange. Something is terribly wrong, he thought. He was tempted to turn his back and walk off but the lure of a new cave just metres away proved too much.

"Alright, I'll have a quick look."

He continued walking down along the edge of the thick covered bush of the gully. He was almost upon Krem Skei when he heard a loud piercing whistle which he was sure was from Morningstar. He was startled and alarmed. His inner sense told him something was not right. He stopped in his tracks, hesitated, and scanned the deep forest cover. Something warned his alerted mind when he heard a faint click. Instinctively he dived into the thicket rolling down the steep slope, a moment not too soon as heard the crack of a rifle. The hair on the nape of his neck froze and he was visibly shaken. He heard movement coming towards him. He was now in battle mood as adrenaline surged through his body. He was in extreme danger he realized. He swiftly got up and ran the few metres into the dark embrace of the cave. Once inside, he took out his headlamp from his pocket and fixed it on his head and as he heard feet running down the jungle to the mouth of the cave he swiftly made his way deeper into the cave. He then crouched behind a boulder and switched off his light. He could clearly see an armed man trying to peer into the dark passage. Thrang waited, watching what the assassin would do; moments later he saw the man shine a torch and cautiously enter the underground after him. Thrang summoned his thoughts as to his next step; he was not unduly worried for there was another entrance he could get out from. Slowly he got up from his crouching position, took off his headlight and cupped it in his hand, shining it along the floor with just enough light for him to creep away. Glancing back he could see that he was gaining on his pursuer, though he was careful not to make any noise. He cursed himself for falling into such a trap; he would have been shot and killed had it not been for the strange behaviour of the boy which alerted his senses. These people are now using little kids to lure him away, alone and vulnerable in the open. He realized that he was a marked man and that he has to watch his back every moment – it was a terrifying prospect to think. As he left the main trunk passage and entered the side passage on his right which would lead him to the other entrance and to freedom just a hundred metres away, he was startled to see someone approaching from that end. He froze and stopped in his tracks immediately switching off his light. He could see that the man was just fifty metres away and that he too was armed. Thrang slowly backed off, back into the main trunk passage, cupping his headlamp close to the ground and hiding the light in front of his body. He hoped the man had not seen his light which would give him an added advantage of a few more seconds. These are local guys he thought, they know the cave well and therefore had it well covered. He hoped and prayed that they were not as conversant with the cave as he was, for he knew of another entrance far ahead, though a very tight one. He now crept along with urgency as if the devil was after him. He felt the tightness in his stomach and the short and laboured breaths he was enduring. What if the crack is choked? With the heavy soil erosion it could very easily happen. Fear gripped his soul as he hurried like a mad man to the little window on the roof that could be his salvation.

He briefly glanced back to see the two pursuers had met and their lights searching for him, all along the passage. Then the lights steadily came toward him. He knew he would be dead meat if the window in the roof is choked. He scrambled, not bothered about the noise any more till he reached the climb to the relic passage. There he had to transfer his headlamp from his hand to his forehead so as to free his hands for climbing. He knew he would be totally exposed and at the mercy of his pursuers. He had to make a quick exit otherwise he was a goner.

He relaxed, taking slow easy breaths and tensed his muscles for the scramble up the climb. His pursuers were very close when he made a dash – up the loose and unstable slope. All the energy that he had left with him was spent on that one mad rush of rejuvenated exhilaration. Rocks tumbled as he clawed up the loose and slippery incline. There was a shot which ricocheted above his head, as he saw them bearing upon him. He slipped and would have tumbled down had he not caught hold of a short and stout stalagmite growing near the wall. Another shot and he was still miraculously intact. The next shot he feared would surely find its mark. With that extra energy born of certain and imminent death he scaled the last few metres to reach the relatively safe haven of the relic passage, where he was confronted with thousands of disturbed and agitated bats. He pressed his body close to the floor, recouping from the exhausted effort. Hearing excited voices beneath him he desperately crawled towards the last little passage that would lead him to the outside world. He felt the strong cool draught flow through the crawl. *It is still there. The window is still open. I am saved*; his heart sang as renewed energy flowed through his tiring muscles. He saw lights bouncing off the roof as the two men attempted the climb. He had to act fast. Once they were over the top he would be slaughtered like a rabid dog.

As he was about to reach for the hole, he noticed a green pit viper resting on a small ledge. He stood still, stupefied at the venomous creature, though he couldn't help admiring its beautiful bright green colour. Transfixed, he wondered what he should do; he had nothing on him to drive off the snake. He couldn't waste time either searching for rocks for the pursuers were closing in on him. He simply had to take a risk and go past the viper, hoping that it was still hibernating and too lethargic to strike at him. Without a second thought he plunged into the narrow crack, pushing himself through slippery mud and rock. He grunted his efforts through the tight squeeze, keeping his head at floor level as he had no helmet for protection. The squeeze was only ten metres long but it felt endless when one is desperately fighting one's way through. He lay limp on his belly, taking slow easy long breaths and then gradually eased his way out inch by inch through the clammy 'devil's throat'. He could almost smell the sunlight out in the open hillside. Getting caught in the belly-crawl would be a catastrophe and a horrible one at that.

A last surge of adrenaline and he pulled himself out of the crack into the warm and inviting sunshine. The familiar surroundings could not have presented a more splendid sight for him to behold. He did not wait to see what was happening behind him. He imagined that the viper would delay them for a few moments longer before one of them smash its head with the rifle butt. Escape and safety was paramount in his mind as he ran into the forest cover of the gully working his way uphill. When he passed Krem Risang he broke cover and ran up the hillside to the road above on the ridge. He was panting and totally exhausted by then but he was not worried anymore. They would not come chasing after him now; they could however take a potshot at him if he was in their sight. Catching up on his wheezing breath he jogged along the road, only increasing his speed when he thought he would be in open view of his pursuers. He stopped when he was sure he was safe and started walking back to camp. He could feel his body quivering with all the emotions of the ordeal he had just gone through. It was then that he realized the gravity of the situation he was in. He was just flesh and blood and friable. Was life worth the risk of taking the might and ire of the miners? In the end would his life be worth anything? But deep in his heart he knew he will always be what he has always been – true to himself and his beliefs. Life has a meaning – a meaning of respect for all life and its environs. He would not in any way willingly be a cause, however minuscule, to the destruction of the only hospitable planet.

What has happened to the boy he thought. Morningstar could not have got involved in this. He is just a kid. But I've got to talk to talk to him – find out who the men were.

From the top of the ridge he saw a crowd had gathered in the now empty camp area; another group was hurrying up the slope, probably going to his aid. When they saw him they stopped and waited for him to come down.

"What on earth happened to you?" Joe exclaimed, seeing him covered in mud that was slowly drying up on him.

"I was waylaid near Krem Skei. Two guys with rifles. I was disturbed by Morningstar's odd behavior – something was not right I'd thought to myself. Luckily enough for me for I hesitated, and in that instant I thought I saw a glint of a rifle barrel. Instinctively I dived and rolled down the few metres to the mouth of Krem Skei. The bullet had missed me. They chased me into the cave but I escaped through the 'devil's throat'. I would have been cornered had this entrance been choked. As it is I barely escaped with my life. I don't know if the two gunmen exited from the squeeze after me or retreated back into the cave to exit from the main entrance. In any case they would have long disappeared by now, I presume."

"This is very serious business. You were very lucky Thrang," Ken said, patting Thrang's shoulder. "We would never have forgiven ourselves had anything happened to you."

Thrang aclnowledged their concern for him.

"But I'm safe and now here with you all," he mumbled, feeling distressing emotions rising inside him.

"Thank God!" muttered Ken.

"Where is the boy?" Thrang asked Ken.

"It was the boy who alerted us. He came running down, shouting and crying. He was unintelligible but after some coaxing we managed to get the story from him. It appears that he does not know the two men. He has never seen them before. He said that the two men wanted to talk to you in private on some urgent matter; that he was persuaded to entice you to that spot. When he refused they pleaded with him and even pressed a one thousand rupee note into his hand, promising him that they would give him another thousand after the meeting. In all innocence the boy was simply persuaded, never imagining that any harm could befall you. He is now devastated thinking that you are dead and it was his fault. Some elders of the village including the assistant headman are down there, about to join us in the search for you."

There was jubilation when the crowd saw Thrang coming down toward them. Morningstar stood up from where he was sitting, weeping inconsolably and clasped Thrang tightly saying he didn't know they were going to shoot him and that he was very sorry for his part in it. Thrang patted his back and told him not to worry – how was he to know. Anyway no damage had been done and so all is well, Thrang consoled him. Gradually the boy disengaged himself after having somehow controlled his sad and sorrowful experience.

"I will show you more caves next year," he said, trying to smile at Thrang.

"I'm sure you will. And I'm looking forward to next year." Thrang smiled back at him.

"Can you tell me something about those men?" Thrang coaxed him.

Morningstar closed his eyes as if in deep thought and then looked directly at Thrang.

"I don't think those men are from this area, otherwise I would have got a hint even if I don't recognise them. Both are young men of not more than thirty years of age and both sport moustaches. One of them however is slightly darker and shorter than the other. They also appear to be quite rich; the dark shorter man took out a big bundle of notes from his pocket and forced me to take a thousand rupee note. It is difficult to describe any of them as there is nothing extraordinary about their appearances; they appear like any other rural village folk. And oh yes, both of them were reeking of alcohol. They were somewhat tipsy."

"Would you recognise them if you see them again?"

"I think so," the boy murmured.

There were discussions as to the identity of the two assassins but everyone knew it would be hard to pinpoint anyone. Most likely they would not be from any of the villages nearby. And they were sure the two men would keep their distance and never show their faces to the boy.

"Bah, I have packed all your stuff and loaded them in the black Scorpio," Ban informed him.

"Thanks Ban."

There were farewells and handshakes all around.

"Bah, go in peace and we expect you back next year. You are a brave man, but be alert always. You never know where danger will come from," the assistant headman said, shaking Thrang's hand. "I am glad nothing bad happened to you. Had you been killed our village would have had to bear the stigma for ever, even though the perpetrators were outsiders. God be with you in whatever you do."

"I will and thank you all for your help, co-operation and goodwill. We will surely be back next year. In any case it was a great expedition this year too. Excellent it was!"

The assistant headman suddenly had a thought.

"Bah, why don't you file an F.I.R. with the police?" He suggested.

Thrang thought for a while, absorbing the suggestion.

"It did occur to me, but what's the point? It will only add to the heavy work load of the district police. Moreover I don't even know who those ruffians were. It will only be a waste of time and effort."

The assistant headman looked unruffled.

"I agree with you. Even then, I think it would be wise to inform the police. At least they would know that such nefarious activities are going on and that vested interests are out to get you."

"Okay, if you put it that way,' Thrang conceded, 'on my way I will drop by the police station and file my F.I.R. Now I think we should really be moving. I have unnecessarily delayed our departure and with the heavy traffic on the national highway, I'm afraid we are going to reach home very late."

The expedition team departed in the big bus, a Tata Sumo and a Scorpio, leaving the Adam-staff behind to clean up and to leave a bit later with all the kitchen paraphernalia in the Mahindra jeep with trailer and the pickup.

It was ten o'clock in the evening when all the equipment were unloaded and dumped in front of the Meghalaya Speleological Group's Office; left to be sorted out the next morning. The cavers sought out their own haversacks and left for their hotel rooms to have a well deserved hot bath, a nice drink at the Bar and a soundless sleep on soft cushiony mattresses with fresh smelling clean sheets.

Thrang spent a long time at the bath, scrubbing himself clean of all the dirt and smell of the expedition, all the while nursing a large peg of Old Monk Rum. He was flushed pink when he came out of the bath. After a quick bite at dinner he sat to catch up on the latest news on the National TV. He didn't get much for he was soon nodding his head. The events of the last month had caught up with him....he was very tired and sleepy. He put off the TV and snugly got in into his soft, warm and familiar bed. He felt at peace and relaxed and as he drifted off to sleep his mind wandered.... *Ri, I am back in circulation.....how are you my love? ...I am dying to see you.*

By ten o'clock the next morning the first of the early cavers had appeared at the office of the Meghalaya Speleological Group to make an inventory of all the equipment and to store them in the store room, after which, last minute marketing and personal contacts were caught up with. The last of the cave data was fed to the laptop, cave plans were drawn and a brief summary of the Expedition Report was printed for the benefit of the local newspapers.

The icing on the cake for every expedition team has always been the farewell parties. These parties have been held every year at different venues so as to give the foreign cavers a feel of the diverse environmental settings and friendly hospitality that is unique to the region..

Jorge, Jon, Andre, Franz, Maya and Thrang were the first to arrive at the farmhouse, twenty five kilometres away from the city of Shillong. Thrang was totally taken aback at the sight before his eyes. The place was lit up befitting a royal function. A Shillong based Band, *The Haunting Devils,* were already on the beautifully decorated make-shift stage, busy arranging and tuning their musical instruments. Across the dance floor was the bar with an arrangement of different brands of whisky, rum, brandy, beer and an assortment of cold drinks.

"Hello!.....Welcome, welcome," Suk came out from inside the house extending his hand in greeting.

"Hello Suk,' Jon returned his greeting, 'What a place you have!"

"Yes, this is absolutely amazing!" joined in Jorge looking at the surroundings and bright lights around him.

"So, how are you Suk? You do look great," said Andre, shaking Suk's hand.

The big smile on Suk's face was enough to show that all was well with him and that he was doing well in life.

"Get yourselves, a drink first," Suk said, inviting them to the Bar.

Pointing across to the left hand side of the stage, Suk said, "And there is the dormitory where you can retire if you want to sleep."

They walked around the farm house enjoying the soft cool breeze of the night. All was calm and quiet except for the chirping of the crickets and the occasional squawk of a bird disturbed in its nest.

Soon the other expedition members began to arrive in their hired sumos and they too expressed their surprise and delight at what greeted them. The stage was ablaze and rocking with the voices of the *Haunting Devils*, as guests started to pour in.

The two barmen were kept extremely busy. The Band belching out number after number of rock, blues and jazz, soon attracted a couple to the dance floor which gradually swelled to fill the floor to capacity. The atmosphere was electrifying with the vibration of the music and the dancing bodies. Bodies and limbs shaking to the music ....the cavers were especially unwinding themselves, letting free their inhibitions. Tonight was their night as was every other night, but tonight was special.

Thrang was nursing his drink of *Old Monk* in a corner at the far end of the Bar, watching the undulating bodies gyrating and envying them for their total sense of freedom. He was not given to such expression in public. He would rather express them in the privacy of his mind; the singing, dancing and whatever. *His mind was his playground and in that playground he would frolic all he want.*

His thoughts were pleasantly interrupted by the sweet flowing voice of the band singing *You look wonderful to me.* His pulses throbbed with excitement as his body swayed to the lilting tune. Sitting quietly with a glass in his hand no one would have guessed what was going on in Thrang's mind. He was totally caught up in the rapture of his intimate dance with Ri, as she rested her head on his shoulder. *What was she doing at this moment*; he wondered *...probably with that simpleton*, and in the midst of such merriment renting the air, his heart filled with the ache of loneliness.

"Bah? May I fill your glass?"

Thrang was brought down to earth from his nostalgic moment. He looked up to see Evermore, one of the bartenders, smiling at him and extending his hand for his glass.

"A small one, please,' Thrang smiled back as he handed his glass to him, 'and fill it up with water."

"Hi Thrang! Why are you not dancing?" Maya enquired, coming over for a breather and sitting next to him, her face flushed and glistening.

Just then Evermore handed Thrang his freshly filled glass.

"Thanks Ever," Thrang said.

"May I have some beer, please?" Maya asked the ever-smiling Evermore.

"Sure Miss," he said, as he expertly popped open a bottle, poured the cool frothy liquid in a glass tumbler and handed it over to her, his lips smiling from ear to ear.

"Cheers!" they toasted to each other.

"Now Thrang, seriously, why are you not enjoying yourself and letting your hair down like everyone is doing?"

"But I am!" protested Thrang, "I am enjoying more than any of you, but in here," as he put his hand on his heart.

Maya looked at him, understanding what he meant and smiled knowingly.

"Thrang,' she softly whispered, 'I hope that things turn out well for you."

Maya took a large sip of the beer and putting down her glass said, "Thrang, wouldn't you ask a lady for a dance?"

Thrang, braving himself to the effort, looked at her mischievous eyes and slightly bowing down, gallantly said, "May I have the pleasure of this dance?"

"I am truly delighted," she said taking his hand.

But the music was all wrong. The Band had now reverted back to one of those fast and frenzied heavy metal numbers which had the dancing floor vibrating with the stomping feet and sinewy bizarre movements of the limbs. Thrang felt out of sorts and ill at ease; his body could not respond to the beat, with such comic expressions. Maya was on a different plane; her body in total harmony with the loud and fast beat and did not even notice his discomfiture. The number did not seem to ever end and when finally it did, Thrang heaved a sigh of relief and excused himself.

"Thank you Maya," he said and even before she could react he had left the floor and was back to his seat in the far corner of the Bar, his unfinished rum no longer where he had left it. He did not bother getting himself another drink, instead he took a short walk around the farm in the dark and letting the cool breeze clear away his muddled mind. Somewhere in the distance, he heard an old song, *When you dream, dream a little of me,* floating through the still air.

Half an hour later he was back to find most of them having dinner. He got himself a plate, dished a bit of fried rice, fried pork with mushrooms, a few slices of cucumber, two leaves of crinkled lettuce and a dash of hot mint paste and sat himself next to Ken.

"Hi Thrang, didn't see you around. This is a bloody good show,' Ken said, taking a big gulp of his beer, '…must cost a fortune" he added.

"Well, this is Suk's style; to do things in a big way," Thrang remarked.

There was no let-up on the music.

"Those guys must be thirsty,' commented Ken taking a large sip of his drink, 'they should take a break to wet their throats. I could smuggle a few bottles to the back of the stage; poor sods!" and he concentrated on finishing the contents of his plate.

Just as suddenly the music stopped for the much needed break. There was a rush for the Bar as well as the dinner place. For a moment the silence was deafening but soon the hum, shout and laughter of the revelers filled the rustic virgin atmosphere. The villages around for miles had never before heard of such a loud and noisy party. They would probably have a sleepless night till the early hours of the morning. Some of the more inquisitive villagers had turned up to see what was going on with a few of them joining in the merriment. For the cavers it was a night to let go…. to drink, dance and shake off the dust, for the next morning they would be off to catch their flight back home. *It was a night they would all want to remember for all the extraordinary events that had taken place and the success they have had.*

It was one thirty in the morning when Thrang wished his caving friends a safe journey back home. Some of them were already dead to the world, bundled inside their sleeping bags in the temporary dormitory.

"Thrang, see you next year,' grinned Ken shaking his hand, '….and if there is anything you need, just e-mail me."

"Will take you up on that, to be sure," Thrang replied.

Thrang turned to Suk, "Thanks Suk, for your hospitality and contribution. This is really beyond me. We never expected such a big reception."

Suk beamed with pleasure, "I hope everyone has enjoyed the evening?" he asked.

"We were all astounded….. really Suk, at this great show you have put up for us," Thrang replied, showing his immense appreciation by putting his arm over Suk's shoulder and tapping it lightly.

"Rightly said! Thrang,' joined in Tim, 'It is the best ever party we have had and all the guys have been very, very pleased and have enjoyed themselves tremendously," as he shook his head in disbelief.

Extending his hand to Thrang and smiling he said, "Thrang, it's been another terrific year of caving; this year more so; with all the happenings and excitement. A sad experience though, the murder. And this party,' he continued, spreading his hands wide, '… is simply fantastic; meeting and making so many friends from Shillong."

He smiled that disarming smile of his at Thrang, "As always, we are leaving more caves unexplored than we could explore, which is good for future explorations." He cleared his throat, "Thrang, thank you once again for everything."

Returning his smile Thrang said, "Yes, it has been a good expedition. In-spite of the problems we faced, it has ended rather well; made us stronger. In fact,' he went on, 'the local people in the villages are more appreciative of our work than ever before."

"So Tim," he cheerfully responded, "all the best. Have a pleasant journey back home and give my regards to Marian and junior."

"I will,' Tim said, 'and thanks once again. And do let me know of the happenings of the case in the Supreme Court."

"Sure, I will keep you informed," Thrang affirmed as he got into his car for the drive back to Shillong, dreading the thought of the hazards he would face along National Highway 40 from the heavy-laden coal trunks and more especially from the empty ones racing back to get another quick trip. *Those empty trucks breathing behind your back at breakneck speed are like hungry monsters…. brashly insolent*, thought Thrang.

The foreign cavers would stay enjoying the party till the next morning or as some had done, catch up on some sleep for a few hours. Suk would provide breakfast for them in the morning, before they leave for Guwahati in their hired Tata Sumos, to catch their flights to Kolkata and thence to Europe and the United States.

PART TWO

What have they done to the earth?
What have they done to our fair sister?
Ravaged and plundered and ripped her and did her,

Jim Morrison

1

The rainbow arched itself across the sky, after the heavy downpour had spent itself; bringing down the temperature appreciatingly to a cool 17 degree centigrade. The last three weeks had been very hot and dry and the vegetation had been crying out for rain. Water supply had dwindled and many a household had to buy water. Watering the garden had become a luxury that few could afford and many a plant had shriveled and dried up. The rain was therefore a blessing, a blessing that everyone had been praying for. Thrang luxuriated in the cool, fine misty spray that kissed his face ever so gently and softly which he felt was more of a tender caress.

He watched the traffic passing by and the people scurrying about their own business after the respite from the thunderous rain. The picture was one of renewed activity. The streets shone bright and clean after the cleansing it had received, with the drains gurgling and carrying away all the dirt and filth, thrown by irresponsible human beings. We are a great nuisance to the planet earth, thought Thrang; creating and building no doubt, but mostly polluting and destroying. In the end, man himself will destroy this habitable planet bringing about his own doom. That will be the inevitable end of mankind.

"Hello Thrang!" the soft, warm and cheerful voice, delightedly broke into his musings.

"Hi Ri," Thrang said, his heart throbbing wildly.

"You look beautiful," he uttered, looking into her eyes.

She blushed. "You don't look too bad yourself, you know!" she said hesitatingly, smiling in reply.

"Come in," he invited her as they entered his shop together.

He had not seen her for a fourth-night or so. She appeared to have lost some weight but it was quite becoming of her. In her light blue body-clinging jainsem and her hair tied neatly behind with a hair-band she looked slimmer still. Thrang could not take his eyes off her. She was stunningly beautiful, he thought. *And to think she is going to marry that…*Thrang stopped himself from thinking awful things about her fiancé.

"So how is business?" She asked him.

"Not too good," he replied, "but I was kept busy updating the accounts, taking stocks and what not, after that one month long caving holiday."

He picked the telephone and rang the restaurant next door for two cups of red tea and one plate of small fried momos, which he knew she loved.

"Business is really serious business," he continued, "and I have to make up for the low sales when I was on holiday. My brother is not a salesman you know. It was kind of him however to agree to look after my business. The two lads working for me are good lads and they kind of helped him in managing the work."

"And what kept you away?" he smiled at her.

"Oh, I was extremely busy with school work and….." she looked shyly at him and went on, "Dondor would come to pick me up from school in his car, and we would go for a drive around, ending up in some restaurant before he would drop me home."

Thrang felt a deep sense of jealousy grip him. *This is not real,* he thought, *this cannot happen to me.* But it is happening and there she was sitting near him and telling him about it. He just wanted to disappear God knew where. He loved her, and he knew that he will always love her, no matter what she did.

The hot steaming fried momos and the two cups of red tea arrived. The restaurant boy carefully laid them on the table in front of them and vanished.

She poured the hot chilly sauce over the momos on the plate and both of them started to eat and sipping their tea at the same time.

"Ri," Thrang said looking at her, "I love you and I will always love you, no matter what….you will always be in my heart."

"Believe me! I shall forever wait for you; even if I know it is useless." Thrang uttered with all the feelings and conviction of his heart. *When all is lost, I will be there for you*, he murmured in his heart.

"Thrang? Please do not make it so hard for yourself. The world is full of so many pretty girls. I'm sure you could find one who would give you the love you so deserve," she softly whispered to him.

"Yes, I suppose so; but it is you I love."

He looked at her and with emotion choking his voice said, "You know sweetheart, you are an angel! I sincerely hope he gives you all the happiness you deserve."

"I am your very special friend; always will be. Whenever you need me, I will be there and will never fail you," he ended, his heart wracked to pieces but with a resolute conviction to live to serve her.

When she left him half an hour later, Thrang busied himself with his work. A number of customers had entered the shop when Ri was with him, but they were attended to by his two employees. In the space of that one hour they had sold a few rolls of Kodak film, two packets of CDs plus six loose ones, eleven DVDs, shot thirty two passport photos and delivered twenty seven packets of developed coloured photographs besides taking a number of orders for burning digital photos to CDs and also for printing of the photos.

Thrang attended to a number of customers during the next half an hour, one of whom bought a 7.1 mega pixel digital camera. By the time the last customer had left and he had counted the day's sales, it was almost 7 PM and time to close shop.

"Well, you two can go. I will lock up." He told the two boys.

They lost no time in disappearing.

He kept about a thousand rupees including all the loose change in the drawer and locked it. The rest he put in his breast pocket which will be deposited to the bank the next day. He then tidied up the shop, checked to see if anything was amiss and satisfied, he began closing up. He carefully checked the three locks on the door and satisfied that they were fast and secure, he walked back home. It would take him exactly eighteen minutes to reach home unless he did any shopping on the way.

Ever since his father had died five years ago, it had become a habit for him to go home straight from work for his mother was all alone with only a maid to help her with the house work. It was a big help that the maid stays at the house. He knew that dinner would be ready by the time he reached home and that his mother and the maid would have had theirs by then, but he would have his only by 9 PM.

"Hi! Mei, I'm home." He shouted over the noise of the TV. It was the maid as usual, watching the music channel. He shrank inwardly from the decibels pounding his mind, but it was a concession he had to give in. *Maid-servants are so hard to come by these days.*

"Thrang?" his mother came out of her room, "had a good day? She enquired.

"Yes. Not a bad day at all. I saw Ri today," he blurted out.

"How is she?" as she looked intently at him.

"She looked good, extremely beautiful!" he said.

"You do love her don't you?" she asked, feeling the sadness, he - her son, was feeling.

"Mei, you know I love her. I love her as no other, except you."

"I feel…" he choked, feeling the lump in his throat, "….as if I was born for her. I cannot understand how she can love someone else."

She put her arm around him. "Thrang, if you were born for her as you said, then you shall have her; somehow, things will work out. You will see." She said it with such force of conviction that Thrang was taken aback.

"Miracles do happen!" and she smiled at him.

Thrang looked at his mother, felt such an overpowering love pouring out of his heart and felt good.

"Yes, I do need a miracle!" he said half to himself.

Thrang felt much better after a hot shower. He took out the bottle of beer he had kept in the freezer before he had gone in to shower, poured the chilled beer into his favourite 350 ml glass tumbler and settled down in the drawing room to relax, reading the latest *Descent* magazine.

"Thrang?" his mother called out, coming into the drawing room, "Please clean up after your dinner, will you?"

"Sure, Mei!" he said, "….and goodnight."

"Goodnight son."

He was the only child of his parents. His mother had him when she was thirty-six years of age and had almost given up hope of ever having a child. No wonder then that she doted on him. For the last couple of years she had been after him to find a nice girl and get married. *After all,* she had said, *I cannot live forever and I want to have grandchildren……I want to see you settled.*

Thrang would have loved to have done just that, but he had never met anyone he would have cared to settle down with; that was until he met Ri. From that day onwards, his attitude towards life changed. He became more condescending, more attentive, more understanding and more helpful to others. His mother had been quick to notice the change……*for the fiery temper that was so explosive had been subdued and actually missing for the last so many months*. She had badgered him about that mysterious lady, whom she thought must be marvelous. In the end he had one evening, brought Ri home with him and had introduced her to his mother.

Initially, Ri had been shy and nervous. Within minutes however, Thrang's mother had broken the ice with her friendliness and hospitality. By the time, Thang was ready to drop Ri home, she was laughing and joking with his mother as if they had known each other for a long time. Thrang could see that his mother approved of Ri, and he was happy.

"Ri, please visit again and give this old woman some of your very lively and beautiful company," she had smiled at Ri. Ri had smiled back, hugged his mother and said, "It will be my pleasure to visit you, I feel so much at home here."

The walk back to Ri's home was quiet as both of them were lost in their own peaceful thoughts.

Your mother is wonderful; Ri had told him when they had reached her house.

For the first time in so many weeks, Thrang felt at peace. The words of his mother reverberated in his mind.....*miracles do happen*, she had said. They were music to his ears and a soothing balm to his heart. He was fast asleep even before his head hit the pillow.

2

The days passed into weeks and the weeks into months. The days were bad for business, for students and for all in general. There was load-shedding for hours on end. The level of the water at the lake which generates almost all of Meghalaya's electricity, had reached an alarmingly low level. It was a spill-over from the year before, when the rains had been very scanty. Moreover, with the rapid industrialization of the State, more and more power was being consumed, leaving little for domestic purposes. It was an ugly scenario; for a state with the world's heaviest rainfall suffering from a shortage of water and power. What an irony! And Thrang felt so helpless.

The future of the state looked bleak. The massive deforestation that had been going on; catchment areas being encroached with settlements coming up; unscientific mining of minerals, of stone and sand; all lend their might to the erosion of the soil and degradation of the environment. The Supreme Court ban on the felling of timber came a bit too late; yet even then, smuggling of timber continued unabated. *If this is the way we treat the environment then what future do we expect*? Thrang grieved. If the Government is so callous in promoting such rapid industrialization at the expense of destroying whole eco-systems in the fragile environment, and in bringing about an imminent doom which has already showed signs during the last few years, what could he do? It appeared as if everyone has lost their senses; seeing only the shine of the green bucks and ignoring the deep chasm in front of them. *What are we going to leave our future generations*? Thrang lamented. *No wonder many a youth had lost all faith in the system and had readily taken up arms. But what was really disturbing was the significant change in the demographic pattern in the city of Shillong and most alarmingly in the rural villages of the state. It is an issue that would have great ramifications in the very near future. And then, wouldn't it be too late!*

The only cave that Thrang felt was safe, at least for the moment, was Krem Mawtynhiang, at Lum Iawpaw in Nongnah. Though not fully explored it is already one of the longest sandstone caves in the world. When fully explored, Thrang was certain, that Krem Mawtynghiang would be the longest cave in sandstone in the world, beating the nearest one by a big margin. Thank God, it is sandstone, and far away in a remote region, where quarrying of sand would not be of much economic benefit. But time and the hour spell the doom, though for the moment, Krem Mawtynghiang, enjoys its idealistic remoteness and not so valuable resource. But for how long? What is not worth an ounce of gold today, will tomorrow be worth more than a hundred times its value. So much for thinking that some areas will always and forever be protected; it is really a fallacy with the unmindful and constant greed to reach out for monetary benefits.

"Hi Thrang!" leaned Ruben over him, "You look so engrossed in your thoughts. What's up?"

Thrang looked up at his friend, smiling down at him.

"Everything is so wrong; the way we live, throwing rubbish in the streets, dumping garbage in the drains and streams; plastic bags littering everywhere. Who bothers?" Thrang fumed.

"Do you remember how pristine Wah Umkhrah was? I still remember as a very small kid, how crystal clear the river was, with anglers lining the banks and boys swimming in the pools; and azaleas blooming along the banks." Thrang's face lit up with the faint recollection of the *Azelea Walk*.

"And what is it today?" His face flushed red with anger simmering inside him.

"A sewage drain, that's what it is! And all along the banks, slums have sprung up."

"Yeah, that's what it is," commented Ruben sadly.

Ruben had come in behind the counter and sat down on a stool.

"So what is happening with your Public Interest Litigation?" he enquired.

Thrang took in a deep breath, relaxed and in a not too happy tone, said, "Things are moving so slow. In the meanwhile massive quarrying of limestone and coal is going on unabated, causing untold destruction to the caves."

One of the boys had brought some red tea in a flask and poured the contents into four cups. Two cups were placed in front of Thrang and Ruben, who slowly began sipping the red liquid. Thrang had really needed it after his outburst.

"And even when the case is still pending with the Supreme Court, more and more cement plants are coming up; and more and more coal is being pumped out of the earth, that the once green hills are now turning into barren deserts."

"You know Ruben," he said, "I feel so bloody damn helpless!"

Ruben smiled reassuringly at him, "No matter! You have to keep fighting them; fight in what you believe in - and if you don't beat them, so what? You would have done all you could."

"But I'm sure something good, will emerge out of this; something that will give some hope for the future."

"I hope you are right Ruben!" Thrang said, feeling a slow warmth of confidence building up in him and glad that Ruben had dropped by.

That evening when he reached home there was a parcel waiting for him. It was from Gautam Roy, an environmentalist, who had helped the Meghalaya Speleological Group in finding an advocate in New Delhi to file a Public Interest Litigation in the Supreme Court. Filing a case in the Supreme Court is a very expensive affair and the MSG would never have been able to do so, had it not been for the interest shown by Gautam Roy in taking up the responsibility. With the influence of Gautam Roy, the advocate had accepted to represent the MSG –without any charge.

Gautam Roy had come to Shillong a number of times to discuss the issue with Thrang and the other Group members. In between, Thrang had been briefing him over the phone and by sending notes, explanations and lots of newspaper clippings, by post and e-mails. Understanding the ground realities of the issues involved in the destruction and obliteration of the caves by the massive blasting of limestone to feed the cement plants and the unscrupulous and unscientific mining of coal was not easy. Moreover, it was an untrodden path, for probably no such cases had ever been filed in the country. It was a challenge that Gautam Roy could not resist. He took great pains to understand the importance of caves to mankind and especially to the scientific community; that they were a valuable scientific resource and should be regarded as natural heritage assets; that they were fragile and easily susceptible to the degradation and abuse of the environment. *He also understood that destruction of a cave is irreversible.* And that was what goaded him to put his might behind the cause.

Thrang tore open the parcel, knowing what the contents inside were. Gautam Roy had rung him up two days earlier and told him about it.

The thick sheaf of papers before him was the affidavit of the Central Pollution Control Board, enclosing within it, the report of the Indian Bureau of Mines on the impact on natural caves due to blasting in limestone caves at Lumshnong.

Thrang was more interested in the report. He went to his study, sat down at his table and carefully read the report, skipping pages which were too technical or of no relevance to him. As he read through, a feeling of pity and anger rose in his heart at the way the study was cleverly done. The very concept of their study was misleading as they had no idea of the subterranean passages underneath their feet. To them, the cave was the entrance only, where they placed their monitoring equipment to record the vibration of their controlled blasting. If the entrance was not effected in anyway, then the cave was safe; so they concluded, ignoring the fact that the cave system runs under the limestone quarries. They were experts in their own fields, but they were no speleologists. *How can they conclude that no harm is being done to the caves when* they *haven't been inside?* Thrang fumed. This is a one-sided report, not taking into account the other part of the story of which they were totally ignorant. *For caves can be destroyed completely just by the mining of limestone which simply remove the cave-roofs, besides other destructive effects like pollution of the underground water thereby exterminating all rare and exotic cave life.* This is a farce, brooded Thrang; how can any agency give a fair and neutral report if it has no knowledge of the subject matter that is being subjected to the effects of their study of expertise. Thrang felt the sweat oozing out of his body and his shirt clinging damply to it. His body itched with the salt drying up on him and he tried to reach with his hand to scratch somewhere in between the small of his back. "This is not good," he muttered under his breath as he got up and headed for the bathroom.

He had a hot and luxurious bath, scrubbing himself clean of all the dirt and grime with the fresh new loofah. With the long loofah he was able to scrub his back especially in the scratchy areas where he could not reach. He closed his eyes and luxuriated in the sensation. When he was all soapy and his body feeling a bit raw from the scrubbing, he opened the shower and stood under it, letting the hot water course over his body taking with it the soap and grime to the drainage. He stood under the shower for a period longer than was necessary. When he felt done, he closed the hot water tap and opened the cold water tap all the way. The moment the cold water hit his body he caught his breath but held himself in place under the cold shower for a few seconds longer. It was something he never did before. He did feel fresh and invigorated after his adventure. *I must do this often,* he smiled to himself.

After a beer and an early dinner, he settled down in his study to read through the affidavit filed by the Central Pollution Control Board. There was not much argument or strong points supporting them except referring to the points already raised by the Meghalaya Pollution Control Board. Thrang concentrated himself in the task in hand in writing a detail counter argument against the affidavit, which would be dispatched by Speed Post the next morning to Gautam Roy, with a copy to the advocate.

The door to his study opened and his mother stood there.

"Goodnight Thrang," she said gently smiling at him.

"And don't sit up too late."

Thrang looked at his mother and wished that his father was still alive. *I don't spend enough time with her,* he realized sadly, *and she must be lonely at times. Ri would have enlivened her life to no end……and with kids in the house his mother would have a new lease of life.*

"No Mei, I won't stay up late. I feel a bit tired today and would like to go to bed early; as soon as I finish my work." He said, gesticulating to the laptop in front of him.

"Night Mei!" he wished her as she gently closed the door.

It was two thirty in the morning when he finally got his work done and went to bed.

3

He woke up to the sound of rain. It was an incessant drumming on the tin roof. The room was dark and quiet. He pulled the blankets closer to his body feeling warm and cosy in the soft warm bed and gave in to the luxury of sleep. The rhythm of the falling rain soon lulled him to sleep again.

He was walking along the edge of a bare and rocky cliff; looking for something.....he knew not what. The cliff was steep and treacherous and he was very careful stepping on the loose stones.....a wrong step and he knew he would be plummeted into the craggy and rocky depths. What am I searching for? He asked himself, stopping on his tracks and scanning the horizon. The far distant crimson horizon was slowly getting darker and darker. I must move on before the dark, silent and ominous night settles in and claims this desolate and creepy place, he gravely deliberated, rubbing and opening his eyes wide as if they were failing him. He continued walking....searching, he knew not what. As far as he knew he was the only living soul for miles around, in that ghostly evil surrounding. He stopped for the second time, looked at the slowly fading light and was about to continue on his search, when he suddenly froze. Just below where he stood, about ten metres from the edge of the cliff, he saw what he was searching for. He knew instinctively, that was what he had been looking for, all the while.....a cave! Even in the gathering darkness he could make out the faint mist coming out of the cave, resting neatly in a small ledge. He grinned, like a kid discovering a hidden box of chocolates. I have no tackle with me so how so I get down there, he mused thoughtfully. He spent a few minutes studying the steepness, the footholds and handholds to the way down and bravely decided to take the plunge. Slowly, carefully, he inched his way down, feeling uneasy and wary at the loose fine debris falling on top of him. It was like lightning when it happened .....the rock supporting his whole weight on his right foot, gave way and he was flung into space. His heart was hovering above his flailing, falling body as his ears split with the shattering and explosion of rocks hurtling past him and crashing down deep below him.

Thrang awoke, his heart thumping wildly to the crescendo of thunder and lightning. *It was just a dream*, he realized, greatly relieved. He fished out his watch from underneath his pillow and looked at the time. It was nine fifteen; he had overslept by more than two hours.

This must be an omen, he visualized, gravely reflecting on the significance of his dream. Thrang was not one given in to superstitions but the nagging prick in his heart sent a tingling chill up his spine. Much against his rationality, he realized that he had to be careful and alert. *I owe at least so much to my sweet mother and darling Ri.*

Thrang was totally soaked, at least from his knees down, when he reached his shop. His two boys were already there waiting for him to open the shop.

"Sorry!" he said, looking apologetically at them, "I stayed up late last night and somehow overslept; what with the rain and all."

"Good morning Bah, we also have just arrived," they smiled at him. They too were not spared by the fury of the rain.

Once inside the shop, Thrang took out the electric heater and plugged it on. He took off his shoes and socks, squeezed the water off his socks and put it to dry near the heater. He himself stood near the heater to dry his trousers.

"You better dry yourselves," he invited the two boys over to the heater.

"And order for some hot tea too," he added.

The tea did not take long in coming and soon they were sipping the hot liquid and feeling much better as their clothes began to get dry.

With the rain not letting up, business that day was dull. Thang was able to catch up on his pending work and bring his accounts up to date and even had some time to start reading a new book he had just bought '*For Who the Cap Fits*', a first novel written by a friend of his.

The rain started to ease off towards late afternoon. Not that the rain ever bothered Thrang. He had always loved the rain; as a kid he would frolic and revel in the rain, splashing puddles in his bare feet. *He remembered those nostalgic days of continuous rain.....nine days and nights of unrelenting rain.... waking up in the morning to rain, going to school in the rain, coming home in the rain, going to bed with the rain.....day in and day out, it was rain, rain and rain. His mother would not be too happy for the washed clothes would not dry and everything was damp and would catch mildew. But to him rain symbolized life, luxuriant life. Why don't we have that sort of rain nowadays? He remembered how he would sneak out of the house and with some of his friends, go for a swim in one of the streams in the Reserved Forest, not far from his house. The water was always warm......when it rains,* he remembered.

"Thrang!" the voice broke through, interrupting his thoughts of childhood memories.

He looked up and smiled at Ri.

What a girl! Beautiful, gorgeous and simply out of this world, he thought.

"Hi Ri," he said, "Good to see you again. Where have you disappeared?"

He had not see Ri for almost two weeks and he had really missed her. He dreaded the thought that one day he would never see or be able to talk to her as he had been doing all along, when she would finally marry that rich ....* baboon. *Pardon me Ri, for thinking so.*

Parting her jainsem neatly behind her, she sat down on the stool next to him. Her hair, strong and fluffy from a recent wash, rested on her shoulders and smelled of sweet, fresh lavender.

"I have been busy, have I?" She raised her eyebrows, faint lines creasing her forehead. "Yes, I have been; busy with my school work and then down with a viral fever."

"But I am still alive and here I am!" She beamed at him, her eyes bright and warm.

As they sipped their steaming special tea, laced with a bit of crushed cardamom, they chatted about a wide variety of subjects. She asked him about his mother and he told her that she's alright.

"Mei also asked about you," Thrang said. "She had wondered why you had not visited her."

Thrang hesitated; then teasingly said, "I told her that you were busy with your wedding plans."

Ri turned scarlet and was left speechless for a few moments. "That is very unfair of you, Thrang! What would she think?"

"She almost fainted," Thrang said quietly. "But its true isn't it? You're getting married soon." Thrang could feel the bitterness bursting in his soul. He wanted to lash out, but he would never hurt this lovely lady, never.

He could see the anger in her face, as she tried to compose herself, looking deep into his eyes.

"Thrang, is that what you want me to do?" She asked in a quiet level tone.

"Ri, I am sorry; ashamed of myself." Thang apologized, bewildered and disconcerted.

"I really mean the very best for you," he added.

Ri mellowed down and smiled at him. "Don't ever say that again," she warned him. "I am confused, you know; and I won't be rushed into anything."

They made their peace and soon everything was back to normal, when Thrang remembered his dream and told her about it. She gravely listened, concern clouding her troubled and worried face.

"Thrang? I am worried and really concerned about your safety. I am scared for you." She softly murmured, closing her eyes and covering them with her hands.

"Ri, you know I love life and I love it more because of you. Don't worry! I will take care of myself," he replied.

She left a short while later, and in spite of Thrang's assurances, she was all shaken up and had pleaded with him to take care. Thrang was amused and rather secretly pleased at her concern.

"Mei,' he called out as he stepped past the door and into the room. 'Mei, I'm home."

She showed her face from the kitchen, greeting him with a smile. "Son, would you like some tea? I have just made some."

"Yes please, Mei," he responded, coming into the kitchen.

She poured the tea into a cup, poured a little milk and added a tea-spoon of sugar. She stirred the tea and handed it to him.

"So how was your day?" she asked him after he had taken a sip and found the tea to his liking.

"Well, it was a rather dull day with the heavy weather, but I'm happy that I have been able to update my accounts and the stock taking."

"And…..' he looked at his mother smiling gently, 'I met Ri today. She came to the shop."

He could see his mother's face lit up.

"How is she?" she asked warmly, looking at him closely.

"She's fine. She was down with some viral fever, but she is okay now." He replied.

"She asked about you and sent you her love. She said to tell you that she will see you as soon as she can," he informed her.

"Ri is a fine person,' she said, warmly and affectionately, 'a beautiful, intelligent, and kind, with a mature, level head on her shoulders."

"I have never come across such beauty and character." She shook her head, looking at her son and feeling his pain and ache of loneliness, which she knew he always tried to hide from her.

"Son?' she said, 'go take a shower and have an early dinner. It's your favourite; brown pork stew and tungrymbai."

"Mei, I love you." He said as he hugged her.

"Now, you listen to me will you?' she scolded him, 'Get some decent sleep. You were up very late last night."

As he left the kitchen she softly said after him, "Why don't you take Ri caving. I'm sure she will enjoy it."

Thrang stopped on his tracks. He had never thought of it earlier. *Come to think of it, I'm sure, she will enjoy caving. Why didn't I think of it before?* A smile lit up his face.

"That is a brilliant idea, Mei." He said excitedly.

"Ri is quite an adventurous girl, so I'm sure she won't need much coaxing." Thrang's mother said a mischievous glint in her eye.

"Thanks Mei." Thrang said, feeling an overwhelming affection for his mother, as he turned once again to go to the shower, trying desperately to whistle a tune, tunelessly.

When he got into bed, it started to rain again. The rain intensified and the drumming on the tin roof became more frenzied and monotonously intoxicating. The wine he had at dinner was a blessed added ingredient to lull him to sleep. It was a sleep free of the dark, lurking devils.

4

It had been raining for the whole week with a few hours of respite in between. Thrang had not seen Ri during that time, except to speak to her on the phone at least once a day. He had not broached her on the subject of caving, for he wanted to do so only when they were face to face. Thinking about it sent a soft glow of excitement to his face, and he couldn't wait to see her. He thought of how she would react......*would she accept his offer of caving instantaneously or would she need a bit of coaxing? I think she will love to go caving......she is adventurous and inquisitive enough to want to go.*

"My! My! Up in the clouds again?" Rueben's voice broke through.

Thrang looked at him. "Just some stray thoughts," he said, guiltily.

"Come in. Sit by the heater so your clothes can dry," Thrang invited him.

Rueben came in, stood his umbrella in the plastic bucket in the corner of the shop, and found his way behind the counter to his usual stool by the heater.

"How's Ri?" he asked Thrang, casually.

"She's as fine as fine can be," Thrang replied.

"Thrang,' Rueben said quietly. 'I would not have come today but it is just because I could not contain myself. I want to know whether what I was told last night is true or not."

Thrang looked at him, bewildered. "And what is it that you were told?" he enquired, his curiosity showing in his face.

Rueben scratched his neck and cracked the fingers of his two hands, nonchalantly. He took out his handkerchief, wiped his nose and put it back in his trouser pocket.

"Last night my uncle visited our home," he said, gravely.

"You know him......Uncle Wesley. Well, he asked me about your case in the Supreme Court and I told him what you had already told me. Then he told me that your advocate in New Delhi had been bought. He said that he had been informed by some very reliable source."

Thrang was astounded. "How can it be so?" he forced himself to say.

"Our advocate accepted to represent us without any monetary benefits, so how can he betray us now?" he said with utter disbelief.

"Moreover, Gautam Roy has not even hinted as much to me. I find it hard to believe in such a thing." Thrang said, with conviction oozing out of his heart.

"I hope that my uncle is wrong, but even then I do believe him. So Thrang, please be alert." Rueben patted his friend's shoulder.

"Thanks Rueben, for your concern. I appreciate it very much." Thrang thanked his friend, rubbishing the idea from his mind.

The talk slowly drifted to politics. As Meghalaya is one of the smallest states in the country, every Meghalayan whether young or old, in some way or the other, would be inexplicably caught up with the politics of the state. It is a subject that one cannot escape from because it affects the lives of each one, rich or poor. No matter how loathsome it is to the majority; they cannot but be drawn into the political discussion at some point of time or the other. Thrang was one of them who were caught up with fighting against the dirty politics of appeasement of political and personal gains, which had scant regard for a cleaner and safer environment for the people to live in. In the name of development, the environment has been sacrificed for the sake of a few rupees. Pristine and rolling landscape with all its natural beauty of life and form, are being disemboweled and led to bleed dry; to be choked with the poisons of greed and wanton destruction. The wounds are then left exposed to the elements of nature, to fester and rot, scarring the countryside; and the once lush and green hills withering into dry, desolate and eroded exposure of dead earth and rock, and looking like wrinkled parchment about to crumble at the faintest touch.

Thrang was particularly pained at the irresponsible remark of a certain minister in the Legislative Assembly who said, "Caves don't give livelihood". It was flashed in the local paper the next day. What really pained him was that no one in the August House objected or raised a voice against such unbecoming remark. It appeared to him that they were all dumb donkeys or simply indifferent and incapable of understanding the havoc being perpetrated on the fragile environment of their own state they were supposed to lead and protect.

"We make the government, why can't we change it?" Rueben voiced, popping a kwai into his mouth.

"Yes we can," Thrang replied quietly.

"But the electorate, poor and illiterate as it is, especially in the rural areas, is easily swayed by the power of money."

Thrang shook his head disconcertingly, "I am afraid that unless certain minimum standards are imposed for election to the Legislative Assembly, we will continue to have legislators who are ill-equipped, insincere and incapable of serving the people and the state."

Chewing on his kwai, Rueben said. "There are a few legislators in the government who are knowledgeable, sincere and upright, you know?"

"I agree with you!' Thrang condescended, 'but they are just a few. They cannot go against the majority and anyway sooner or later they will have to fall in line with the rest."

"Rightly so," Rueben acquiesced, getting up and spitting out the kwai juice into the spittoon outside the door. Coming back in he asked, "How do we get a government that will perform for the welfare of the people and of its state?"

"That is the million dollar question," Thrang ventured, gloom clouding his face.

"There must be a way to attract the right people to form the government; energetic youth who are intelligent, upright and willing to serve the people, to take up politics as a profession,' Thrang opined 'people who are willing to sacrifice and to give their best."

Rueben was not convinced. "How do we ensure that these young intelligent people when elected and are in the government, will not fall prey to corruption?" he asked.

Thrang nodded. "We don't really know. But if the electorate were educated and sensitized to the issue of electing the right candidate without being swayed by money or muscle power, then there could be some hope. A government comprising of such legislators would, I believe, be less prone to corrupt practices. They would govern better and give the people a fairer deal on the civic amenities," Thrang responded, reaching up with his hand to rub the lobe of his right ear to relieve an itch he suddenly felt.

They had some tea, after which Rueben left.

When Thrang reached home that evening, he noticed that his mother had a smug and pleased look about her. She burst out the moment she saw him. "Ri visited me today. In fact she left just half an hour back."

"She did, did she?" Thrang was incredulous. "Why was I not informed? I could have come home earlier." Thrang said dejectedly.

Looking at him she smilingly teased, "Ri didn't want you to drop her home. She said she had to visit a friend on her way home. Anyway we had a good one hour of beautiful time together; full of jokes and laughter. She is so much fun, Thrang!"

Thrang was happy seeing the joy and happiness exuding from his mother.

"I'm glad to see you happy, Mei." He said, putting his right arm across her shoulder and gently kissing her cheek.

"She brought me some pastries too; so kind of her." His mother told him, the smile lighting up her face.

"You can have the pineapple pastries, Thrang," she said, as he was about to go to his room. "......Ri knows you love them."

Thrang felt good.

"Thrang?' He heard his mother call out through the door. 'You haven't invited Ri to go caving with you, yet?"

"No Mei. Not yet. But I will, as soon as the weather clears up," he shouted through the door, a smile lighting up his face.

As he entered the shower, the rains burst forth again with such force and ferocity that he imagined that nature was conspiring against him, to keep his caving date with Ri, if there would be one, at bay. Just as suddenly, the breeze that had been blowing all evening picked up speed and turned into a howling wind, splattering the raindrops against the window panes and banging open-doors shut. Thrang hated the wind in as much as he loved the rain. The wind to him, always evoke a sense of fear and doom but not tonight. Tonight, the wind was a blessing for he knew that the rains would soon stop. *Such winds do blow away the dark rain-bearing clouds.* He was already thinking of his caving trip with Ri. *But what if it doesn't blow away? What if it is a depression in the Bay of Bengal? Then the rains will continue for at least a week delaying the time when I can even think of asking her. Can I afford the wait, when I am so anxious to take her caving with me? No, the wind has simply to die down.*

5

Sometime during the night the rain had stopped and the wind died down too, after a while. When Thrang woke up the sun was smiling in the sky. He got up and went into the backyard and was amazed at the greenery. The grass, thick and overgrown and still wet and juicy from the rains, needed mowing; as also the lustrous camellia leaves outgrowing the neat dome-shape pruning that Thrang had recently done. Everywhere he looked there was growth, luxuriant growth. *Yes, I do love the rain…..it gives so much energy to the plants and they just grow overnight. But I have a lot of work to do now, especially weeding the flower beds.*

The air was fresh and exhilarating and Thrang took deep breaths, soaking the warmth of the sunrays on his back. A lovely sunny morning, made more pronounced by the whole week's deluge.

Ri made her appearance that afternoon.

"Hi Thrang," she said, sweeping into the room.

Thrang looked up at her from his work, a smile instantly appearing and lighting up his face. He fell in love with her, as he always does, whenever he sees her. His pulse quickened its beat and he felt heady. *What is life if love cannot be fulfilled?*

"Hello Ri." Thrang said, getting up from his seat.

"I just missed you last evening."

"Sorry,' she apologized, 'but it was getting late and I had to meet this friend of mine."

"And …..' she continued, looking softly at him, 'I cannot be seen too often with you."

Thrang was flabbergasted. He looked at her incredulously, jaws agape.

"Dondor is jealous," she said quietly.

Thrang was speechless and didn't know what to say. His world suddenly gave way under him.

"Ri,' he finally managed to say, 'you know I love you; will always love you, no matter if you marry him or any other." He felt the emotions welling up inside him, racking his heart.

He suddenly felt so alone; totally deflated, totally numbed.

He had wanted to ask her to go caving with him.....now could he? He mused sorrowfully.

"I thought of asking you to come caving with me this Saturday,' he ventured bravely, 'but I would understand if you couldn't."

Thrang wished he were far away, somewhere where he wouldn't hear her abject refusal.

"Are you asking me to go caving?" She asked, taken aback with surprise, not hiding the pleasure showing on her face.

"Yes, I am!" Thrang admitted, still unsure of her reaction.

She combed her hair from her forehead to the back of her neck with her fingers and fastened it with a hair clip.

"Thrang? I am delighted. Can I bring my friend along?" She said.

Thrang's heart soared. He was ecstatic.

"Sure, you can bring him along," he said nonchalantly.

She put down the cup of tea she was sipping from, on the vacant stool.

"It's not him, if that's who you are referring to." She said, looking at him incredulously.

He could see the smile in her eyes as she said, "I am bringing Lakyntiew, my best friend."

Thrang heaved a sigh of relief which was not lost on Ri.

"Ri, I will be delighted if you bring any of your friends; I will be honoured. I really mean it." He said, feeling the sincerity of his own words, strong and pure, in his heart.

"In that case, I will ask Clarissa, Lakyntiew's younger sister, too," she said.

"That will be wonderful," he said, grinning from ear to ear.

She prepared to leave, picking up the novel *For Who the Cap Fits* from the counter, which Thrang had given her.

"Ri?"

She looked at him, seeing the adoration and happiness in his eyes. *I love you Thrang, but I must win my mother's approval.*

"Thanks!" His eyes said it all.

"Bye," she said, feeling a pleasing sensation in her own heart, as she left, leaving Thrang stupefied and mesmerized in the heaven he had just carved for himself.

6

Thrang always believed himself to be a very patient man. That week however, proved to be too much for him; the days were agonizingly long and Saturday seemed to be far away. The last couple of days had been dry and warm with clear blue skies; in fact the clearest blue that he had ever noticed, for the rains had washed the polluted atmosphere of all its dust. He hoped that by Saturday, the river sinking into Krem Mawmluh would have lessened, to enable them to cave.

Last evening after returning back from his shop, he had opened the store room, where the MSG equipment were stored, and selected two sets of caving suits, Wellington boots, neoprene socks, belts, gloves, helmets with carbide lamps, LED lights, a small rope ladder and a short length of rope. He had carefully selected the smallest pairs of boots and suits to fit the two ladies; Clarissa would not be joining them, he had been informed by Ri. Breaking the large lumps of carbide rocks taken from the container, into smaller pieces, he had filled the two generators just a little over half full. He packed the two sets of equipment into the two tackle bags. Everything was ready for Saturday.

His own caving equipment was always packed and ready at a moment's notice. After every caving trip it was his habit to fastidiously wash and clean all the gear, dry them out and pack them back into his tackle bag.

He had even got the cave plan xeroxed and laminated so he could take it with him into the cave, to show the two potential cavers where they were inside the cave, while exploring.

Now the long wait!......while every night he would visualize that dream of a long sought caving trip.

His mother had smiled at him. "You are already set for Saturday, son?"

"Yes Mei," he had said.

"I just hope the weather stays like this the whole week."

It was a glorious morning.

Thrang woke to the delightful songs of the bulbuls, excited at the start of a new day and eager to begin their quest of life afresh. He marvelled at the many varied songs and calls the birds made. He had never really noticed it before. He lay in bed, giving in to the warmth of the blankets and tuning his mind to the melodious and sweet notes. *Beautiful creatures*, he thought, *but there was a time when as a kid I would shoot them with a catapult. I could never imagine doing so today...... not any life; maybe, fishing only.*

To attract the birds he had planted some berry-bearing bushes in a corner of the courtyard and placed a bird-bath also for them, making sure that it was always cleaned and full of water. It attracted three different types of birds with the bulbuls making the most of it. Every Sundays, relaxing at home with a glass of chilled beer, he would be completely mesmerized by the sight of those exquisite birds splashing themselves in the bath, and then ruffling and preening their feathers to dry themselves. A smile would light up his face as he watched them swarm the bushes, picking up berries, bigger than their beaks would hold them, and sucking all the juices from within, leaving the skins and the seeds scattered on the ground to dry in the sun. Those were the moments he would treasure.

He looked at his watch. It showed 6 AM. Time to get up, he thought. He lay flat on his back, stretched his legs and arms wide and tightened his muscles. He repeated the exercise for a few times and then slowly got out of bed. He was almost naked except for his undies. That was the way he always goes to bed even in the dead of winter. He put on his jeans and slipped his feet into a pair of slippers before he disappeared into the bathroom. Twenty minutes later, he was out, having done his toilet, shaved, brushed his teeth and had a face- wash. He squeezed some sun-screen lotion on the palm of his hand and applied it to his face and arms. Fastening the laces of his sneakers, he put on a black tee shirt with the MSG logo embossed on the front and then combed his hair.

He silently went to the kitchen and put the kettle with enough water for two cups to boil on the gas burner. In no time it was boiling and he put some tea leaf in. He poured the red tea into the two cups, added a tea-spoon of sugar to each cup and stirred. He took one cup to his mother who was still in bed. It was only on such rare occasions when he would get up early that he would have the opportunity to serve bed-tea to his mother.

He knocked on his mother's door and slowly opening it, entered.

"Morning mei. Your tea," he said cheerfully, as he carefully put it on the side table by her bed.

"Good morning son. You ready to go?" She smiled, looking up at him.

"Yes," he said. "I think I can hear the vehicle outside."

He returned to the kitchen and gulped his tea in three swallows. He then got the three neatly packed tackle bags and carried them out to the front of the house, where the yellow Tata Sumo was waiting. The driver helped him to put the bags in the back seat. He went back into the house.

"Mei! I'm leaving now," he said as he bent down to kiss her cheek.

"Have a nice time, son. And take care of her," she said.

"Thanks! I will have a great day, I'm sure." He said, exuding such carefree happiness that shone in his eyes.

Ri and Lakyntiew were already by the gate by the time he reached. Both were wearing slacks, tee shirts and sneakers. *Ri was absolutely stunning*, thought Thrang. *The slacks and tee shirt bring out the best of her form.*

"Good morning, Ri." He said, as he got out of the vehicle, his eyes transfixed on hers with complete adoration.

"Morning, Thrang!" She smiled with excitement, her eyes quizzically answering his.

"Meet Lakyntiew!" She said, as she introduced him to her friend.

"Nice to meet you!" he said shaking her hand. "I shall call you La, for short."

Lakyntiew smiled, "My pleasure, Bah Thrang. Yes, please call me La, everyone does."

"Call me Thrang," he softly told her, as he opened the door of the Sumo for the ladies to get in.

He sat next to Ri.

Driving to Cherrapunjee or Sohra as it is known locally, has been and will always be a very pleasant drive for Thrang, especially on such a beautiful and sunny morning, and with two beautiful ladies with him. *This is life, to be out in the open countryside with the girl of his dreams and not cooped up in the suffocating confines of his shop*, he smilingly reflected. They stopped somewhere halfway at a view point on the *Duwan Sing Syiem Bridge,* where they had some tea and snacks and spent a few moments enjoying the view of the deep incised valley.

It did not take them long to travel the fifty kilometre and odd distance to the hamlet of Mawmluh, where they stopped just before the main gate of the Cherra- Mawmluh Cements Limited. They got out of the vehicle and heaved the tackle bags unto their backs.

"It's just nine o'clock, so we will be back by about two." Thrang told the driver. "You can go wherever you wish to in the meantime."

"No Bah, I am not going anywhere. I will wait for you here." The driver responded, a smile lifting the corners of his lips.

Thrang led the way, along the grassy bank and then across the river, where they followed the river downstream along the dry part of the sandstone bed of the river. Ri had taken out her camera and had handed it to him, so along the way he had done his best to photograph them. When they reached the part where the effluents of the cement factory joined the river they stepped out of the river bed into the grassy bank and continued on to the sink.

Ri stood transfixed at the sight of the sink, where the water entering the cave is no more clear but a dark filthy colour. Thrang could understand her abhorrence.

"Ri," he said looking at her and pointing to the mouth of the cave. "You cannot enter through that entrance. You have seen that sludge coming out of the cement plant? It forms a deadly quicksand at the cave entrance where you could sink up to your waist."

Pointing up to a dark hole, three metres above the surface of the river, he said. "That is where we enter from."

They quickly changed and got into their caving gear. Helmeted, suited and booted the two ladies looked terrific. He took a few photos of them. He then took out an empty plastic bottle, filled it with water from the cleaner part of the stream, and filled the water container of their generators. Adjusting the water-flow into the carbide section, he lighted the lamps. With the flames burning brightly and lovely, they were ready for their adventure.

Thrang hesitatingly stepped into the dark murky waters. That little bit always repel and disgusts him. Carefully, he crossed the few steps to the other side of the stream. Climbing the three metre height into the bye-pass from the oozing sucking mud underneath his feet, was no easy task, but he had two ladies watching him. Using all his ingenuity and strength, he somehow scaled the small climb making it look easy to those watchful feminine eyes. He took out a five metre rope ladder from his tackle bag, anchored it to the rocks above and dropped the other end into the slimy waters below, to where Ri and Lakyntiew were, having also crossed over. They easily climbed up and were soon with him. He freed the ladder and put it back into his bag, for they would probably need it again to get into the *Gold Fish Pond.*

Thrang led the way in through the upper level bypass. He could sense the excitement of both the girls for they had never been in a cave before.

"Here is where you get wet." He turned, grinning at them.

They gingerly followed him into the water. It was cold. The water reached up to their bums. There were squeals and shrieks behind him.

"It's cold, this water!" Ri shivered.

"You'll get used to it. And as we keep moving you won't feel the cold." Thrang assured them.

Soon after a low hands and knees crawl, they were into the main trunk passage with the sound of the stream in their ears.

"Wow! This is big," Lakyntiew exclaimed, marveling at the size of the passage.

"It gets bigger further down." Thrang said.

Pointing up to the roof, he said, "Do you see those bits of debris hanging up there from the ceiling?"

They looked up and nodded in unison.

"Well, during the monsoons, this passage gets flooded up to the roof, twenty-five metres high."

They looked aghast.

"Hard to imagine," Ri managed to say.

They continued leisurely downstream, the passage becoming wider and higher. Suddenly, Lakyntiew pointed and said, "I can see a small waterfall."

Thrang smiled and gently replied, "That is no waterfall."

When they came up to the "waterfall," Thrang touched the wall, "See" he said, "It is just some kind of white powdery stuff. I am not too sure whether it is moon-milk or something else."

They were thrilled at that amazing sight.

"This is really beautiful." Ri ventured.

He took a couple of photos of them by the "waterfall;" they could fool some of their friends.

At *Horn Junction* they turned east, for the passage continuing straight ahead ended in a sump. As they explored further into the nice walking size passage, Ri touched Thrang's shoulder from behind and said. "You seem to have names for all the passages. So what's this called?"

"*Christmas Canyon*," he said looking at her. "And I think you can guess why it is called so."

"Because of all those candle formations?"

Thrang nodded.

After a low aquatic crawl, they were into bigger size passage with a false floor that had lots of clean holes and aptly named *Swiss Cheese Passage.* Continuing on straight ahead, they came to the *Gold Fish Pond.* They got into the pool. The water was clear, cool and invigorating. Up to her waist deep in the pool, Ri was reveling in the water, splashing herself and cleaning her suit from the wet muddy crawl. Ri was clearly the more adventurous of the two, climbing up wherever possible, looking and poking her head into holes, crawling into tight squeezes and generally soaking up the wonders of the dark underground. The joy of happiness and inquisitiveness seemed to shine through her eyes. *She will make a good caver........fit, agile and blessed with an enquiring mind*, thought Thrang smilingly to himself.

Out of the pool, they retraced their steps back along the *Swiss Cheese Passage* and Thrang led them into another part of the cave, the famous *Gebauer Strassse,* named after a noted Indian cave explorer. Ri and La were ecstatic, seeing the numerous formations all around them, some of which were sadly broken and lying dejected on the rocky floor. Thrang managed to take many photographs of them amidst the formations, some of which he knew they would be proud of. He did however take some very special photos of Ri alone, capturing the sheer magic of bliss emanating from her being.

La suddenly shrieked. Bats, disturbed by the fumes of their carbide lamps, started flying in circles around La's head.

"Let's leave," Thrang said. "We are disturbing those bats."

He pointed them out to Ri; the thousands of bats hanging upside down from the ceiling; nice furry gentle creatures for some but obnoxious blood sucking creatures for others. La allowed her eyes to travel to the ceiling and was terrified at what she saw. She was ready to bolt.

They retreated, with Ri lingering at every fascinating spot, mesmerized by the creative heavenly sculptures wrought about by the infinite patience of Nature in the eternal darkness. *Only the wisdom of God can bring about such exquisite beauty in the deep, dark womb of the earth,* envisaged Ri, *and am I glad and privileged to be a witness to all this?* She suddenly felt a surge of emotional longing and love for Thrang flowing through her heart. She realized with a touch of guilt that she had always taken Thrang for granted.

The sweet realization of her true feelings for Thrang overwhelmed her as she let her heart overflow with the warm sensations of the chemical reactions taking place inside her. She looked at Thrang as he bent down to pick up a pebble. As he straightened up, it happened. There was a loud but distinctively diffused explosion. The vibration raced along the length of the cave, as loose rubble fell from the ceiling. She cringed in fearful anticipation of a dreadful disaster in the dark subterranean womb. La's face was ashen as her knees gave way and she sat down huddled and whimpering in a corner.

Thrang put his arms around Ri. "It's alright, Love." He consoled her.

"The cave is stable enough, but how long will it last with this brazen and unmindful blasting of limestone over the cave system? I don't think it will last much longer."

Ri felt the anger in Thrang's voice. Her fear dissipated as she felt his anguish coursing through his taunt and lean body. She held him close. It was a moment in eternal bliss.

Ri understood and appreciated the real significance of Thrang's Public Interest Litigation in the Supreme Court. *These industrialists are downright criminals......murdering and obliterating our God-given blessings,* she cried within her heart. *They are raping the earth in sickening frenzy ......destroying, murdering in ecstatic madness, to burst in a euphoric moment of self indulgence of greed and lust.*

They were nearing the exit and Thrang who was in the lead could faintly discern daylight; another thirty metres or so and they would be out of the cave. He had hardly taken another three steps when something whizzed past very close to his ears shattering some rocks behind him followed by the sound of a bullet shot. In that fraction of a second he saw two men at the entrance, one of whom was pointing a pistol at him.

"Down!" he shouted to the two ladies, "Run back into the cave."

Even as he turned round, another shot reverberated through the dark atmosphere, shattering pieces of rocks which stung his face.

They hurried back into the dark depths sensing that their lives were in danger. When they were well inside, Thrang bade them to stop and rest behind a huge boulder.

"What happened?" Ri inquired, her face writ with fear.

Thrang could see that La was equally confused and frightened.

"What was that? Someone shot at you?" She blurted, her body shaking violently.

Thrang was rather shaken himself; he felt the rage building inside his heart for he knew he was the target. He could not begin to answer; he tried to compose and calm his racing heart. His life was in serious danger as also the two ladies with him.

After thirty seconds or so which to Thrang seemed an eternity, he spoke as softly and as calmly as he could.

"They are after me. I was lucky enough, for the bullet missed me by a few inches only. They must have followed us from Shillong on orders from vested interest I'm sure."

"How will we get out?" Ri wanted to know.

"Won't they come after us?" La asked nervously looking back up the dark passage to the outside world.

"No! They won't come after us for I'm sure they would be scared entering into a cave they know nothing about. Besides they would have only a little torch if they have one at all. They would reason that they would be vulnerable to surprise attack inside the dark cave even when armed with a weapon. They would therefore wait at the entrance where they were, waiting for us to come out. Why risk their lives when sure that we have to come out at some point of time?" Thrang replied soberly.

The two ladies looked apprehensively at him in the dim light of his pencil torch as they had all put off their headlamps a while ago.

They had spunk these two ladies, he thought; but getting caught in a dark underground cavern with murderers on the loose is a terrifying proposition to accept, even for the bravest of hearts. Yet Ri and La did not panic.

Thrang cleared his throat suddenly feeling dehydrated. He took several sips of water from his water bottle. Offering Ri and La the bottle he told them that there was a way out of the cave, in fact four ways out as he corrected himself.

"Yes' he assured them, 'we will have to go back all the way to *Swiss Cheese Passage*, then down to *Gold Fish Pond* from where the passage gradually winds upwards into *Cave Pearl Canyon* before we are out of the system."

Ri and La smiled at him in the dim light, their faces reflecting hope and happiness. What a boon to be delivered from certain death. They would live to see the day yet.

Thrang stood up slowly stretching his limbs; his muscles were getting cramps and he was feeling a bit cold.

"Come, lets us get out of the cave," he urged them as he put on his headlamp. Ri and La clicked on the igniters of their carbide lamps, all too eager to be off.

Their pace was hurried though tired, stumbling over rocks some of which were slippery. They were quiet; concentrating on their steps and every few seconds looking fearfully back in case the goons had followed them.

They had not gone a hundred steps when there was a loud crash behind them; they froze in their tracks. Even as Thrang turned around another smaller rock had dislodged from the ceiling and crashed into the boulders on the cave floor.

"We were very lucky," Thrang murmured more to himself than for the benefit of the others.

"There will be a cave-in soon; it cannot hold much longer,' he told the frightened ladies, 'do you remember earlier when loose rubble fell from the ceiling after that explosion?"

"Yes' answered Ri, 'but isn't that the same place where we had just sat down?"

"You are right; it is the exact spot and we could have been killed. Just a couple of minutes separated us from certain death and nature could have done the goons a favour," he said gravely.

"Oh God!" La uttered, in total disbelief and shock.

The choking dust from the crash of the rocks spread through the dark air and they started coughing.

"Let's hurry, it's not a safe place anymore," he said as he strode away with the two behind him.

The urgency of getting out of the cave was much more pronounced then; danger was coming at them not just from men who were out to kill them but also from natural disasters caused by man unmindful of their acts. The one thought on their minds was to be out on the safety of the surface again which was reflected in their determined steps.

The low aquatic crawl proved no problem at all as they swiftly passed it like experts. They were hurrying to the point of running, breathing heavily, till they reached the edge of *Goldfish Pond.* Thrang helped them climbed down into the pond up to waist deep water where they waded to the other far side into a passage strewn with small rocks. The passage then slowly climbed and Thrang had to help them over some awkward climbs till they reached *Cave Pearl Canyon.* That part of the cave was a beautiful section scattered with tiny cave pearls yet the ladies, intent on their exit, did not appear to appreciate any of it.

"I see day-light," suddenly shouted Ri.

Thrang smiled. "Yes, just a few more metres of awkward crawl over the top and we will be out in the sunshine," he said, relief spreading over his face.

Five minutes later, one by one, they were out in the blessed light of day.

The sun was bright and strong but not where they were; they had exited into a jungle-clad doline where the sunrays could not penetrate. All the same it was a beautiful feeling to see the warm sunshine up on the ridge; to feel safe, secure and free in bright and unhindered space.. They quickly got out of their dripping clothes, the ladies doing so behind a huge rock, to change into dry apparel.

"I am famished," Ri said.

"I am too," La rejoined.

"Any of you been to Laitkynsew?" Thrang asked.

"No," they both responded.

"Then let us drive down to Laitkynsew; it is only fifteen kilometres away. We can have lunch at the Cherrapunjee Holiday Resort. But first we have to get to the vehicle."

Climbing out of the doline, up the steep slope through bush and thorn was exhausting. It took them twenty minutes to reach the ridge where they rested for five minutes enjoying the sunshine. It took them another half an hour to walk down the other side of the ridge to the motorable road, circuiting the Cement Factory and to where their hired vehicle was parked.

When they reached the vehicle, they saw the driver fast asleep inside. Thrang knocked on the window and he jumped up guiltily, hastily opening the door.

"Must have fallen asleep," he said, smiling sheepishly.

"Good! Now you will be fresh and alert to drive us back," Thrang smiled back. "But first we go to Laitkynsew for some lunch. You must be hungry yourself."

"Well, I did have some tea at that tea-shop there," he replied.

"By the way did you see two suspicious guys passing through here?" Thrang asked him.

"Fifteen minutes or so after you left two guys came and walked past my vehicle going in the direction you took. They came back half an hour ago walking hurriedly down the road. A few minutes later I heard the start of a car engine; it must be them leaving. Why, is there anything wrong?"

"No, I was just curious," Thrang said.

The pleasant and scenic drive to Laitkynsew was a great treat to Ri and La. They were lapping up all the beautiful experiences that were unfolding before them that splendid day. All too soon, they were at the Resort.

"Hi! Denis." Thrang raised his hand in greeting to a middle aged gentleman coming out to meet them.

A broad grin appeared on his face as he recognized Thrang.

"Great to see you, Thrang."

Thrang introduced him to Ri and La.

He shook their hands, beaming with pleasure.

"It is my great pleasure to welcome you both to my humble resort," he said.

"We have been caving today, Denis," Thrang said, "and we are very hungry. What do you have for us?"

"I will get some food ready in no time. You go and freshen yourselves first," he said, going to the kitchen.

"How about some chilled beer?" Thrang shouted after him.

"Coming!" he shouted back.

Soon he was back with the beer, which he poured into fairly large glass tumblers and handed them around.

"Cheers!" They toasted to each other as they went about to quench their parched throats. The beer was refreshingly cool and sweet and the glasses were emptied in no time. Denis, watchful as ever and proving to be the perfect host, refilled them immediately.

"The beer is on the house," he offered.

"So how's business?" Thrang asked his friend.

"It is picking up very well now. And we have had a lot of foreigners this year." He smiled. "There were days when we had to pitch up tents to accommodate some of them."

Thrang was glad to hear his friend was doing well, after all those hard times he had gone through.

"There comes your lunch." Denis got up to help the two young girl waiters with laying the food on the table.

The food – rice, fried chillie chicken, pork cooked in ground black sesame seed, dal, salad and a variety of pickles--was excellent, especially after a hard and hungry day. Even Thrang, who was disciplined in his food habits, gave in to have a second helping.

The ladies were having a ball, giggling and laughing away, enjoying some joke or other. Thrang could see their happiness emanating from their expressions and he was pleased. Ri especially, he could see, had not been able to contain her excitement, for she was on her third glass of beer and second helping of the delicious food, which astonished Thrang, for she was always a poor eater. He was glad that the ugly incident of danger they had experienced was behind them.

Thrang quietly narrated the events of the day to Denis whose face suddenly took a serious turn.

"Did you inform the police?" He asked Thrang.

"No, what was the point. The goons have long gone and it will be just a waste of my time."

"But the goons could lay in wait for you when you go back?"

Thrang shook his head.

"I don't think so,' he said, 'they would have fled to escape identification and being caught; better to try their luck next time."

"You have to be very careful Thrang; these guys are very dangerous," Denis said, a worried and alarmed look on his face.

"Yes, I think you are right Denis. Thrang must watch his back every moment of the day and night. I am really scared for him" Ri joined in.

Thrang smiled at them.

"I appreciate your concern for me, but don't worry; I will be that extra bit careful and alert at all times. There is so much in life that I want to achieve. Besides,' he confided somewhat shyly 'beautiful days are still ahead of me."

Denis gave a knowing smile with Ri and La not missing the point made.

"Let's open up another couple of beers shall we" Denise said getting up to fetch the bottles.

The afternoon quickly wore off as sunset slowly faded into a silvery moonlit night, filled with the sounds and chirping of the night insects and beetles. Thrang paid Denis for the food and thanked him for the hospitality.

"Thrang, when you come next time please stay the night," he invited.

"Sure will," Thrang promised.

He shook Denis's hand, "Where is Kong Mary? I didn't see her."

"She had to go to Shillong this morning. But she will be back tonight, coming by the last bus that arrives at about eight o'clock."

"Give her my regards," Thrang said.

"Yes, I will tell her," he nodded.

"And take care," he shouted after Thrang.

The drive back home was quiet. They were all tired; the excitement of the day's caving, the life-threatening danger, the resort, the beer and the splendid food having taken its toll on the ladies. The ladies were soon drowsed off to sleep. Ri, ever so gently, leant against Thrang, her head on his shoulder. He could feel the sensuous wisps of her hair on his face and lips. Conscious of the warmth flowing through his body, he dared not move for fear she should wake up and remove her head from his shoulder. *What a wonderful day I have had*, he dreamily contemplated, *this is a day that will be etched in my memory.*

He dropped La to her house first, and then the vehicle stopped by Ri's front gate.

"Thrang? Thank you for such a beautiful day. I don't remember enjoying myself so much, as I did today." She tiptoed and gently kissed him on his cheek.

He was stupefied and dumbstruck as he flushed with excitement at the warm and soft lips on his cheek.

"You are welcome, Ri," he whispered.

"I have enjoyed myself tremendously," she whispered back.

"In spite of the life-threatening incident we faced?

"Yes, in spite of that."

"And please don't tell my mother about that unfortunate incident inside the cave, for it will only worry her every time I leave the house, okay Ri?"

She hesitated, then smiled, "I won't for now, at least; but eventually one day I have to tell her."

"Thanks Ri. You are very adorable, you know?"

"Am I? Well, good night, Thrang!" she said, as she closed the gate, "and please take care of yourself."

"I will, more so now; and good night Ri," He said, watching her disappear into the house.

He would have loved to have held her in his arms, had he not seen the front door opening and her mother framed against it. *A protective mother, still concerned with her grown up daughter*, he mused.

7

The days passed by in a blur. Thrang was caught up in the daily activities of his own business, which was doing very well. He had managed to increase his stock and the two lads with him were kept busy all day. They were happy, for Thrang had given them a substantial increase in their pay. He considered himself to be fortunate for his two employees were good, hardworking and trustworthy.

He had not met Ri since the day they had gone caving to Cherrapunjee, although he had spoken to her everyday over the phone. He had never bothered to get himself a mobile phone, thinking that it was just a bit of an extravagance. Lately he had felt the need for one. *I must buy a set and get a connection either from Airtell or Reliance,* he decided; *today itself.*

"Aiban," he called, "Please go to the Reliance Outlet office and collect an application form."

The younger lad responded with a "Yes, Bah" and was off, to return a few minutes later with a form. Thrang filled it up and signed. He rummaged in one of his files and took out the last paid telephone bill, again sending Aiban to get it Xeroxed. He pinned the Xeroxed copy of the telephone bill to his application form and sent Aiban to deliver it to the Reliance office together with the required amount of money. Thrang would like to believe that he never put things off but attend to them immediately. Probably sometimes, he was not too laid off.

The telephone rang and Thrang picked it up immediately. He could never stand the continuous shrill of the telephone.

"Hello?" He said.

"Hello Thrang!" It was Gautam Roy.

"I received the newspaper clipping you sent me. It was a good piece and it will help in our presentation to the Court. But what I need are more photographs of the coal mining activities and the limestone quarries in and around the cave systems." He cleared his throat, hesitated, then ventured. "Why don't you come over to Guwahati this Sunday and we meet at the airport? I will be there by eleven in the morning. We will have a few hours time to discuss our matter before I take the next flight back by 3 o'clock. I need a lot of clarifications from you."

Thrang thought for a few seconds, and then said, "Okay! I will be there."

"Bring your MSG seal also for I need your signature on the affidavit we have to file."

"Right!" replied Thrang, "See you Sunday."

That evening, on his way home, he entered an electronics shop and bought himself a Siemens A52 mobile set. He was not prepared to buy a sophisticated and expensive one as yet. All he needed was something to contact people with. The set he had just bought would serve his purpose well.

"Thrang! Thrang!"

The voice was familiar, as Thrang turned round to see how it was.

"I wanted to meet you and had gone to your shop. But it was closed," Eddie said, a wry smile on his broad and round face.

"Lucky to catch up with you," he added, trying to catch his breath.

Thrang was bemused, for Eddie was not actually a friend or someone he would like to befriend. To put it mildly, Eddie was more of a con-man and a kleptomaniac to boot. Thrang had lost a number of articles from his shop whenever Eddie was around, trying to con him of a few rupees.

"So what is it you wish to see me about?" Thrang replied nonchalantly, walking along towards his house.

"Just wanted to know what has happened to your case in the Supreme Court," he said, as smoothly as he only could, trying to keep pace with Thrang's stride.

"The Court is taking its own sweet time," lamented Thrang. "But I believe the next hearing will be held very soon."

"Thrang?" Eddie touched his arm to slow him down. "Do you realize what you are up against? Big, powerful people! You or your Organization has no chance at all."

"Yes, you may be right." Thrang admitted, sadly, shaking his head.

Caching in to Thrang's admission of defeat, Eddie warmed up to Thrang, "Then listen to me. These cement company guys want to meet you, to sit and discuss things over. They are willing to accede to whatever demands you may make. You know what I mean."

"It's a win-win situation for both parties. And I can arrange the meeting, if you say so." He added with a smug look on his face.

The blood rose to Thrang's head and he felt the anger rising in his heart. "I or my Organization is not interested to meet anyone, connected with the destruction of any eco or cave system."

"There is nothing to discuss! For the areas they are interested in are the areas we want to be protected." Thrang fumed his eyes riveting with the dark smoky countenance of a hurricane, on the sly moon-faced Eddie.

"But your life could be in jeopardy. Moreover, they have immense political clout and unlimited money power. You will be no match against them; so why not make the best out of it. Your case is as good as lost, but before that happens, why don't you come to a compromise with them and come out a rich man yourself. You have nothing to lose but everything to gain." Eddie stammered, lamely.

"My life is my life. I will live and stand for what I believe in. It doesn't matter if I die, but I will not compromise on this issue. This is something I have thought long and hard." Thrang shouted, against the backdrop of the honking vehicles as they reached Thrang's front gate.

"Think about it, Thrang. There is no sense in being brave foolishly," Eddie said, his face clouding with dejection.

"If you change your mind, let me know. And for your own good I think you should seriously consider what I have just said. There is no need to be so stubborn and risk your own life. You can look around and see that everyone connected with them have been well benefitted."

"Fat chance, that!' Thrang retorted, 'I am not for sale." He opened the gate, entered in and looked at Eddie full in the face.

"Anyway, thanks for the warning and goodnight."

His mother was there at the veranda, waiting for him.

"What was that all about?" She asked him.

"Nothing; Mei," he said, smiling at her.

"Don't lie to me, Thrang," she said gravely.

"Is it something to do with your case? Are you being threatened?" she demanded to know, her face showing alarm.

Thrang looked into her eyes and confided, "Eddie is trying to be a go-in-between, between the cement industrialists and me; wanting me to agree for a meeting with them to sort matters out. I told him I am not interested."

"He said something about your life being in danger?" She gazed closely, probing his eyes.

Thrang cracked the fingers of both his hands letting out loud pops and faced his anxious mother. "Mei? There's nothing to worry about. There may be threats floating around, but I sincerely don't believe anyone would go about murdering people. Besides,' he went on, 'I cannot back out now. I believe I am standing up for the good of the people in general and not for the few, bent on making money at all cost."

"Mei, don't you worry. I will take care. I want to live and enjoy life too. I have so much at stake."

They entered the house together, his arm around her shoulder. *I have such a wonderful mother,* he thought, feeling a soft warm glow in his heart.

8

Thrang got up very early that Sunday morning. After the necessary toilette and a quick shave, he made himself a cup of tea. His stomach would not allow him to eat anything that early. He may stop for a bite on the way to Guwahati, at Nongpoh probably. His mother had told him before going to bed, not to make any tea for her that early. The maid, who would be getting up a bit later, would bring her morning tea.

At Khyndai Lad, the place was abuzz with travelers, newspaper boys, roadside breakfast vendors and touts shouting for passengers going to Guwahati.

"Guwahati, sir?" asked one of the touts, ready to whisk him to one of the many waiting cabs.

"Airport," Thrang said.

"Come sir," the tout said, leading him to a Tata indica vehicle. Thrang got into the front seat beside the driver. The three seats at the back were still empty. They waited for another forty minutes before the three seats were filled and they were off on their way.

The drive to the airport was uneventful, except for a few snarls on the highway due to repair work being done. They made a twenty minute stop at Nongpoh but Thrang was content not to have any breakfast. The vehicle picked up speed once it reached the plains and on the highway from Beltola to the Lokpriya Nath Bardoloi Airport. It was getting warm and sultry and Thrang could feel the sweat running down his back. He looked at his watch and saw that it was five minutes past eleven. He should reach the Airport in another ten minutes. *Gautam would have landed by now*, he guessed.

He got out the moment the taxi stopped and hurried to the arrival section. Security was very strict with a lot of armed guards manning strategic points. The Airport Authorities were alert to the dangers posed by the ULFA who had a few days ago, engineered a number of blasts in and around the city which had killed six people and injured more than twenty.

Thrang strained his eyes through the glass wall from a distance, searching for Gautam. He noticed him immediately and waved and made signs that he would meet him inside. He bought an entry ticket from the counter and entered the Departure Section just as Gautam joined him. They shook hands warmly.

"Let us go to the Airport Restaurant, where we can sit and talk," Gautam said, carrying a black case containing his laptop.

They chose a table closest to a fan and a waiter immediately attended to them.

"Not now," Gautam told the waiter. "We will order in a short while. But bring us a large bottle of mineral water."

They got down to business the moment the bottle of chilled water was brought and place on their table.

Gautam poured himself a glass of the chilled water and kept it aside for the water to lose some of its chillness. He cleared his throat, wiped his perspiring face with his handkerchief, and said. "We have to file another affidavit. So you have to brief me again on certain points."

Thrang handed him a CD disc and said, "You can have a look at this first. It is a video of the coal mining activities all along the base of the Shnongrim Ridge."

Gautam took out his laptop and played the CD, with Thrang explaining each and every scene as it appeared on the screen.

"You can see here these deep pits they have dug and the water being pumped out; there, you can see the trees being felled and the forest cleared; do you notice those tin shacks the miners live in with all the filth and rubbish littered all around and absolutely no sanitation? Can you imagine the stink emanating from these hovels?" Thrang pointed them all out to Gautam, feeling sick at heart.

"I have to make some still photograph copies out of this CD for submission to the Court," stated Guatam, when the video was over.

They were silent for a moment, before Thrang said, "Let me start with Lumshnong. You better take notes."

Gautam took out a ball point pen and some white sheets from the case.

"OK! Go ahead." He said pen and paper ready as he signaled for a waiter to come over. "Shall we start ordering?"

"Okay by me." Thrang replied, who had not eaten anything since he had his one cup of tea in the morning.

"We can start with a soup." He said, looking at the menu, but there was hardly any choice. The best bet seemed to be chicken corn soup which they ordered. It did not take long in coming and as they ate their soup, they were engrossed with their own business at hand.

"Let me start with the Lumshnong area," Thrang began.

The loudspeaker inside the restaurant started blaring out in Hindi: "....Flight IC 717 is ready for departure and all passengers are requested to proceed to the bus for boarding." Before Thrang could begin, it blared again, this time in English. He waited till the announcement stopped.

"The main problem here is the limestone quarries and not the coal mining. The massive blasting of limestone is actually removing and destroying the caves in the area. Some have had their entrances blocked and choked with the debris while others have been totally obliterated. I wonder if Krem Umkseh is still in existence. It will be a tragedy indeed if it is so for Krem Umkseh is a beautiful two kilometre long cave which superimposes the lower reaches of India's second longest cave system. With nine to ten cement companies coming up in a fifteen kilometre stretch in the Lumshnong area, I dread to even think what will happen in just a few years' time, let alone the safety and existence of the caves." Thrang delved into his bowl of soup, and continued. "The cement companies argue that they have the state-of–the–art technology to control environmental pollution, but the fact remains that they are removing the rocks that house the caves." Thrang remained silent for a few seconds, visualizing the ugly scene the area would present a decade later, if it lasts that long.

"In a few years time when the limestone is finished and the caves are just a memory, then what? Who is going to own up to all this unmindful madness? Who is going to answer to our future generations about our brazen greed?" He choked on the picture he saw in his tormented mind.

Gautam stopped writing, troubled and worried as he could slowly comprehend the environmental disaster that would unfold in the not too distant future, and shuddered.

They finished their soup and ordered some vegetable fried rice, some paneer masala and a plate of noodles. There was hardly any choice in the restaurant, not even *fried chilly chicken.*

The waiter dished out the fried rice and paneer into the two plates. Before they could start on their lunch the power went off. The restaurant became dim, except for a few low voltage lamps and the fans totally stopped. They endured the sultriness enveloping them in near darkness as they went about picking on their plates, leaving the noodles untouched. It was a lunch half eaten and totally unenjoyable.

"Now," started Thrang, when Gautam was ready with pen in hand and shifting his position to get as much light as possible. "The Shnongrim Ridge is an area that is unique and needs more protection than any other area; it has more cave density than any area in India, besides boasting of having the country's longest and third longest cave systems. Some of the caves are so ancient that they merit conservation for their scientific value. It has also been observed that some of the troglobitic animals found deep inside these caves are new species and not found anywhere else in the world."

"Like what?" interrupted Gautam.

"Well, so far, we know of a particular fish – a loach rather and also a spider." Thrang informed him. "The loach, small and white, is blind or rather has vestigial eyes and has been documented as Schistura papulifera; and the spider which is bigger than the span of my hand has been documented as Heteropoda fischeri. There could probably be other forms of rare and unique cave animals just waiting to be discovered and studied."

"The Ridge as it is is a great place that could very well be conserved as an eco or adventure park - an ideal place for camping, trekking, and Para-gliding. As an eco/adventure park and a tourist attraction, it could just be the solution for providing a sustainable future for the local people."

"The existence of this unique and beautiful spot in the country……." and Thrang stopped in mid-sentence as the loudspeakers blared again, this time informing passengers traveling to Delhi, to go in for security check. *This was irritating; the Airport Restaurant was not the place for any business transaction or quiet conversation.*

Thrang had a few sips of water to wet his throat and continued.

"As I said, the Ridge today is threatened, by the very rich resources it possesses. The coal miners are wrecking havoc all along the base of the Ridge, sinking deep pits and boring deep into the mountain, thereby lowering the water-table of the Ridge and making the life of the villagers miserable. The paddy fields which sustain the life of the villagers are rendered useless because of the sulphur leached from the coal dumps. Yet, those simple village folks have no say, for they cannot stand up against the might of power and wealth. Their rights are totally disregarded and trampled with."

Thrang noticed that Gautam was furiously writing trying to keep pace with what he was saying. He waited for Gautam to finish, and then continued at a slower pace.

"Whereas, the coal mining is destroying the region in subtle ways, there is however, a far greater menace that is looming up. These are the cement industries. With their massive mining of limestone they will simply remove large chunks of the Ridge and take the caves away. And a huge multi-national company has already received permission from the State Government to set up their plant on the Ridge. Can you imagine the environmental consequences that may follow? Already, the forest cover is being destroyed and the bare rocks exposed, for exploitation."

The power came on, and the restaurant was flooded with light and the whir of the ceiling fans. Thrang and Gautam heaved a sigh of relief. *This International Airport should be fitted with air-conditioning and an un-interrupted power supply,* they reasoned.... *and the loud-speakers removed from the restaurant or to reduce the volume to an acceptable and pleasing level.*

"You know Gautam; there is a troop of hoolock gibbons living in the area. They will be driven away to God knows where – probably to die for want of living space. They need the tall trees and thick forest cover. These apes are an endangered and protected species, under the Wild Life Act; yet we are all blind for the sake of quick and easy money." Thrang clenched his fists and tightened his muscles as he voiced his pain, anger and frustration.

"No one really cares," he said, embittered.

Gautam looked at him and said, "I feel for you; your sincerity and your commitment. That is why I agreed to help you."

He rummaged in his case and took out a copy of the Report on the investigation of the pollution of the River Lukha, which Thrang had sent to him earlier.

"I want some clarification on this report," he said.

Thrang took the Report from him, and opened the page showing the sketch of the rivers flowing into the Lukha which had been poisoned.

"See here,' he said, pointing out with his index finger, 'This catchment area is the coal mining area which includes the Ridge. It had very heavy rainfall prior to the incident. The ferrous-oxide released from the coal is washed by the rain-water into the streams and rivers and into the Lunar River, making it highly acidic. On the other side here,' he pointed, 'is the area which had no coal mining activity and also no rain during the period in question. The Lukha River flowing through this area was therefore clean. But because there was no rain in this part of the region, there was less water flowing and therefore had no effect in being able to dilute the polluted water from the Sutnga and Shnongrim/Nongkhlieh areas, at the confluence of the two rivers. Thus, beyond the confluence of the two rivers, the water had turned highly acidic, which had suffocated and killed thousands of fish on the river, and deprived the local fishermen of their livelihood."

"You know,' Thrang added, 'while the Lukha River runs blue because of the acidic water reacting with the limestone along its path, the Litein River runs yellow; in fact even the rocks on the river and on the banks are all painted yellow."

"Why yellow?"

"Well, I suppose it's because the Litein River runs along sandstone banks where the acid does not react. I don't think anyone would really dare immerse his foot in that water. Never have I ever seen such yellow waters anywhere and I dare say that it is highly acidic. Yet there is no hue and cry about such blatant pollution."

"Do you have any photographs of the two rivers?"

"Sure," Thrang said, handing him the photos.

"Okay! That's it," Gautam said, satisfied.

They took a respite when the loud speakers burst into life again, and found their way to the men's room to freshen themselves up.

Back at their table some minutes later, Gautam produced a neatly typed sheet of paper and handed it to Thrang.

"Please put your seal and sign on this affidavit," he said.

Thrang read the affidavit, put his seal on the appropriate place, signed and handed it back to Gautam.

Gautam looked at his watch. "It's almost two thirty,' he said. 'We don't have much time."

"I'll make it brief," Thang replied.

"There are two other places that warrant protection; the first is Siju Dobhakol or the Siju Cave. Being the most researched cave in India, it is also probably the most well known. A very comprehensive biological study of the cave was undertaken by Kemp and Chopra of the Indian Museum, Calcutta, as far back as 1922; venturing only twelve hundred metres into the cave they have produced a voluminous report of their findings. This cave is home to tens of thousands of bats and with its easy accessibility it is attracting a lot of tourists. The setting up of cement plants in the area would adversely destroy a very important heritage asset of the country; besides of its proximity to the Bird Sanctuary, the Butterfly Park, the Reserved Forest etc."

Thrang drowned the remaining half glass of water and continued.

"The second is Krem Mawkhyrdop or Mawmluh Cave located in the hamlet of Mawsmai, near Cherrapunjee. We all know that Cherrapunjee is the main destination of tourists coming to Meghalaya, and this cave could be an added attraction. Yet, we are bent on destroying this precious asset, by the massive exploitation of limestone over the cave for the last forty and odd years."

"Now, to end, I would like to clarify that our opposition to the mining of both coal and limestone is not a protest against the attempts to industrialise the state of Meghalaya. Development has to take place and the growth and prosperity of the people has to be taken care of. The objection is rather towards the destructive and uncaring method adopted in the search for development. Firstly, the steps taken are totally in violation of all norms against protection of the environment. Secondly, no respect has been paid towards the historical heritage of the state. Thirdly, development cannot be sustainable if it is done at the cost of the poor as is the case here. It is on these grounds that the protest is being made."

"That's it?" Gautam asked, as Thrang appeared to have ended.

"Yes, that's it."

"Oh, no! There is something else I want to tell you," Thrang said suddenly remembering.

"The greed for amassing wealth is so great that there is open war among the villages. Can you ever imagine the villages which had been living in peace and harmony for centuries to suddenly turn hostile and fight with each other? And all for the sake of coal? Now suddenly villages are fighting over possession of community lands which are not even theirs. When I say village I mean certain vested interests forcibly claiming community lands as belonging to their village when in reality it belongs to another village. For example the village of Samasi claimed a certain tract of forested area as theirs when everyone knew it belongs to the village of Pala. So there was great tension between the people of the two villages; people were killed creating a fear psychosis among the villages. It is so bad that a person from one village would not dare go near the other village. Some villages have even constructed gates which are kept twenty four hours under lock and key. Not content with that they also place steel traps all along the perimeter of their village – to trap not animals but man. During our expeditions we had to be very careful coming back from the day's caving in the dark; for on two occasions two of our members were almost caught in the traps. I say it is shameful when brothers and sisters become enemies; and all for what? For the few greedy unscrupulous mafias who dictate terms? This is utter madness and beyond comprehension, when community lands which have for centuries remained intact and respected have all of a sudden become bones of contention."

Seeing that Thrang was worked up with anger, Gautam offered him a glass of water, which Thrang gratefully accepted. He drank the glass of water in one continuous spell. Finished, he looked at Gautam, "Sorry Gautam, I have forgotten myself."

"I understand your feelings, Thrang. You have every right to be angry. I would too in your place."

He helped himself to a glass of water, while Thrang sorted out his stuff to put in his bag; he had finished letting go his emotions.

"What about the police? Aren't they sorting out the mess?"

Thrang shook his head.

"The police I'm afraid, are stretched to their limits. With so many bigwigs in the fray, sometimes it's best not to know anything. I believe the police in the district are a harassed lot."

Gautam got up collecting his laptop and briefcase, realizing he had to hurry.

"It happens, especially when big, influential and powerful people want to have their own way. It is not confined only to your state."

"Thrang? It would be very good if you could come to Delhi for the next hearing," Gautam said, as he was about to go for security check, for his flight back to Kolkata.

"Let me know when the hearing will be,' Thrang said. 'If I can make it I will surely be there."

"By the way,' he rejoined, 'Please be careful, will you?"

"Don't worry! I will," Thrang said, smiling at him.

Thrang hired an Indica taxi back. The driver, a young man, seemed to be in a hurry to get back to Shillong. He drove as if the devil was behind him, and almost rammed into the back of an auto-rickshaw which seemed to take ages to get out of the way. Thrang had stretched out his legs before him ready for the impact. He was relieved when the auto-rickshaw got out of the way just that fraction of a second earlier. Thrang was sure that the driver of the auto-rickshaw must have cursed out loud or thanked his lucky stars that he had moved out of the lane just in that nick of time. His driver however seemed unperturbed and unmoved as if the incident was just part of the game, like racing in the Grand Prix circuit. Thrang cautioned him to slow down, which was obeyed for approximately two minutes only. The vehicle zoomed, passing everything within sight. His heart was in his mouth most of the time and his body tensed like the thong of a bow stretched tight. The thought of reading a book on his way back soon fizzled. He just prayed that he would reach home in one piece.

Thrang was alarmed as the taxi raced towards a mass of vehicles snarled on the Shillong-Guwahati national highway. His body braced for the impact, but the driver had coolly controlled the engine and slotted in behind an LPG truck. Thrang gesticulated at the driver, telling him to slow down as he was not racing for time. The driver smiled, nodded his acquiesce but old habits die hard. Thrang felt that this driver's days were numbered; he just hoped that it would not be that day. Thrang was sure that only a very small error on the part of the driver would send both of them on their way to heaven. He did not disturb the driver anymore; he must be driving this way every day and so far he had had his luck. Maybe today too, would be one of those normal days, he hoped. He asked the driver to stop at Nongpoh for some tea; not because he was particularly thirsty but more for the respite from the tension he was undergoing. A much needed breather - to soothe and calm his shot-up nerves.

When they came to the long winding climb before reaching Nongpoh, Prem, the driver whose name, Thrang had elicited a few moments earlier, had decided that if he were not fast enough, the tea waiting for them at Nongpoh would grow cold and insipid. It was a nightmare of an experience for Thrang, swerving round the curves. Not that he was scared of speed, but of the incoming traffic and more dangerously of vehicles trying to overtake and coming towards them. He wondered at the chances of an accident-free drive along this hundred kilometre long stretch of heavy-traffic road, at the speed they were they driving, and concluded they had less than fifty percent. A frightening thought indeed!

As the taxi came to the straight, a truck stalling by the side of the road suddenly burst into life and almost rammed into the side of the taxi. It was only the quick reflexes of the driver and his tremendous pressure on the gas that saved them from an imminent catastrophe. Prem swore with the choicest of expletives in Hindi and Nepali; he was rattled and nervous and Thrang could feel that Prem was really frightened, for the vicious and hungry looking truck was still bearing down on them, bent on flattening them out. Prem was confused as to why that mad truck was after him, and tried desperately to get away from that monster. But the monster would not be shaken off and was almost licking the rear of the taxi. Thrang urged the taxi to speed up; earlier he had been holding on to the edge of his seat, now in the presence of the ominous threat he felt the urgent need for greater thrust. Prem's eyes were bulging with fear and anxiety as he mumbled incoherently, calling out to the gods. About to overtake a fully loaded goods truck, he barely escaped a Tata Sumo zooming in the opposite direction, by ducking back in the nick of time, into the back of the goods truck, to be out again in the fraction of a second after the Sumo had zipped by. The crazy truck almost collided with the goods truck, as Prem maneuvered the taxi out of danger. He raced away like mad. Thrang heaved a sigh of relief – they were out of immediate danger, but for how long? The truck would reappear again to finish its job of destroying the taxi or more precisely him. He was sure of it, though he did not tell Prem of his suspicions.

His body shook with the realization that he had almost been killed, but for the expert driving of his taxi driver. That truck which had unloaded its twenty four tons of coal at Baridua was on its way back to the coalfields of Jaintia Hills. That it belonged to one of the coal barons was a certainty. The driver or the other person inside the truck must have seen and recognized him in the taxi and had decided to get rid off him. They had almost pulled off the job, he acknowledged in anxiety to himself. The taxi would have surely been smashed on the side he was sitting on, and would have hurtled over the railings to the gorge down below. He shuddered at the scene in his mind. Good chap, Prem! He acknowledged. *I owe you my life.*

"Woodland, sir?" the driver asked. He had been very quiet, concentrating on his driving after gaining distance from the assassin truck.

Thrang shook himself and realized that they had reached Nongpoh.

"Yes, Woodland," he answered.

Thrang went straight to the toilet, relieved himself and washed his sticky face, before he entered the restaurant. He was joined by Prem a few minutes later.

"I saw the truck passed by just now," Prem informed him.

"Did they see you?"

"I don't know."

"We have to be very careful now,' Thrang advised him, 'it is better to drive very slowly and keep out of the truck's sight."

Prem's face, serious and inscrutable, appeared to be deep in thought.

"Yes, but the truck could very well lie in wait for us somewhere along the road, you know," he uttered in fearful anticipation.

"Could be. In that case if we have to pass the truck, we do so in the company of other vehicles. I don't think they would take the risk in front of witnesses."

"Alright, we'll see what happens on the way," he murmured, taking a long drink of the water in the glass.

"But why are they after me? Why do they want to destroy my vehicle? I haven't done anything wrong nor do I know them," he fumed in consternation.

"Or are they after you?" He asked on second thoughts.

Thrang looked straight at his quizzical eyes.

"No, I don't think so. What business would I have with them? I'm certainly at a loss," he lied. "In any case, the reason is of no consequence at the moment; what is important is that we must reach Shillong, safe and in one piece."

None had any appetite for any food. They had tea, in fact two cups each, to quench the dryness in their throats. They whiled their time in the restaurant, giving enough time for the truck to be far ahead of them.

"We could file an F. I. R. with the police," Thrang suggested.

Prem shook his head in rejection of the idea.

"We would only be wasting out time. Moreover, the truck has not even scratched my taxi and it would be our word against theirs."

Thrang left it at that.

Unlike the first half of the journey, the second half was like driving in a park; slow and easy. Thrang was sure that Prem was itching to press on the accelerator but for fear of the lunatic truck. It must be telling on his nerves controlling his inanimate habits. Now it will be a test of his character, as the taxi slowly winds its way towards Shillong, letting vehicle after vehicle overtake him. This was against his grain, Thrang was sure. They drove in silence.

"I believe they are going to convert this road into a four lane expressway," Thrang broke the silence.

"It would be very good, then. Good driving, less accidents and faster." Prem smiled at the thought.

Thrang could almost feel the train of thoughts passing through Prem's mind – how he would enjoy driving unhindered.

"And they would also complete the Shillong Bye-Pass," Thrang added.

Prem gave a snort. "That I doubt; it's been almost two decades since the project started and it hasn't got anywhere. Nothing seems to see the light of day in our state," he concluded.

"I suppose you are right. We never seem to conclude any project within the scheduled time nor within the budgeted estimates. You know what, we are a very irresponsible and indiscipline people. That is what we are really."

When they were about three kilometres to Umsning, Prem suddenly sided the taxi and stopped.

"What's wrong? Why are we stopping?" Thrang inquired.

"I just want to check on the truck ahead of us on the next bend," he answered, stepping out of the car and walking cautiously along the edge of the road.

He came back after five minutes with a grin on his somber face.

He nodded at Thrang, "Our truck is waiting there for us."

Thrang was silent. What should, they do now, he wondered, as they waited apprehensively in the car?

They waited as many vehicles passed them by. Soon they heard a truck approaching. Prem waited till the truck was in sight. He started the engine and as the truck passed them, Prem drove his taxi staying close behind the truck. Thrang understood what Prem was doing; the taxi would be out of sight till the last possible moment. As the truck passed the assassin-truck, Prem pressed on his car horn continuously. The truck sided off to one side, letting them through, even before the assassin could react. They were free and raced away. Prem let out a sigh for he was now in his elements. It was a delight to see the triumph on his face, as he gave a little chuckle and never looked back.

At Umiam Lake they came to a standstill; an ugly mess of a traffic jam. While the trucks were lined all along the left hand side of the road, and the outgoing vehicles on the right hand side, the smaller vehicles pushed their way through the centre. There must have been a breakdown somewhere, reasoned Thrang, for no vehicles moved even an inch, either way. There was talk that the traffic jam was as far as Mawiong, six kilometres away. Thrang was fretting, waiting for the vehicles to start moving. But nothing moved and as the minutes ticked by more and more vehicles piled in behind them. He was not worried about his pursuers, for the truck would be lined far behind and if there was any chance of movement it would be the smaller vehicles that would have the right of way first. It was annoying however, telling on one's patience, to wait out this stalemate. Then it rained, keeping everyone inside their own vehicles. Thrang's impatience grew for he surmised that with the heavy rain, the policemen would not come out and sort out the traffic snarl. They would be stuck on the highway for many hours. Curiously enough, Prem slept with his head on the wheel. He has had a horrifying day, Thrang admitted.

Suddenly there was a stir as vehicles to Guwahati started their motors and slowly begin to move. Ten minutes later, their long line of vehicles to Shillong started to move, ever so slowly, leaving the trucks stranded where they were. They had been immobilized for almost seventy five minutes. At least they were now moving, slowly increasing their speeds.

It was nine thirty by the time Thrang reached home. He paid the driver his fare and gave him an extra five hundred rupees. Prem was elated with the generous tip and thanked him profusely.

Giving Thrang his mobile number, he asked Thrang to ring him up anytime he should need a vehicle to go anywhere. Thrang promised him that he surely would.

That night Thrang slept a fitful sleep, dreaming of an anaconda about to devour him. He woke up with sweat oozing from every pore of his body. He went to the bathroom and relieved his swollen bladder. After a glass of water, he retired back to bed and slept peacefully. He woke up very late the next morning.

9

There were days when Thrang would lose heart, and feel sorry that he was born at the wrong time, seeing the utter contempt and sheer disregard of the Government in the protection and conservation of the environment. The environment always loses out to the exploitation of natural wealth for the so-called development of the area. A more progressive and far-sighted Government would balance the positives and negatives, giving more weight-age to environmental conservation, before acquiescing to the setting up of any red-category industry or unregulated mining. *But is there such a Government today in the state?* Thrang fumed. *The Government is bringing wealth and prosperity to the state and its people*, so they say. But at what expense, Thrang reasoned.

The populace, by and large, are deeply conscious of their surroundings but are timidly put down and ridden over by the unscrupulous few. Rules and laws have no meaning for such hell bent mafias. The lure and greed of the quick buck is all that matters. Thrang felt defeated and deflated at such times.

Thrang and his Group were fighting a lone battle. It hurt and angered him to realize that no group or individual had openly voiced their support to him or his Group. *Why this loud silence*, he had often bitterly asked himself.

That Thursday morning however, as he read the *Meghalaya Guardian*, he smiled as he felt a great relief overcoming him. Somewhere on the front page he read, slow and easy:

"The Wildlife and Environmental Protection Group (WEPG) has urged the Centre to impose a blanket ban on lime stone mining in Jaintia Hills and Garo Hills and also to prohibit the State Government from issuing fresh licenses or permission for setting up of cement plants in the State.

In a letter to the Secretary, Union Ministry of Forests and Environment, the group appreciated the recent action taken by the Ministry in controlling forest damage in the State which is caused due to limestone mining by the Lafarge Company.

The letter stated that Jaintia Hills, which is very rich in caves and monolith rocks, was once covered with forest but recently, with mushrooming of cement factories and random limestone mining, most of the caves and monolith rocks are destroyed. They also said that the district is now almost a barren land with hardly any trees around.

The WEPG said that due to the release of toxic wastes from the cement plants there was massive death of fishes in one of the biggest rivers of Jaintia Hills.

Stating that in the whole of India there are only two bio-diversity gateways, the Western Ghats and the North Eastern Region, the letter said Jaintia Hills has been identified as an ecological hotspot as it contributes a major percentage of it. Recently, a new eye-less fish species was discovered by a group of cave explorers in the district."

The same news appeared in The Shillong Times too. Thrang's heart soared. *There are people after-all, who do feel the way he does.* Buoyant with the news, he bought another copy of the paper and made a cutting of the item, a copy of which he would send to Gautam, immediately that very day itself.

That afternoon, he left his shop in the able hands of his two assistants, to check up on his mail at the cyber café, just across the road. He hadn't checked his mail for the last couple of weeks and he expected there must be quite a few. He was not disappointed, for there were five of them, discounting all the junk. One of them was from Tim, who had sent a list of twenty six names, twenty one of whom had confirmed their participation in the next expedition while five are as yet undecided. *My, how time flies. The next expedition is already at the doorstep; he must start preparing soon*, he realized.

He replied to three of the mails. The other two would have to wait, till he had collected some facts. He left the cyber café, realizing he had spent about an hour or so. When he entered his shop, he saw Ri sitting on the stool, waiting for him. She smiled the moment she saw him.

"You look bright and happy," she said.

"Do I? It must be because of your presence," he grinned at her.

"Seriously! The papers have done wonders, bringing about that rare sunshine on your face."

He blinked, for a moment not comprehending what she was saying.

"The papers? Oh, yes," he said, beaming a radiant smile. "That news item this morning is great, isn't it?"

"I'm glad for you," she responded, a gentle smile playing on her lips. "Now you have someone supporting you."

"Yes. It's good to know that you are not alone."

"Well, I have sent a clipping of that news item to Gautam this morning. It is going to help us in our case," he revealed, as he sat down next to her.

"Aiban?' He called out, 'can you ring up for some tea and potato chops, for all of us."

They sat, talking and enjoying each others company as they sipped their tea and relishing the hot and fresh chops.

"Thrang?"

He looked up at her, seeing the shyness creeping into her face.

"My mother asked about you. Why I don't invite you to our house."

Thrang was taken aback. This was something he had never expected. *Today must be my lucky day,* his heart sang.

"You are not joking, are you?" he asked, half afraid it was so.

"No Thrang. I am not joking."

"How come she has a change of heart?" he enquired, feeling the quickening of his pulse.

"I don't know!" she admitted.

"But what I feel is that she was not really against you. She favoured Dondor because she knew his parents very well and thought Dondor would make a good husband for me. But the idea has somehow worn off, seeing me not too keen on the prospect of marrying him."

"Isn't she afraid of the *Thlen* that I am supposed to be rearing and worshiping?" he asked her, gravely.

"No! She never believed in it. It was just an excuse." She sighed.

"Thank God! For that," he rejoiced. "Now I have the field to myself."

She gave him a smile that held all the promises of heaven.

"Ri? I love you," Thrang whispered, wanting to kiss her but dared not, in the presence of the two lads attending to some customers.

"I could drop in this evening, when I close shop?" he said, expectantly.

"No. Not this evening," she said resolutely, taking up her handbag, preparing to leave. "Make it tomorrow. I will tell her first."

"Bye, Thrang. I will expect you tomorrow then," she said, with a tinge of heightened excitement lighting up her face.

He stood, transfixed. His heart pumping wildly, his mind traveling the expanse with the billions of stars, as he murmured, 'I will be there Ri, I surely will.'

It was ten fifteen when the phone rang. Thrang had just finished his dinner and his two pegs of rum. He thought he would read a novel, *The Camel Club* by *David Baldacci*, for an hour or so before he went to bed. The sudden shrill of the telephone jolted him from his exuberance.

He picked up the telephone.

"Hello?" He said.

"Hello! Is this Thrang?" a heavy accented male voice spoke.

"Yes, you are speaking to him."

Before Thrang could even ask him who he was, the rasping voice said.

"You better come quickly. There appears to be a fire inside your shop. We are trying to break open the door. We have also informed the Fire Brigade." With that, the telephone went dead.

Thrang was confused. Could it be a short circuit? He quickly put on his sneakers and a light jacket ready to run to the scene, when his mother came out of her room.

"Anything wrong, son?" She enquired.

"Well someone on the phone just told me that my shop is on fire. I'll have to run and find out," he said hurriedly. "Don't worry Mei; I don't think it is anything serious. I will be back soon."

"Take your mobile with you, so that you can let me know, otherwise I would worry," she said, looking worried.

"I have it, Mei." He glanced back at her as he opened the door and hurried out.

There was a light drizzle and the cold black-topped road glistened under the street lights. The street appeared to be deserted, except for some stray dogs and the odd vehicle passing through. He ran, slowing down after a while to catch his breath and tried to push himself harder. *The sedentary life of a shop-keeper is not good for him. He needed more exercise,* he realized. He kept on, lapping up the metres, and careful with his steps on the slippery footpath. He was soon in view of his shop. As he neared, he noticed the huge mound of building-sand on the pavement which had been dumped there before he had closed his shop. He slowed down, sidetrack unto the main road to avoid the heap of sand, and that's when it hit him in a flash. *His shop was in darkness and everything was quiet. There was no fire!* In that one split second, he instinctively dived into the sand, as he felt the speeding car whisk by him, missing him probably by just a few centimeters. Sand got into his eyes and he furiously rubbed it off with his hands. He scrambled to his feet when he heard the car screeched to a halt. *They are after me.* A chill went up his spine and the hairs on his neck stood on end. His blood surged to his head at his own stupidity and he ran the opposite way. He thought he heard two loud noises but kept fleeing from the imminent danger to his life, not knowing that one of the bullets had hit his thigh. He fleetingly saw the blinding headlights of a white Maruti Gypsy bearing down and screeching to a halt. *The Police!* He gratefully acknowledged, at the same time hearing in the turmoil of his head, the car speeding away to escape into the darkness.

Thrang had slowed down and stopped. He could feel that his trousers were wet and sticky and heavy. He felt his trousers with his hands and realized he had been shot. He suddenly felt weak and giddy, ready to collapse.

"He has been shot." He heard the Police Officer say.

Thrang felt himself being supported and half carried by two policemen to the Gypsy.

"What happened?" The portly Inspector asked.

Feeling the searing pain on his left thigh, Thrang managed a wry smile and said, "I had a phone call telling me that my shop was on fire. Without thinking, I ran to find out, fearing for my shop. I was almost run over by a speeding car when I neared my shop. Then I was shot and that's when you happened by.'

'Thank you, Inspector. If you hadn't come then, I would surely have been dead." Thrang shuddered at the thought.

As the Police vehicle sped towards the Civil Hospital, the Inspector immediately alerted all police out-posts to check all vehicles leaving the city, with suspicious occupants, probably carrying firearms. Having conveyed his message, he turned to Thrang, smiled and said. "You can thank your mother. She rang the Laitumkhrah Beat House informing us of the fire, though why us? She should have informed the Fire Brigade." Realizing the gravity of the situation, he shook his head and gently said: "Man, you are one lucky bloke."

At the hospital he was given a private room, with a doctor, on emergency duty, and two night-duty nurses, attending to him. The nurses cleaned his wound, some anti-septic ointment applied to it and it stung. He didn't know if the doctor had done any stitches nor did he care to ask. When they were done and his thigh neatly bandaged, he was given a blood transfusion.......he could see the 250cc bottle of blood hanging over his head. The blood given from the hospital stock would have to be replaced in kind, he was told.

"You are very lucky; the bullet just went through flesh and didn't hit any bone. You will be alright in a few days time," Dr. Dkhar smiled at him.

"You take these medicines. You can also take one of these pills. It will put you to sleep which will be good for you. You need all the rest you can."

"Thank you, Doctor," Thrang weakly smiled at him, as he left.

One of the nurses helped him with the two different pills which he gratefully accepted.

"No!" he told her when she gave him the sleeping pill. "I will take it later. First I will have to ring up home and inform my mother."

Seeing that he was comfortable enough, the nurses left with a cheerful glint in their eyes. At the door, one of them told him to ring should he require any thing or any help.

Alone in the stillness of the room, he suddenly had the shivers. He realized the enormity of the dangers confronting him. He could so easily have been killed, had it not been for his foresighted mother, who had the coolness and reasoning to inform the police. He could feel his body trembling and he let it so. When it subsided somewhat, he picked up the mobile from the side-table which the nurse had placed, and called his mother. It was past midnight but his mother would be waiting, worried about him.

"Hi! Mei." He said, trying to sound jovial, when she was on the line.

"Thank God, Thrang. What happened? The police told me just now that you had been shot."

"Calm down, Mei," Thrang consoled her in a cool and even voice. "I am alright. It was just a graze on the thigh; no bones broken."

He felt his mother heaved a sigh of relief, and he said: "The doctor and nurses are taking good care of me. I am quite comfortable."

"I will see you in the morning, son," she said, happy in the knowledge that he was alright and that he would be out of the hospital in a matter of days.

"Goodnight son."

"Goodnight, and sleep well," he said, knowing that his mother would not sleep well but would worry the night, waiting for the day to dawn.

"Mei?" He added quickly, before she put down her phone, "Don't tell Ri. It is too late and I don't want her worrying the whole night. I will ring her up in the morning." An overpowering feeling of love crept over him as he thought of Ri, now probably fast asleep.

He popped the sleeping pill into his mouth and swallowed it with a half glass of water. He felt the burning sensation on his thigh lessening as he gradually drifted off to sleep.

He woke the next morning to the nurse calling, "Bah, wake up."

He opened his eyes and he realized where he was. It was no dream. His thigh hurt and he could feel the bruises on his hands and knees.

"Have your breakfast first before I can give you your medicine." She said, as she helped bringing the tea and toast with jam closer to him. *He was probably asleep when breakfast was brought in.* He noticed that the bottle of blood had been replaced by a bottle of saline water.

Feeling a bit hungry, he devoured the two thin slices of toasted bread smeared with jam and followed it up with a big long gulp of the now tepid tea. The nurse removed the tray to a corner of the room.

She took his pressure, noted it down, and handed him his two pills which he dutifully swallowed.

"Do you want to pee?" she asked him, matter of fact.

"Yes," he replied, blushing.

She reached under the bed, took out the urinal and lifting the blanket, placed it under him. He closed his eyes as he relieved himself. When he was finished, she took it out and disappearing into the bathroom, dumped his refuse into the toilet and flushed the cistern.

The time on his watch showed nine o'clock. Ri would be in school by now, he thought. He instead sent her a message to ring him up when she was free.

He then rang up home asking his mother to bring him a pair of pajamas, which he did not normally use at home, and the novel on his bedside-The Camel Club.

A junior doctor doing the rounds visited him at about ten. The doctor studied the medical report, asked him a few questions and left, satisfied. The saline in the bottle above his head was almost exhausted, when a nurse came in, stopped the flow from the bottle, and extracted the needle from his arm. She cleaned the area where the needle had penetrated with some stinging lotion; put a wad of cotton wool over it and used a band-aid to keep it in place.

At eleven thirty the hospital doors were opened for visitors. A few minutes later there was a light tapping on his door, which gently opened as his mother stepped in with the maid in tow, carrying a heavy bag.

"You don't look too bad," she said, bending down and kissing his cheek. The maid deposited the bag by the lone chair and voiced his mother's concern.

They sat down, his mother close to his bed-side.

She emptied the contents of the bag- a bottle of his favourite apple juice, a packet of cream crackers, a jar of horlicks, toothpaste and brush, a pair of pale blue pajamas, a pair of slippers, a towel, soap and the novel, *The Camel Club.*

"If there is anything more you need I will bring in the afternoon," she said.

"I was so scared last night, until I heard from you. Now, tell me son, what really happened."

"Mei? That telephone call last night was just a ruse to get me to out of the house. Like a fool, I swallowed the bait to find myself in a trap." He smiled at his mother. "If it were not for your good sense I would have been a goner," he admitted.

"Yes, I know what you are thinking, Mei," he said, his face, deadpan. "You think my life is in danger. Yes, I suppose it is but not to the extant of hiding. I have to be alert and careful, that's all. And after last night I will be extra careful," he promised her.

"You told Ri?" she brightly enquired.

"No Mei. I could not ring her up as I woke up late. I just sent her a message to ring me up when she is free."

His mother attended to him as she would a small child, wiping the sweat off his brow with a face towel and pouring a glass of apple juice for him to drink.

They chatted on for some more time till the bell rang for visitors to leave.

"I will come again in the afternoon," she said, preparing to leave.

"No, Mei!" Thrang said. "You better rest at home. I am alright, as you can see. Besides, Ri will visit me then."

His mother smiled. "As you wish, son," she said, "but I will be back tomorrow morning. And keep me informed."

He got a sudden jolt when he felt a vibration under his pillow. It was his mobile ringing. He fished it out and realized it was Ri.

"Thrang?" she said hesitatingly, "What is it?"

"Ri Darling, I had a bit of an accident last night," he blurted out.

"What? What kind of an accident?" she asked, bewildered and suddenly anxious.

"First of all I was almost run over by a vehicle, and then someone from inside the vehicle took a shot at me and hit me on the thigh. I scrambled up and ran, not knowing I was hit; luckily, the police patrol vehicle appeared and those murderers raced off. No serious damage done, Ri. I am alright and doing fine at the Civil Hospital."

"How come you didn't inform me?" she asked, slightly agitated.

"It was too late, Love; I didn't want to worry and disturb your sleep and besides I was not seriously injured," he replied. "I wanted to ring you up in the morning but I overslept."

"I'll come see you straight after school," she said, breathlessly.

Thrang spent the afternoon quietly; reading and napping. He had a little bit of lunch which he found to be too bland for his liking. Not that he had any complaints; he was never a good eater.

He scratched his chin which had a day's growth of beard. He was so used to shaving every morning, and he felt a bit old and unclean; and he had forgotten to ask his mother to bring his shaving set.

There was a tap on the door, which opened even before it stopped. Ri entered and closed the door behind her. She turned her gaze on him, paused for a second and in four quick steps was by his bedside.

She bent down and swiftly kissed his cheek, ever so lightly.

"Don't I deserve to be kissed properly?" Thrang said aggrieved, offering his lips.

"No! Not now," she said mischievously.

"We shall see, when you can walk again and are back home."

"But don't you see? Your kiss will be like a balm to my wound. I will heal much faster," he said in a very seductive voice. "Besides, it will be like a bright sunshine lighting up the lonely night I have to spend, in this inhospitable and desolate room."

She smiled, her attractive wide lips becoming wider still, as she graciously bent down again and this time kissed him full on his lips, but was quick to disengage herself from him before he could hold her.

"There now, be content. You are too weak for anything. You need to rest to become your normal self again," she admonished him, as she presented him with a bottle of Active Apple Juice and a Get Well Card.

She sat on the edge of the bed by his side.

My, isn't she beautiful? Thrang thought, as he looked lovingly at her.

As if reading his thoughts, she smiled and said.

"Now tell me what actually happened."

Thrang narrated in detail the incident of last night and of how, like a stupid fool he was duped into almost losing his life but for the coolness and foresight of his mother in informing the police.

"Thrang? You are very lucky. You could have lost your life."

She took his hand in hers, holding it tight, and he could feel the fear filling her mind as her body trembled.

"Ri? I have been lucky, thank God! But I never really imagined that I would be a target for murder. However, I believe that whoever is behind this act, will not proceed further." He tried to console her.

"Thrang? Please be careful," she pleaded.

Thrang looked at her, full in the face. "I will, Darling. I have so much to live for."

"Ri, I hate to see you leave but you better go home. It is getting dark outside and soon it won't be safe for you to travel alone."

She got her handbag and gave him another kiss on his lips, this time a little longer and with some intensity.

"Goodnight, Thrang,' she said, 'and sleep well. I'll see you again tomorrow after school."

At the door, she looked at him and winked mischievously, before she disappeared.

"Goodnight, my Princess," he murmured, at the door which had closed softly behind her.

The next day after his mother had left visiting him, the police Inspector turned up.

"Good morning." The Inspector said jovially, "You look good."

"Good morning, Inspector. I guess I am okay. Nothing serious, just a flesh wound."

After a bit of a chit chat, the Inspector got down to his purpose of visit.

"I would like you to tell me in detail, exactly what happened that night, and please do not leave out anything that you may think irrelevant," he said, in the professional manner of an investigator.

As Thrang narrated the events of that fateful night, the Inspector noted it all down in his notebook, interrupting now and then with some questions.

"Do you recognize the voice on the phone?" he asked.

"No. Absolutely not!" Thrang said.

"And the vehicle? Did you recognize it?"

Thrang shut his eyes, trying to recollect and said hesitatingly, "I don't really know. It was dark and it happened in a flash. I think however, it could be a dark coloured Tata Sumo or even a Bolero, but I'm not sure."

"And I suppose you didn't see who shot you?"

"No! Sensing my life in danger, I scrambled to my feet from where I lay sprawled, and just ran. I didn't even know I was shot at, until later when you arrived and I felt my trousers sticky and wet. Only then did I feel the pain."

The questions carried on for another fifteen minutes until the Inspector felt he had everything recorded that was worth recording.

He was released from the hospital after four days. By that time he was able to walk around, but with a slight limp. The wound had yet to heal properly, but that was no problem. He rested another three days at home after which he started attending to his business at the shop, and his life gradually reverted back to his normal habitual cycle.

10

The days in the month of November had become shorter and the nights longer. Thrang was immersed in his own business and did not notice the fleeting days pass by, and the incident of his being shot had become history, with only the big ugly scar to remind him that his life was not yet out of danger.

He had visited Ri's house that month, when he no longer showed any trace of a limp and had met her parents. Her father, a Professor at the North Eastern Hill University, taught History. Thrang was rather taken up with the soft spoken gentleman whom he found to be very interesting and quite witty.

Her mother, a no-nonsense and down to earth woman, was the soul of the home. Thrang was at first shy and afraid of her, but soon shed his apprehensions altogether. He found her to be level headed and very jovial and enjoyed her company. A warm and kind hearted person, actually. *What would she have thought of him had she known his earlier impressions of her?* He chuckled inside his heart.

"Now Thrang, you are the only son?" She had asked him.

"Yes, Mei," he had replied.

Thrang had noticed her slight start at his calling her "Mei." She, however, looked pleased and he was encouraged.

"I have seen your mother on a few occasions. She is a very pretty woman, Thrang." She had said, smiling at him.

"Thank you, Mei. But you yourself are no less pretty." He had smiled back, somewhat embarrassed by his bold compliments of her.

"You lost your father long ago? That's what Ri told me," she had softly enquired.

"I lost my father when I was only ten years old. He suffered from leukemia. I don't really remember much about him."

Just then, a young pretty girl very much like Ri, entered, carrying a tea tray. She carefully placed the tea and cakes on the table.

"Ailinda? Say hello to Thrang, Ri's friend." Ri's mother had said.

Ailinda looked up, blushed and offering her outstretched hand had said. "Hello? Bah."

Thrang had taken the proffered hand, smiled and said: "My pleasure to meet you, Ailinda. I didn't know Ri had a sister. She never told me."

"You never asked me." Ri responded, all the while having kept silent.

He had, had a wonderful evening that day. The cake baked by Ailinda was delicious and he had complimented her, to which she had blushed, feeling rather pleased. Thrang had felt so much at home with that wonderful family.

The phone rang just when he was about to close his shop. He picked it up.

"Hello?" he said, alert after the close call he had had.

"Hello Thrang. Gautam here."

"Oh hello, Gautam. How are you?" Thrang broke in a smile.

"I am alright," he replied.

"Do you remember, some time back I had told you of the pressure and influence that money has?"

Thrang suddenly felt uneasy; something was coming up, he felt.

"Yes, I do remember it well," he said.

Gautam was somewhat apologetic when he said: "The money-power of the industrialists and miners has won over our advocate. We have to let him go."

Thrang was silent, not knowing what to say. *This is disgusting! The way money can buy and corrupt. It is unfair.*

"Thrang?" Gautam's voice crackled over the line.

"I have managed to persuade another Advocate, a Mr. Natarajan, to take up our case. Let's pray that he does not leave us halfway. The big problem nowadays is that no one is willing to fight for a cause without being paid. And the fees, asked by the advocates in the Supreme Court are astronomical."

Thrang knew too well the amount of money that would be needed to file any case in the Supreme Court of India. He realized that he and his Group were very lucky to have met up with Gautam, who had genuine interest and the wherewithal to get the case filed in the Supreme Court, without any paise being spent, so far.

"Well Gautam, what can I say. I trust your judgment explicitly. Whatever you decide to do is okay by me and our Group."

At the other end of the line, Gautam was trying to get through the faint and heavy loaded line: "Thrang, I am sending a typed affidavit tomorrow morning by Speed Post. The moment you receive it, please put your seal and sign and send it back to me, immediately by Speed Post."

Thrang assured him that he would do so, the moment he received the affidavit, and the line went dead.

PART THREE

What would the world be, once bereft
Of wet and wildness? Let them be left,
O let them be left, wildness and wet;
Long live the weeds and the wilderness yet.

Gerard Manley Hopkins

1

"Bah? How many vehicles do we need this year?" enquired Ban.

The year had come full circle and the year's cave expedition was on hand. Thrang had been having meetings all the week with his trusted lieutenants; Ban, Lung and Aseem, the chef. Provisions for the expedition had already been finalized and ordered, to be delivered a day before the camp staff would leave for the base camp. That day, Ban and Lung had bought four large tarpaulins to replace some of the old and torn ones, which had provided many years of service.

"I think we could make do with three vehicles, to be stationed in camp throughout the expedition period," Thrang answered to Ban's query.

"We could use the bus to ferry the cavers from Shillong to base camp and back again at the end of the expedition; and if necessary, we can hire Sumos as and when required," he added.

"Good! I think I will bring my Pick-up," Lung said, taking a sip of his drink.

"So when do we leave to set up camp?" Ban asked, looking up from his jottings on his notebook.

"Let me see," Thrang said, looking at the calendar on the wall.

"I think you should all leave on the 31st, that is a week from today; that way you will have two clear days to get the camp ready, for most of the foreign cavers would be arriving Shillong on the 31st and we will all be at the camp on the 2nd of February. That okay with you all? I have already contacted Hawa and he has begun his work at the campsite this morning."

The three nodded in agreement.

"What about the letters to the headmen and the Daloi?" Ban asked.

"I will get the letters ready by tomorrow; also the letters to the Deputy Commissioner and the Superintendent of Police, Jowai, for their information about our activities. You can deliver them on the way," Thrang assured him.

"Oh, before I forget, give me the registration number of the vehicles that are going to be with us during the entire expedition. Because of the state assembly elections the district authorities have already started requisitioning all commercial vehicles. So I need to write to the Deputy Commissioner to spare our vehicles from such requisitioning."

Lung and Ban exchanged glances, realising that they had somehow overlooked a serious issue which could have jeopardised their expedition.

"I'm sorry Bah that I have forgotten about the coming elections,' Ban said rather sheepishly, 'anyway let me confirm about the vehicles tonight. Then tomorrow morning I can give you their numbers," Ban said.

"Good. But we shall have to get everything ready by tomorrow."

"Yes, and by tomorrow evening all the provisions would be delivered here," Lung confirmed.

Aseem, the chef, warming to the spirits he had been helping himself, asked Thrang if he would like anything special for dinner the day they arrive at camp.

Thrang smiled broadly, "Yes! What I would like is dohkhlieh."

Aseem's smiling face fell, for he was a Muslim.

"No! Bah Thrang. I will not touch pork," he said, incredulity written all over his face.

"In that case, you can cook us anything." Thrang smiled at him triumphantly.

Aseem burst out in a guffaw, and taking the bottle, poured himself another drink.

"Bah Thrang,' he said, giving a mock box on Thrang's back, 'You are pulling my leg."

The expedition camp was pitched on the same spot that was used during the last four expeditions. The nearby villages on the Ridge had got so used to seeing the big expedition camp every year and the cavers of different nationalities occupying the tents dotting the hillside. It had always aroused curiosity and excitement amongst the rural folks, especially the children.

The sun had just disappeared and darkness had enveloped the camp when the bus and a Sumo, carrying the twenty five cavers arrived. Ban and Lung had already got a big bonfire burning brightly to invite them. Soon, the camp was filled with activity, with everyone trying to find his own bunk or to pitch his own personal tent. Many of the cavers are well versed with the routine, except for a few of them who have come for the first time. With another eight joining in the coming week, the camp population would rise to forty six.

While the cavers were settling down, as was the custom, Thrang and Tim went to pay their respects to the new Daloi and the headman of Shnongrim village. Over tea at the Daloi's house, they discussed about the tremendous potential of caving on the Ridge, the environmental degradation caused by the coal mining and of Cement Plants that would be coming up on the Ridge. Thrang also briefed the new Daloi about the latest position on the Public Interest Litigation filed by the MSG. Thrang and Tim returned back to camp, full of confidence with the Daloi's support and of the many more new caves to be shown, over the next few weeks.

After the next day's programme was chalked out, the night was given to merrymaking. Thrang had his tent pitched close to the store-room where it was generally quieter and closer to the camp staff.

The twenty five days on the Ridge passed off so swiftly that no one had time to realize that the expedition was on its last day. It had been a good year for the cavers; thirty two new caves were discovered, 17.65 kilometres of new cave passage explored and mapped, and Ken's theory of a vast cave system under the Ridge slowly proving to be a reality, with the connection of Krem Liat Prah-Um Im- Labit System to Krem Rubong and Synrang Ngap, making it a system of over thirty five kilometres.

"This is great," Thrang said to Tim.

"Yes, it is. You know, we could spend years here on the Ridge, discovering more and more cave passages, and still, not yet fully doing justice," he said, like a man, appreciating and in-love with the Ridge.

Thrang had not ventured into Krem Khung that expedition; he had spent most of his time assisting Dr. Sorenson, in surface survey of the Ridge. During their excursions, they had discovered a sink which they did explore and left it still ongoing at the end of the expedition.

Krem Khung was extended by another 1.2 kilometres, but with little prospect for further extension; Krem Tyngheng however, was still ongoing after 2.4 kilometres was added to its earlier surveyed length of 9.2 kilometres. And the Humming Bird Cave? It was descended over a series of magnificent clean washed shafts to a depth of -110 metres, explored and connected to Monkey Skull Cave, another newly discovered cave, to create a single system - named Humming Monkey System; the system yielded almost five and a half kilometres of cave passage with a superb river passage which exited at the foot of the ridge near Umthe village. Thrang never had a chance to explore the system, much to his dismay. However, a few days later on a recce, he was thrilled to discover a big horizontal cave and he thought to himself, how come no one had discovered such a big cave with an entrance of no less than fifteen metres wide. This was too good to be true, he thought. Contemplating on starting the survey, he suddenly noticed a white spot on a protuberance on a large rock at the entrance. He was not sure whether it was a survey point or bird shit. He entered the cave to confirm whether the cave had been surveyed at all. Sure enough, on the most likely spot he discovered another white mark; a white fluid eraser mark. His heart sank! The cave had been explored and surveyed. Nevertheless he ventured further into the cave to admire the huge passage and the magnificent underground river, wondering all the while what cave it was. It was only at camp later in the evening, that he realized it was the lower horizontal passage of Humming Monkey System. Though he was not a party to the mapping of the cave, he had however inadvertently 'discovered' the resurgence and seen some portion of the magnificent system.

With the underground secrets of the Ridge slowly being unravelled, Thrang realized the importance of conservation and protection of that very significant area. *Yet, what I see before me today is very heartbreaking. I cannot sit and see this Ridge destroyed.*

The expedition that year had been very noisy and somewhat disturbed for the cavers as it was the election month. Hoards of village people canvassing for their respective candidates were moving around the countryside in a long convoy of vehicles, shouting and singing and generally merrymaking throughout the day and late into the night. And with free liquor being supplied by the candidates the village menfolk had abandoned their farming to enjoy once in five years, a two week long picnic of free booze, free food and a handsome daily wage, just for roaming throughout the constituency intimidating the other candidates. There were drunken brawls, threats, intimidations and even murders. The villages were mostly dead during the daytime. The cavers learned to keep away at a safe distance from those crazy election canvassing mobs, more so as one of the candidates was a well known coal baron, who it was believed would stop at nothing to sway the voters in his favour. He was blantantly showing his prowess by distributing vast sums of money; it was believed that he had already spent not less than ten crores. The general prediction of the people was that he would win hands down. Thrang could well understand and believe such a claim; for this ruthless man had been giving money even to voters who were known supporters of his rival – requesting them that even if they would not vote for him they could just stay home and not cast their votes at all, thus increasing his own chances of being elected by buying negative votes. Elections in the coal belt areas of Jaintia Hills were a very dangerous and risky business, meant only for those unscrupulous big spending mafias who would not hesitate to resort to unfair means.

It was a delicate balance for the cavers and Thrang was well versed to the demands of such situations. It was a great relief for them when the elections were over, bringing back normalcy to the region; and the villagers back to their daily chores of tilling the land for planting. By then however, the expedition had also ended and they were headed back for Shillong.

On the last night in camp Thrang received a visitor.

"Kymno Bah?"

Thrang looked up from his task of noting down all the expenses incurred for the expedition.

"Oh hello Hawa. Good that you have come tonight. I may as well settle your bill." Thrang welcomed him with a smile as Hawa found himself a seat. The young man from the village of Shnongrim had been associated with the expedition for the last four or five years ever since the expedition had shifted their camp to the ridge. It had been his job to construct the camp – sleeping quarters for those who don't use tents, work cum dining space, kitchen, store rooms for caving equipment and provisions, toilet facilities and bathing cubicles. He had also been very useful as a guide in finding caves for the expedition. This year however except for setting up the camp he was far too busy with the elections to have any time to be involved with the expedition.

"How come you never showed your face all these weeks?" Thrang asked him though he knew the reason.

He gave a sheepish smile, scratching the back of his head.

"Canvassing. I had to help out and they were very hectic days; leaving home very early in the morning and returning very late in the night. I am still feeling the strain."

"So, your candidate will win?"

Again the head scratch. "I'm afraid not. The chances are extremely dim."

"Who then do you think will win from your constituency?"

"There is no doubt as to who will win. Everyone is sure it will be Ma Thor; he has spent crores of rupees to distribute to all the households in his constituency. Further his close aids and hired goons are using threats and intimidation to frighten the opposition."

"And who is this Ma Thor?" Thrang asked.

Hawa looked surprised.

"You don't know Ma Thor? He is the richest coal mafia in Jaintia Hills. And he is determined to become a cabinet minister in the next government. He will too at that."

"God help us all then," Thrang commented, rather sarcastically.

"Yes," Hawa said, scratching his head again. Thrang knew he had something on his mind.

"Last night, a day after the elections, there was a massacre in the Briwar area," he began in a low conspiratorial voice.

"Where is Briwar?" Thrang interrupted him.

"On the next ridge north of here. Not too far away. That's where the coal seams are thicker and richer. That's where the mafias are congregating and fighting to grab as much of forest land as they could with whatever means they could deploy. There it is that might rules. Even surrendered terrorists have joined in; openly carrying AK47s and grabbing a piece of the cake. Anyway, what I was trying to tell you is this: last night a group of miners from a nearby camp attacked another camp at around midnight when the labourers were fast asleep. Some were hacked to death in their sleep; some escaped in the dark night with severe injuries; some succumbed to their injuries running away in terror. The head labourer of the attacked camp was wounded but managed to flee only to collapse at the edge of the paddy field. In the morning he was discovered dead – bled to death during the night."

"What happened this morning then?" Thrang enquired.

"This morning? The place was swarming with policemen and now section 144 of the CRPC has been clamped. The area is quiet and controlled now but for how long? When the police force is withdrawn trouble will brew up again. Briwar is the most dangerous and highly volatile area in Jaintia Hills today – it is a boiling pot simmering and seething like a volcano rumbling in its depths. And one day you will be going to that area for there are many caves there too."

"How I wish these hills were as quiet and peaceful, green and pristine as they were two decades ago," Thrang murmured his nostalgic thoughts aloud.

"But it is we who are living here that has to bear the brunt of all the spoils and the lawlessness that has become the order of the day," Hawa complained, his hand travelling to the back of his head. "We are masters no more of our own lands. These immigrant labourers especially the Bangladeshis walk and trample around as if they own the place. All businesses mostly in the shanty towns have been taken away by these strange and uncouth outsiders and we are reduced to second grade citizens in our own birthland. I would never have believed that this would happen to us one day. A great shame has befallen. I can't even go fishing; there are no more fishes to catch."

Thrang took a sip of his Old Monk. Then he fished out a bottle of Budweiser from the carton box next to him.

"Here, I think you need this," he said handing the bottle to Hawa.

Hawa popped the cap out and raised the bottle to Thrang, "Cheers."

"Shakiya" Thrang responded, raising his own glass.

He watched in awe as Hawa drank more than 300ml in one long gulp.

"Very thirsty. I was out in the sun the whole day today and I didn't have any water with me," he explained, trying to control the belch that was forcing its way out.

Thrang nodded with a smile at his Shnongrim friend, who though standing less than five feet tall is nevertheless considered a braveheart in his village.

"Now, I too grieve at the sad plight of these hills which I dearly love, as much as you. My heart cries in silence every time I see new scars appearing in green forested slopes. I feel so helpless and defeated. What more could I do, what more could I do. I am just a puny little being against the might of organised plunderers of the earth. Only You oh God, know the anguish I suffer in my heart. I bleed, oh I bleed as much as the soil that is torn from its roots."

"Can I have another beer please, Bah?"

"Sorry Hawa. Sure you can have another one," Thrang apologised handing him another bottle.

He took a sip of his Old Monk before he continued again.

"I fear for these hills. I fear because it is an ecologically fragile environment and the damage that is being perpetrated upon it will have a very long term ecological impact. Many of the villages will be unfit for habitation and will need relocation. Then the people will weep – when they have lost everything; when they realise and fully comprehend the significance of their despoiled and degraded serene environment; when their children look at them with shame and sad accusing faces at the massive erosion of their rightful inheritances. *Why didn't we stand up for our rights,* they would lament then; but it would be too late. The guile and persuasion of the devil is too smooth and overpowering for most to be able to resist. Only when everything is gone would they come to terms with themselves."

"Bah,' Hawa interrupted, 'we have been resisting selling our land for the last one year; now we know that the miners have got into our coal seams from underneath. There is nothing we could do, to either stop it or even prove that they are stealing."

Ban appeared. "Bah, dinner has been served," he said.

"Alright Ban, but I'll have mine in the kitchen, later with Hawa."

"Tell me Bah, are the other districts in the state as bad as ours?"

Thrang smiled, seeing the interest in Hawa's face.

"This part of Jaintia Hills is the worst affected – totally ravaged. Next is Garo Hills. They would have destroyed Siju Dobhakol had it not been for an NGO working in the area. As it is the thousands of heavy loaded coal trucks have made a mockery of the roads in the region. The next of course is West Khasi Hills and what is very alarming is the pollution of the River Ranikor. A beautiful river known for its sporting fish, the golden mahseer – where a 50 kg catch is not unheard of. This river has attracted anglers even from other states. Now if the coal mining in the upper reaches is not stopped immediately, that river will go the same way as all the rivers in these parts; an unthinkable and unpardonable proposition. And Sohra? The once beautiful and scenic road leading to it is now an eyesore with scarred hillsides and choked streams. And the state's most beautiful and picturesque tourist attraction which is also the most ecologically fragile landscape is allowed to be mined indiscriminately; that too in the only catchment area in the region – the Lawbah Ridge. I personally believe that Sohra should be declared a no mining zone as the area is all eroded and denuded of topsoil. Are we going to mine Sohra out thereby killing it, or are we going to promote clean and eco-friendly tourism for the region for which it is best suited for?"

Reeling under the revelation, Hawa sat wide eyed and silent, too stunned for words.

"Yes Hawa, this state of ours is sold, and the powers that be are all mute spectators, happy with their little cuts."

"What I'm hearing is very depressing," Hawa managed to murmur.

"Hawa let me explain further. It is a known fact that the costs of the negative effects that occur out of mining, far out weigh the benefits arising out of mining. The negative impacts on the people especially those at ground zero are highly jeopardized and all for the sake of a few individuals who aspire to become billionaires overnight. Are we still living in the dark ages where might is right? Where the poor and unwary are trampled upon?'

'What has the state government done to prevent such devastation? Nothing! They brush away their responsibilities by admitting to their inability to control the rampant and unscientific mining on the grounds that the lands being mined are private propery. This is utter nonsense! If the Supreme Court of India could ban the felling of timber in the state how could the state government shirk its own responsibility? If mining in one's own private property causes pollution, degradation of the environment and affects the lives and livelihoods of the people in the region then there is no question of not stopping such mining activities or regulating and monitoring the activities on sound and sensible methods. Do we not apply for building permission on our own private property on rules and regulations as laid down by the government? Am I being baised in my judgement?"

"Absolutely not! You have always been fair in your judgements. But what I don't understand is why no one is standing up to fight this corrupt system?"

Thrang merely smiled and took a sip of his drink.

"You know most of the time I feel that all is lost – that neither you nor I could do anything to stop it; that all of us are corrupt. Let me tell you a story.'

'Last year I went on a recce to the village of Khahnar near the River Kopili, to assess the caving potential of the area. I met the headman and the secretary of the village and we had a very fruitfull discussion, where I was informed of many caves in the area. I also discussed with them the importance of protecting the environment, as the coal mining operrations were getting closer to that village. They were very enthusiastic about the idea and even pointed out to me a vast tract of forest land which they said belonged to the village. They told me that the village dorbar had decided to conserve that forest area; they had therefore approached the Forest Department with their suggestion and offer – that is for the Department not only to protect the area but to restock it with wildlife. I was naturally thrilled, realizing that here at last was a village standing up to protect and safeguard its own environment and surroundings. In my discussions during the year I had always cited this village as an example of courage – not falling prey to greed, threat and intimidation. How wrong and heartbreaking it was for me to discover that greed overshadows everything, including commitments made. Last week I visited Khahnar again and I was utterly shaken to realize that the community forest land had been divided and demarcated into as many households as was present in the village. This meant only one thing – the villagers could now sell off their new acquired plots to the coal mafias who were now almost at their doorsteps. I was devastated and did not even bother to seek clarification from the headman. It was pointless. It was then that I realized, no matter how upright and strong of conviction we are, we can all be bought; the limit when we begin to succumb will depend on the strength and feelings of our conscience. I was so creastfallen that when I left them, they must have realized my disappointment from the gloomy expression I wore."

"Yes, I too know about this,' Hawa nodded, 'the village has already been approached. And it appears that our would-be minister, the coal baron has the upper hand; there is talk that he is negotiating for acquiring the whole chunk of that forest land. His agents are already camping in the village."

Thrang picked up his glass, was lost in thoughts for a while, then put back the glass on the upturned mustard oil tin without having a drink.

"Okay then, let us finish with our business; now tell me how much I owe you."

"Thirty two thousand five hundred" he said, taking out a piece of paper from his pocket and handing it to Thrang.

"Isn't that a bit steep?"

"Well, the bamboo poles are very costly nowadays for there is a great demand from the miners. Labour costs too have gone up. In fact prices of everything have skyrocketed."

"No worry Hawa, I am not complaining; just making a statement."

He counted the notes and handed the amount to Hawa, thanking him again for the help he has been extending to the expedition for the past many years.

"Bah, next year you are coming back here again?"

"Sure! This ridge has much more to offer. I'm positive we will return to the ridge next year and the next five years after that. It is indeed a superb karst area, unparallel in the sub-continent."

"So I'll make the camp in the same spot?" He asked Thrang.

"Yes, we will again have our camp here; for it's the only place with some water from that little spring over there," Thrang said, pointing in the general direction of the spring. "This has been an ideal camping site in close proximity to all the caves on the ridge."

"Come on, bottoms up. We have to go for our dinner. I don't like cold food."

The expedition farewell party was held in a resort by the picturesque lake, where everyone let go of their inhibitions and gave in to a wild night of entertainment.

The year's expedition had unravelled many secrets and had opened up new and exciting vistas for future cave explorations, so much so that all the seven new comers in the expedition had expressed their desire to come back the following year.

Ten days after the end of the expedition, as he was about to take stock of the day's transactions, Thrang received a call from Guatam, informing him that the Supreme Court had sat that day and after having heard arguments from the advocates of both parties, had agreed to the plea of the Meghalaya Speleological Group for the constitution of an expert committee to study the impact that the coal and limestone mining had on the destruction of caves and on the environment as a whole.

"This is great news, Guatam!" Thrang said, excitedly.

"Yes, this is a good omen for us," Guatam replied, pleased with the outcome of the Court proceedings.

"You better get ready,' he continued, 'for you are one of the members."

"The other six members are: a representative each from the Central Pollution Control Board, the State Pollution Control Board, the Indian Bureau of Mines and the British Cave Research Association; Dr. Mainul Ahmed, Professor of Environmental Studies, Delhi University, and Mr. Ashutosh Mazumdar, a retired Supreme Court Judge who will be the Chairman."

"Guatam? I am overwhelmed and honoured to be nominated to the committee," Thrang simply said.

"Just be ready. Letters will be dispatch by tomorrow. Better get in touch with your friends in the UK, so that the BCRA will be alerted and will be in a position to send someone immediately the moment the request is received by them from the Office of the Supreme Court."

Thrang could almost imagine the sparkling and merry eyes of Guatam when he said: "The Chief Justice has expressed his deep concern at the environmental degradation in the state, caused by the unscientific and unregulated mining and had ordered that the Committee submit its findings to the Court within two months from today."

"This is marvelous. It is what I had hoped and prayed for."

"Yes, it is going our way isn't it?" Guatam interposed.

"Bye, Thrang and be careful, seriously. You can't pretend it is otherwise."

"Sure will, Guatam, you have given me such great news I'm absolutely ecstatic," Thrang said, and hung up.

2

On his way home that evening, Thrang had stopped by the cyber café and e-mailed his friend Dr. Tim Warren about the latest happenings in court and the Court's request to the BCRA to depute a reputed speleologist as a member of the expert committee for assessment of the impact mining had on the environment and the safety of caves. The request letter he said would be dispatch in a day or two.

That night, Thrang felt a deep soothing satisfaction in his heart. He couldn't have asked for more; that the Apex Court had constituted a Committee to assess the ground reality of the damage being perpetrated by the miners and industrialists speaks highly of the serious view taken by the Chief Justice. Thrang felt vindicated; what the MSG and he himself had stood for had not proved in vain. *At least they were being heard, and all is not lost, not yet; for there were times when he thought that they were up against a brick wall and that they were fighting for a futile cause. Political and money power could never be overlooked – they were two extremely potent forces that could destroy and undermine the basic values that we believe and uphold.*

Thrang slept as one dead to the world; innocent and uncaring. He may have dreamt the night, but he did not know or remembered. When he woke up he was refreshed with vigour and vitality to a bright sunny morning, with promises of exciting adventures in the offing.

Over breakfast, Thrang read the local newspapers which gave a mention about the Supreme Court's orders and elaborating about the impasse between the miners and the cement companies on the one side and the cavers on the other. He was glad that things were moving, though so very slow for his liking. But that's the way things move in this country he thought – either it needs greasing of the palm or the department is overburdened or the machinery is totally unconcerned and indifferent to efficient and quick deliverance of duty, which in effect is indispline and irresponsibility.

That afternoon, Rueben made a visit to his shop.

"Hi! Thrang," he said, brandishing his presence in front of Thrang.

"Oh! Hello, Rueben. It's been some time since we last saw you."

"Yeah! Almost two months," Rueben replied. "I was in South India; I had to accompany my mother for my sister's treatment at the Vellore Christian Medical College. We came back only yesterday."

"And how is she now?" Thrang enquired.

"Alright," he said. "My sister appears to have responded very well to the treatment."

"Glad to hear of it. Give her my regards, will you?" Thrang said, smiling at him.

"Sure." Rueben said, taking out three rolls of film.

"I want these developed."

Thrang handed them to Aiban, who made out a receipt.

"What has been happening, while I have been away?" Rueben asked, sitting down on his favourite stool.

"Well, things have moved, though slow." Thrang said. He told Rueben about the Apex Court's orders. "Yeah! Things which I have dreamed about are now slowly taking shape. And I couldn't have asked for more."

"I'm glad Thrang," Rueben said, smiling at him.

"But you should know Thrang, despoiling and degradation of the environment is not just happening in Meghlaya. It is prevailing in many other states of the country, for example Karnataka, where illegal mining of iron ore is rampant. A few people are literally raping the earth, with the knowledge and protection of powerful politicians. These barons, who have amassed huge wealth, in the shortest time possible, are totally unconcerned with the destruction they are causing to the environment and the misery being meted out to the poor people. It is really no different from what is going on in our state."

Thrang let out a sigh of exasperation.

"You are right, Rueben; but here in Meghalaya they are also destroying these wonderful caverns that nature has bestowed upon us; assets, the destruction of which is irreversible. Moreover, I'm more concerned with the destruction that is being wrought about in my own state and the sufferings our people have to face. If each state can protect the environment in its own territory, then the country as a whole will have a well preserved and healthy environment. Don't you think so, Rueben?"

"Well, yes. But I don't see such a thing ever happening, at least not in the near future."

"I think democracy has failed in our country, what with a large proportion of the population undernourished and illiterate and easily swayed by rhetoric or money. Look at our legislators in parliament – many of them with criminal records and abysmal level of education. What can we expect? In my mind, democracy would flourish only in highly industrialized countries like the United Kingdom and the United States of America, where people are well aware of their rights and know what they want. Our country I'm afraid to admit is many generations behind; it would take many, many years for our country to reach the level or standard of a true and real democracy. I am of the opinion that our country would be better off under a dictatorship. A dictator who is strong, honest and sincere, ready to sacrifice for the welfare of the people; a personality with well meaning intentions - striving for the soundness, security and prosperity of our country, India; with every thought and action aimed at the conservation and protection of the rich natural environs that we are so proud of."

"A dictator will always be a bully, a plunderer, a self egoistic moron," Rueben snorted.

"Yes,' Thrang admitted reluctantly, 'where would you find such an ideal dictator anyhow? People initially tend to have good intentions, but once in power they inadvertently lose their equilibrium. Power, somehow or other, corrupts even the strongest of minds."

They chatted for the next half an hour before Rueben left.

3

When one is eagerly waiting for, or looking towards a particular day or event, time crawls so agonizingly slowly, and patience is at a premium. But the day eventually arrived, when the Chairman of the expert Committee, Mr. Ashutosh Mazumdar, arrived and was lodged at the Pine Wood Hotel. Thrang was ecstatic; he just couldn't wait for the Committee to start its intended fact finding mission.

Thrang closed shop half an hour earlier to meet with Mr. Mazumdar.

Mr. Mazumdar was a big man, bigger still at the waist; age however was catching up, furrowing deep lines on his flabby face. Thrang could see that he had trouble breathing. *Now what the hell*, thought Thrang. *How will he be able to tramp across the countryside, to see the disaster areas and also visit some of the caves which are in imminent threat?*

"Good evening, Mr. Mazumdar. I am Thrang Mawlong," Thrang said extending his hand.

Mr. Mazumdar broke into a wide grin as he shook Thrang's hand with a very firm grip. "Good evening Mr. Mawlong. So you are the guy who filed the Public Interest Litigation?"

"Yes sir. I represent the Meghalaya Speleological Group," Thrang said simply.

"Well, do come in," he invited Thrang inside his suite.

Thrang settled himself on a heavy, well cushioned chair, sinking a few inches in the seat. A couple of minutes later, Mr. Mazumdar having called room service and ordered some tea and pastries, came in and sat opposite him.

"Have you ever been to Shillong before?" Thrang asked him.

"Yes, a long time ago. Probably thirty years ago," he said.

"It has changed a lot; so overcrowded, noisy and busy. It took my vehicle more than an hour to reach the hotel just from the outskirt of the city. The city traffic was a total chaos." He shook his head. "No, I don't think I would like to drive here. Absolutely nerve-ending it is; with most of the taxi drivers having no road etiquette."

Thrang smiled, sympathizing with him. "Yes, it is bad, especially at the peak hours. And the government does not have the will to crack the whip on erring drivers or even enforcing discipline and civic sense among the people."

There was a knock on the door and a waiter entered carrying a tray with tea and pastries, and put it on the table. As he poured the tea into the two cups, Thrang enquired if the other members of the committee had arrived.

"Professor Ahmed was with me on the same flight, but decided to stay the night at Guwahati with his in-laws. He will be here by mid-day tomorrow. The others also will all arrive by tomorrow; Mr. Gurpreet Sondhi of the Indian Bureau of Mines, Dr. Avinash Pathak of the Central Pollution Control Board and Dr. Daniel Harper of the British Cave Research Association. Your State Pollution Control Board will be represented by Mr. Kyrshan Lyngdoh, Senior Scientist, who had phoned me just before you came."

Over tea and pastries, Thrang gave a brief update of the mining scenario and of the many more companies being given licenses to set up cement plants, in the state. What was once all green hills and valleys is today turned into dusty, barren and desolate ugly sites, and potable drinking water is becoming a scarce commodity, he told the retired judge.

Thrang left soon after, after confirming his presence in the first meeting of the Committee the next day at five in the afternoon, in the judge's suite.

All the members were seated by 5 PM. They had arrived fifteen minutes earlier and had met and introduced themselves to each other. Thrang had found Dr. Daniel Harper or Daniel as he preferred to be called; a friendly and down-to- earth person, with thirty-five years of caving experience and an authority on cave fish, having published many scientific papers on the subject.

"I met Tim before I flew here and he briefed me on the prevailing situation with regard to the mining in the cave sensitive areas," he had told Thrang.

"Besides, I have been reading in the Descent about your expeditions for many years now and I have always wanted to visit Meghalaya and see your wonderful caves," he had added.

"Well, you're here now, and during our investigation I'm sure we will have a lot of cave visits to do," Thrang had replied, warming up to him.

Thrang jerked himself back to the present when he heard Mr. Mazumdar, the committee chairman, say: "You all know why we are here. Our job is to visit the mining sites and assess what damage if at all, is being done to the destruction of specific caves, the environment as a whole and the problems faced by the villagers by such mining and cement companies."

The chairman shuffled some papers lying on the table before him, before he continued.

"I need not stress that we should not be biased or impartial in our duty and that our assessment or report to the Supreme Court should be objective and constructive, rather than pulling down one side."

He took a sip of water, looked at Thrang and said, "I call upon Mr. Mawlong to brief the Committee, on the specific areas which the committee, need to visit for on-field assessment."

Thrang blushed, feeling a sense of extreme importance thrust upon him, in the presence of such learned and distinguished persons.

"Mr. Chairman Sir,' he began, 'I think there are four areas that this committee need to visit. The areas of Lumshnong and the Shnongrim Ridge in Jaintia Hills District, Cherrapunjee in East Khasi Hills District and Siju in South Garo Hills District, will suffice to give a clear picture of the pollution and degradation of the environment in its entirety and the wanton and imminent destruction of ancient and important cave systems."

Thrang looked at the members and smiling said, "We also need to get into some of the caves."

"I am definitely out of it," the chairman said, pointing to his girth and age. "The caving could be done by some of you who are younger and fitter. At crucial times we can divide into two groups, as and when required."

"How many days do we have before we have to submit the report?" Daniel enquired.

"I am afraid we don't have much time; just about three weeks, in which to visit the effected sites and to write the report," the chairman lamented.

"So we leave tomorrow, leisurely after lunch, for the Jaintia Hills first as Thrang has suggested. We have two vehicles at our disposal and our rooms at the Circuit House at Jowai have also been booked."

"Gentlemen, I think we are all ready to begin our task," he ended, as the members nodded in agreement.

From their base camp at the Government Circuit House in Jowai, for the next three days, after breakfast, they travelled the sixty kilometres to the village of Lumshnong, where they visited the cement factories and the quarry sites and interviewing the company officials, the labour force, the villagers, farmers and even the youth of the area, eliciting opinions of everyone.

"Do you see the spilled-over debris from the quarry filling up that little valley? That's where the entrance of Krem Kharasniang was," Thrang said, pointing out. "They have choked a beautiful two kilometre cave; a cave that could one day be linked to Krem Umlawan, which if it does happen, would increase the total length of Krem Kotsati-Umlawan system to more than 23.5 kilometres."

"And just there you can see one of the vertical entrance of the Kotsati-Umlawan system, where the debris is being dumped, filling up the cave and choking the water outlets, thereby creating backwaters filling up the passages to almost near the entrance." Thrang spread out the cave plan and pointed out to Daniel and Gurpreet, who had both been with him inside the cave the day earlier.

"The cave system is definitely under the quarry," Daniel agreed.

A hundred metres further up, Thrang showed them the remains or what was left of the once stunning resurgence cave, Krem Umkseh.

"Here is where the locals would come to bathe and wash their clothes. Now where is the water?" he choked, his heart filled with remorse at such devastation.

The sad plight of the once sleepy village now turned into a cauldron of noise and dust, with its demographic structure now dangerously turned upside down by the flow of cheap outside labour, was soon sickingly revealed to the Committee. The poor, simple, rural villagers were slowly feeling the brunt of exploitation at their doorstep.

What was more alarming to the Committee was the existence of five cement companies in an area of just five square kilometres, with more companies waiting at the doorstep for clearances. How could anyone justify the setting up of so many cement plants in such a limited area? This beats all logical reasoning. The area will be devastated and ruined to an unrecognizable and desolate wasteland.

They spent another five days at the Shnongrim Ridge, returning back to the Circuit House every evening.

Everyone was impressed with the Ridge; they realized the uniqueness of the area and the potential it held for tourism, especially with Krem Kut Sutiang in the vicinity, the last fortress of Kiang Nongbah in his fight against the

British. They were taken aback with the ugly scene of the coal mining, which was sucking up all the water from the Ridge, and the deforestation that went along with it. Erosion of the top soil exposing the shale was evident everywhere. The local villagers complained that their paddy-fields were destroyed by the acid leeched from the coal and that blasting and extraction of limestone which had picked up in the last few months was making their lives miserable.

Thrang, Daniel, Gurpreet, Kyrshan, Dr. Pathak and Professor Ahmed visited Krem Liat Prah. The Professor, who had never been in a cave before, was awestruck by the size of the main trunk passage. Daniel, who had over the years explored hundreds of caves the world over, and seen some magnificent ones, was in no doubt impressed with Krem Liat Prah.

"This cave is definitely ancient," he had said, excited at the secrets it held of the geology and geo-morphology of the area.

"And this is the cave where you all found the cave fish, which I believed is a new species?"

"Yes," Thrang had answered.

Pointing up to the ceiling, the Professor had enquired, "What are those iron rods or pipes up there on the ceiling?"

"Oh, they are the Geological Survey of India's steel drills and sheaths improvidently dropped in through an unlikely situated borehole in the ceiling." Thrang had replied.

"They are diamond tipped, if you can get up there," he had added, smiling at the idea of trying to reach thirty metres up the ceiling.

The new Daloi of Nongkhlieh Elaka, Mr. Welborn Sukhlain, with the headmen of the different villages, met the Committee members and implored upon them the urgent need for the protection of the Ridge, which would ensure the wellbeing of all the nine villages on the Ridge.

"Thrang,' he had said, 'if you cannot help us now, then we are doomed. We will have no future. Subsequently, we will have to shift our village to a new place."

The expert committee then travelled to South Garo Hills to the village of Siju, where the famous Siju Cave or Siju Dobhakol as it is locally known, is situated. Daniel was thrilled; for when he had done his own research work on cave fish, he had studied the research papers of Kemp and Chopra on the cave life of that great cave. Except for the chairman, all the six members explored the cave. As they entered the Bat Chamber a great stink permeated the air, which almost knocked the breath out of the Professor.

"Don't look up!" Thrang had warned them

But Kyrshan already had his face turned up, his mouth agape, looking at the thousands and thousands of bats hanging upside down from the ceiling. Even before Thrang's warning had ended, Kyrshan had bent down and rubbed his face with a handkerchief.

"Kyrshan, you have been bombarded with fleas and piss from the bats," Thrang informed him, unable to stop his glee.

Everyone had a good laugh, seeing Kyrshan's eyes popped out with utter disbelief and repugnance and spitting out whatever he thought he had in his mouth. The caving became more lively and enjoyable after the incident, much to the disgust of Kyrshan.

During the four days they stayed at the village, they also visited the Bird Sanctuary close by, across the river Simsang and every evening at camp, they would individually update their own observations which were handed over to the chairman. The chairman, who had stayed out of all those underground trips, had busied his time writing up the draft of the report.

Two days was all the time they spent at Cherrapunjee, concentrating their time and resources in the hamlet of Mawmluh, before they returned back to Shillong, to sit and finalize their Report.

The on-field study and findings of the Expert Committee on the impact of the coal and limestone mining on the environment and its effects on the local population and also the destruction being caused to the caves, was completed three days before their scheduled time. Having accomplished its task, the Expert Committee ceased to exist. The following day Mr. Mazumdar, Mr. Gurpreet Sondhi, Dr. Pathak, Daniel and the Professor left Shillong for Guwahati to board their respective flights back home. Mr. Mazumdar had with him the Report which he would submit to the Chief Justice of the Apex Court. Thrang heaved a sigh of relief; *now the future of the caves rests with the Apex Court.* He had done his bit; the rest is up to the powers that be.

4

It was a very busy day at the shop. For the last two hours Thrang and the two boys were busy attending to the customers, non-stop. He had forgotten his tea, which when he did remember, was cold and looked insipid. He threw away the contents of the cup.

His back ached. The moment the shop thinned of customers, he went out the door for a breath of fresh air and to stretch his aching muscles. The sky was clear after the heavy rains that had started last night and ended just an hour ago. Thrang rejoiced in the romantic feeling of spring. Trees looked resplendent in their green and shiny tops and flowers blossomed in their varied and coloured hues. Thrang could almost feel the sweet flowery smell but for the rains that had killed its scent. He was suddenly attracted by the excited chirping of birds. He looked and saw the reason why. The April downpour had flushed out the termites from the ground; they were just waiting for the rain, to energize them for their flight out into the open sky to begin their cycle of life. As they flew out in their thousands they were plucked from the skies and gobbled up by the congregation of frenzied and hungry birds. *These termites are crazy,* he thought, *flying right into the jaws of death. Yes, but they are actually braving death in answering to their basic instinct of finding a mate to ensure the continuity of their genes.* For the birds it was a splendid feast of pure protein; for the termites it was a fight for survival, either to be eaten up or to survive, find a mate and reproduce. But are we any different from them? He reasoned. Every step we take, everything we do, every pursuit we follow, every interest we have – all is fraught with danger; the unknown danger that lurks for the opportune moment. In that way, we are really defenseless, for we cannot guard ourselves every second of our lives. And are we not bravely, sometimes insanely, pursuing love, with an intensity that is electrifying no matter how awesome the danger presents? When it comes to love do we not all lose our senses and often times do foolish things? Love is a chemistry that only God can explain and we are more than willing victims. From where he stood, Thrang could see some boys scurrying about trying to find the hole from where the termites were popping out of the ground. He smiled to himself, remembering that there was a time when he had done the same; catch the termites as they pop out of the ground and put them in a plastic bag. When he reached home he would transfer them to an earthen pot partly filled with small pieces of paper and close the lid, making sure that the termites got enough air circulation. That way they would stay alive for at least a week and in that week he would have a chance to go angling. His face lit up as he remembered the many thrilling times he had had, hooking fish after fish with those very tempting termites. *A beautiful sport,* he reflected, *but I find no time for it today......with my work and caving. Anyway the pristine rivers are gone – dead and suffocated.*

As nightfall was beginning to settle down and the western sky tinged with a soft crimson hue, Thrang turned back towards his shop, reluctant to leave such splendour and joy outside. *Why do I not linger some more time outside, where I can see the bustle and activity of life?* But I have my own work to attend to and that is the reality of life.

The hours flew swiftly and when the last of the customers had been attended to, Thrang realized it was eight o'clock and half an hour past their usual closing time. He took the sale proceeds of the day and felt good. It was a great day - business-wise. He dumped the cash inside the iron safe and locked it. He would sort it out first thing in the morning.

"Kupar! Aiban! You better go. It is late. I will lock up after you."

"Good night Bah," they both said in unison.

"We can wait for you to close up," Aiban volunteered.

"It's alright. You go. It'll take me just a few minutes to tidy things and lock up," Thrang said, smiling at Aiban.

"Goodnight," he called after them, as they departed.

Thrang took the tea-cups which were still lying on the counter, uncollected by the restaurant boy, and put them in one corner of the shop. He took a cloth duster, doused it with a bit of water, and tried to wipe off the tea stain from the counter. Satisfied that the counter was clean and free of any stain marks, he opened the drawer to retrieve the shop keys. He had better hurry or his mother would start worrying. Being tuned to a regimental life he knew he was late going home. He was looking forward to a supper of pork and mustard leaf soup with his favourite tungryngbai - an early supper that's what it should have been.

He looked up, as the half-closed door creaked opened and two men stepped in. He was about to tell them that he was closed when one of the men, a bearded, dark and muscular looking individual, quickly crossed the room and had him pinned against the wall with a large ugly looking knife at his throat. Thrang was utterly taken by surprise at the turn of events. Who were these men? What do they want of him? There must be some mistake somewhere, he thought. He dared not move or shout for the point of the dagger was pressed just below his Adam's apple. The other man had locked the door from inside and joined the first one. He was also dark and bearded but it was his eyes that frightened Thrang. They were glassy and un-emotional; dead, yes dead. Thrang knew that this man was dangerous and would slit his throat without even blinking an eye-lid. Between the two of them, they bound his hands and feet and taped his mouth shut with plaster tape. The 'dead, glassy eyed-individual', turned off the lights and they sat in the dark, waiting and talking in hushed tones. *They are Bangladeshi ruffians working in the coal mines,* surmised Thrang and a shiver ran up his spine. *What will happen to me now? Why didn't I let Aiban and Kupar wait for me?* Thrang flexed his muscles but it was no use; he was securely bound, like a pig snared in a pig-basket.

Thrang lay on the floor, hands and feet bound and feeling very sore and numb. The street sounds outside seemed to have lessened. *That's it! His abductors were waiting for the street to empty so that they could bundle him out without attracting any attention.* Thrang thought and suddenly realized that the longer they waited the better it would be for him, for his mother would seriously begin to worry and would start ringing soon to find out.

The sound of a vehicle stopping just outside the door alerted Thrang. *This is it!* He felt he heard the vehicle doors open. Just as soon, there was a quick succession of three knocks and a name being called out. One of the men un-bolted the door and slowly opened it. There was a brief exchange of words between them which Thrang could not make out. Just then, Thrang felt the vibration in his trouser pocket even before he heard the ring tone. But he could not get his mobile out. He prayed that they would not hear. The muscular one did. In the dark, he fished the mobile out of Thrang's pocket, switched it off and put it on top of the counter, away from Thrang's reach. He then disconnected the landline, letting the instrument dangle over the desk.

There was a hushed whisper from the door, and the two men took hold of Thrang and lifted him up and between them, half-carried half-walked Thrang out to the back seat of a silver Tata Indica with tinted glass. They also got into the back seat, sandwiching him in between. The third man, who had come knocking at the door, locked the shop with the keys he found on top of the counter; having done so he gave the keys to "Muscles" and got in the front seat next to the driver. 'Muscles' put the keys in Thrang's pocket. As the driver started the ignition, the "dead glassy eyed" man on Thrang's left, took out a black cloth hood from his pocket and put it over Thrang's head. Thrang froze; he wouldn't know where they would be taking him. He would be helplessly carried away in the blindness of the dark terrorized night.

As the car sped into the night, Thrang tried to picture in his mind the direction they were travelling; not that it would do him much good. In a short while however, he gave up. He was utterly confused. The drone of the car and the twists and turns became monotonous, as he sat slumped and aching; the hood over his head adding a new dimension of fear. He lost all sense of time; the journey seemed endless. He must have fallen asleep for a while for he suddenly woke up to a bumpy stretch of road. He could hear heavy loaded trucks pass by. He strained his ears to hear the noises outside. *Tatas and Shaktimans! I must be in the coal mine areas; Jaintia Hills. That's where I am,* Thrang visualized. The significance of his abduction became clear, as he dreaded what was to follow.

After what seemed to be an eternity of slow and painful bumps, the car finally came to an abrupt halt. He heard the doors open and the men get out. He was roughly pulled out of the car. He was so numbed and cramped that he almost collapsed on his feet. "Muscles" steadied him for a while till he could stand firmly. On the journey he had felt a great need to urinate, but had somehow contained himself. At that moment he was about to burst, more so when he heard the others relieving themselves. With his secured hands he fumbled awkwardly with his fly and just managed to free himself to blissfully urinate in the dark open void. It was pure bliss, letting go, not knowing where.

When he was finished and his fly zipped, he was led into the confines of a room or a house. He heard the door shut and latched. The hood was removed from his head. He blinked in the dim candle light, as he realized he was in a tin-shack, with a mud floor.

It was a one room shack about two hundred and fifty square feet in area. At one end of the room a bamboo platform serving as a sleeping bunk, stretched the entire width. The other end served as a kitchen, with a kerosene stove in one corner. Thrang was unceremoniously shoved and made to sit on a bare rickety wooden bed, next to the sleeping bunks.

The driver got busy emptying the contents of a packet he had brought with him into two large aluminum plates. Thrang could clearly make out the chapattis and the vegetables. 'Muscles' asked him if he would like some food. Thrang shook his head. He was damned if he would eat; besides he was not hungry. The four men ate the cold food, with apparent appetite; washing it down with water from a plastic bottle.

Having eaten, the men without much fuss, climbed into their bunks to sleep. 'Muscles' offered him a blanket but Thrang refused. He would rather shiver the night than used that filthy, lice infested blanket. 'Muscles' checked the ropes around his legs and hands. Satisfied, he climbed into his own bunk, leaving the candle burning.

Thrang lay on his back on the hard wooden bed, with nothing to cushion his head. He felt tired; his body ached with pain and cramp. With his mouth firmly taped for so many hours, he felt his jaws locked. There was no way he could escape for he was sure "Muscles" would be alert. Somewhere, he heard a cock crow. Dawn was about to break. He wondered about his mother: *She must be terribly worried, upset and fearful for his safety. She would have informed the Police*, he was sure. In the stillness of the softly creeping dawn and the frightful events of the night, and in the most uncomfortable position that he was in, he somehow drifted in and out of sleep, with the demons of the netherworld conjuring up dark and frightful scenes.

Thrang's mother did not sleep the whole night. When Thrang did not respond to her ring, she tried calling him up on his landline. It was engaged. She kept trying for a few more times with the same result. She tried dialing his mobile again. The response from his mobile was that it was switched off. She dreaded the thought that something bad had happened. She could almost feel it in her heart. With trepidation she contacted the OC at the Police Beat House, and was told that a team would be sent to his shop to investigate.

She fretted all the while, waiting for news from the OC. Almost to the hour; she was informed that her son's shop was locked and that nothing seemed to be amiss. *Probably your son is partying out with his friends*, the OC told her.

She was shocked. "No!" she shouted.

"He would never go anywhere, or stay out so late without informing me. I am sure he is in some sort of danger." She banged the telephone in its cradle, and almost immediately, she lifted it up again and dialed the Director General of Police himself on his mobile.

"Hello, Frankie?" she blurted, when he was on the line.

"Thrang is missing. He hasn't come home yet. This is unlike him."

"Are you sure, Aunty?" The DGP softly asked.

"I am absolutely certain that something bad must have happened to him."

"Aunty? Don't worry; I will find out what has happened and I will keep you informed," he assured her.

What he didn't tell her was that, that very evening, the Government had, on the directions of the Supreme Court, decided to give security to Thrang. The orders would have been ready and sent to the concerned department for implementation, the next morning.

By the time the seriousness of the situation had sunk in and Police teams deployed to man strategic points on the National Highway 42 and 44 and other main roads in and out of the city, Thrang and his abductors had almost reached their hideouts.

The aroma of the tea boiling in the kettle wafted over to Thrang's nostrils even before he was awake. His parched throat was crying out for a cup. He tried to rub his eyes with his bound hands, managed to get up and sit down on the edge of the hard bed, all the while adjusting his eyes to the dim light in the room. The time on his watch showed ten fifteen. Streaks of sun light penetrated the locked hut through gaps in the corrugated tin walls. He was aware of the loud noise of an engine motor. *I'm sure that is a crane, lifting coal from the shafts. I've heard that sound too many times not to recognize it and it's a sound I've learned to hate.*

'Muscles' indicated if he wanted some tea and he quickly nodded his head. A cup of red tea was poured, one tea spoon of sugar added, stirred and 'Muscles' brought the cup and placed it on the bed, by Thrang's side. 'Muscles' then took hold of a corner of the tape on Thrang's mouth and in one swift motion pulled it free.

Thrang felt as if his lips and the area around his mouth were raw and devoid of any skin, but greatly relieved to be able to move and open his lips and mouth, though hurting. He tried to take the glass cup in his two hands but it was too hot. He had to wait till it cooled down a bit. His lips hurt as he slowly sipped the tea. The tea was excellent, maybe because he was so thirsty and probably dehydrated. He asked for a second cup. "Muscles" smiled and poured him a refill. Thrang nourished the second cup, soaking the pores of his throat as it passed through.

Feeling the muscles of his bladder expanding, he asked 'Muscles' if he could go out for a pee.

"Na!" answered 'Muscles', going out and bringing in an empty, dirty five litre jerry can.

"Pissab, yaha karo," he said, keeping the can under his bed.

Thrang tried to control his urgent need, but not for long. He got up, picked the jerry can and slowly shuffled to a corner. He put the jerry can on the floor, unzipped his fly and lifting the can again, awkwardly managed to let himself go. When he was finished, he put the can underneath their bamboo bunks.

'Dead glassy eyed' was furious; muttering some obscene words to Thrang, he took the can from underneath his bunk, opened the door and simply threw it out. *Got to be careful with him*, Thrang reminded himself, *but why did I antagonized him? I should not provoke him,* Thrang reminded himself. *This sadistic ruffian would not hesitate to slice his throat at the slightest excuse, not that 'Muscles' would not do the same. He was no angel either, but it was just that 'Dead glassy eyed' with that maniacal look would relish the prospect of bleeding him to death.* It was a close call and a stupid one at that he realized.

Thrang sat on the edge of the bed, feeling the heat of the sun warming up his body, through the corrugated iron sheets of the roof. He watched his four abductors sit huddled in the kitchen section, talking animatedly amongst themselves in hushed tones, with casual glances at him from time to time. He pretended to be least bothered with his own condition.

Soon, the driver and the third man stood up and left. He heard the vehicle start and drive off. 'Muscles' and the 'Dead glassy eyed' continued talking. Thrang was bored; he lay down on the bed, trying as best as he could to make himself comfortable. He has to conserve his energy, for whatever lay ahead. Foreboding thoughts they were, as Thrang realized that he was completely at the mercy of those unscrupulous hired killers.

After an hour or so he heard the sound of the vehicle returning. 'Muscles' opened the door for them. They came in carrying two jute bags filled with food supplies. One of the bags was emptied off its vegetables. The two of them immediately got down to the onerous task of preparing food. 'Dead glassy eyed' shoved his hand into the other jute bag and produced six bottles of beer, which he placed on a rickety stool. He opened four bottles, one for each of them. "Muscles" looked at Thrang and offered him one of the un-opened bottles. Thrang shook his head and said, "No!"

Thrang's stomach growled; he was hungry, he suddenly realized. The aroma of the dal and the vegetables being cooked made it worse. But he was damned if he would give in and eat. When the food was finally done, he pretended to be fast asleep. He heard them drinking and eating, amidst some small talk. He wanted to give in to the demands of his belly, but his pride would not let him. He was determined to survive the night.

The day passed by so perceptibly slow. Thrang had slept and woken, slept and woken again – a sleep filled with apprehensions, worries and fears. He was exhausted and utterly miserable. His abductors had also taken a siesta. At one point of time he was about to scream his heart out, hoping that someone would hear him and would come to investigate. But he knew that would only hasten his end; they would have no hesitation in murdering him in the shack, these merciless and unscrupulous cut-throats. What really irritated and unnerved him was 'dead glassy eyed', who kept brandishing his wicked looking knife as if to goad and provoke him into some rash act. He had ceaselessly over the day, been sharpening the blade on a small piece of corundum stone and seemed to be relishing the work. The knife gleamed in his dark hand as he admired and acknowledged its razor sharp edge. Thrang shuddered, looking at that repugnant man, who he felt had no qualms in strangling a baby in the crib if he had to. He was the one to watch out for – no emotions, no fear, compassionless and totally indifferent. Thrang watched in horror as 'dead glassy eyed' pretended to slice through his throat with the razor-edged blade. Probably a maniac, who would enjoy seeing blood flow and life ebbing out, Thrang thought sickeningly. The best he could do was to wait for an opportunity which would present itself, if he was alert and diligent enough. Thrang felt it in his bones that they were actually waiting for the night; the dark envelope of darkness and stillness that would supposedly cover all misdeeds and throttle all sounds.

5

Thrang could feel the cold creeping over his numbed body. He shifted on his side, trying to keep warm. The dial on his watch showed fifteen minutes to ten. The abductors had prepared and eaten their dinner half an hour back, and didn't even bother to offer him any. 'Muscles' however, made two cups of tea for him, which he had gratefully accepted.

He watched the quartet whiling away their time, playing cards and warming themselves by the chullah filled with red, hot glowing charcoal. He could smell the carbon-monoxide emitted by the burning charcoal; just as well the shack had a lot of gaps along the ceiling through which the gas could escape, otherwise they would all die of asphyxiation. Thrang was uneasy though, seeing the glinting knife with its sharp point embedded in the stool. *Maybe the fumes would make them unconscious and he could make his escape.* Thrang brightened at the thought of such a prospect happening. He also saw that they were drinking; drinking whisky. There was a 750 ml bottle of AC Black at the foot of the stool. *Is this good or not? For his safety, that is.* He wondered. He sensed that something, very soon, will be happening to him. *They are going to murder him, in the dead of the night when all is quiet. But they could have done it last night or early this morning. Why didn't they?* Thrang's head throbbed with migraine. He felt suffocated with the stench of unwashed bodies and dirty unaired clothes and he longed for the cool fresh air outside. His belly growled and he suddenly felt sick and it was only by sheer willpower that he was able to control himself from throwing up; not that he had much inside him.

His hands were raw and bleeding, where the ropes had cut the skin. He ignored the pain. He thought of his mother and Ri. *How are they taking his disappearance? Are the police looking for him? Will he be denied a long and fruitful life with Ri?* Tears formed in his eyes and rolled down his cheeks. He could not contain himself any longer; he wept. *Oh Ri, I love you.*

Through the haze of frustration, pain and the inevitable prospect of death, he heard them stop their card game and get up. The driver opened the door of the shack and went out. A few minutes later he heard the rev of the car engine. The moment he dreaded had come; he was roughly hoisted up on his feet by 'Dead glassy eyed', who, with a length of tape sealed his lips together and put the black cloth hood again over his head and face. He was then literally dragged and pushed into the car, with 'Dead glassy eyed' and 'Muscles' on either side of him. He knew that the third abductor was beside the driver.

The car drove slowly over the bumpy and slushy road, if it was a road at all. Thrang did not hear any vehicles passing by. The road was all theirs. No one spoke in the car, as it negotiated obstacles in its path, which Thrang could only imagine. How was he going to get out of this predicament, he prayed? Suddenly, the car stopped. It was stuck; try as he did, the driver could not move the car out of the rut or slush. He heard the car doors open and the three men got out. Thrang heard them search for stones to fill the rut made by the car; they worked in silence, eager not to attract attention. After a few minutes, the driver started the engine, and as the car raced the three men pushed. The back tyres spun furiously and Thrang could smell the acrid smoke of burning tyre. The driver stopped the car engine, as more stones were collected and pushed into the rut in front and behind the tyres. Thrang prayed that the car would remain stuck and that someone would eventually come by and he would be saved. But the men were desperate; they had to free the car somehow and be off on their way. The second time when the car raced full throttle with the three pushing from behind, the tyres got enough traction and jumped out of the mire to be free. The driver stopped for the three to get in and the car drove off again over a terrain that must still be awful. That monotonous and endless drive finally came to a stop, after Thrang had finally lost count of the time.

They got out; Thrang was dragged out of the car and the hood was pulled off his face. He breathed the cool fresh air and looked around, adjusting his eyes to the darkness. In front of him was a dense jungle, climbing up; behind was a plain, flat open space with hardly any trees – a paddy field, he realized as he made out the terraces. A torch was switched on; "Muscles" took out a knife, bent down and cut through the rope around Thrang's legs, freeing them. Thrang took a few steps, testing his feet. He could feel the pain on his legs where the rope had cut and bruised the skin. His legs now free, Thrang felt a surge of confidence enter his heart; he could make an escape should an opportunity present itself. That hope however vanished, when "Muscles" secured Thrang with another rope around his waist and tying the other end around his own fat waist, separating them by about two metres.

The driver and the third man led the way along a very narrow jungle path, climbing up the hill. 'Muscles' followed them with Thrang in tow behind him. Thrang was nervous with 'Dead glassy eyed' right behind him. The path led steeply up the hill. The undergrowth had reclaimed stretches of the path making it tough going for all of them; more so for Thrang, who could not use his hands to protect himself from the sharp thorns. His face stung, especially when the sweat of his exertions trickled over the wounds. With his hands tied securely together, Thrang used all his concentration to keep his balance in the dark menacing climb. "Muscles" was panting with exertion and stopped every now and then to catch his breath.

But where are we going? Why don't they do away with me right here, in this deep dark jungle? Why take all the trouble to go somewhere far and out of the way? And why take so much trouble after all and risk chances of detection? Thrang was utterly confused at what lay ahead for him.

Suddenly he froze. He realized that they were going straight up towards Krem Khung, approaching it from the western flank. A chill went up his spine. *These bastards are going to kill me and throw my body into the shaft. I would have just disappeared from the face of the earth and no one would find my body or know what has happened to me,* as he realized that the next expedition would not explore Krem Khung, for Krem Khung has been considered to be more or less finished. *Very smart bastards,* he cursed under his breath. *No! They will not kill me and leave a lot of blood on the rocks around the entrance. They are going to do a clean job; just push him into the gaping hole. How brilliant the idea; but for Thrang, it would be death in the most horrendous form. It will be a long, long drop into the dark abyss.*

He felt his body quiver with anger and helplessness. The unimaginable fear of falling through space, down the deep, dark shaft and to smash into the depths below, was a nightmare that he never imagined to ever occur to him or to anyone for that matter. An unimaginable fate, to push a man into dark space and let him be entombed in the dark depths of the earth. He wanted to scream but he could not; he wanted to run but he was secured to 'Muscles'. He had escaped death on a number of occasions; could he do it again? Or will the law of probability catch up with him? No, he will not die; he cannot afford to lose his life when it is just beginning to open up for him – the wonderful life ahead with Ri. He must bide his time and act the moment there was the slightest of chances. Surprise, yes that's what it is; I must take them by surprise, when they least expect it. I must steel myself and rise like a Phoenix to be able to make my escape. And break from their clutches I will, Thrang vowed in the desperate and deep recesses of his soul.

On they laboured up the hill, through bush and thorn. Thrang's head boiled with confusion and frustration. He tried to calm himself down and to conserve his energy which would be required, if he were to make a dash. He composed himself and plodded behind "Muscles". He could barely see his steps for there was only one torchlight, held by the third man who was leading the way. Suddenly he stepped on a loose stone and with his hands bound tightly behind his back he was completely thrown off balance. He would have hurt himself had he not been tethered to the big heavy-set 'Muscles', who somehow or other barely managed to stand his ground. Nevertheless, he landed on his face scraping the vegetation and thanking his lucky stars his face didn't hit that loosed rock. But 'Muscles' was furious alright; and in a rage of obscene language he gave a mighty kick at Thrang's ribs. Thrang had seen it coming and tried desperately to roll away, escaping the full force of the kick. Nevertheless, he still felt a sharp pain on his side, knocking the breath out of his lungs.

"Get up, you dog!" 'Dead glassy eyed' shouted, prodding him with his filthy sandaled foot.

Fearing more kicks from the both of them, Thrang painfully balanced himself on his knees first, before he slowly got up on his feet. He was still smarting from the fall and the kick. Inside his mouth he tasted warm blood; his teeth must have bitten his tongue or the insides of his mouth when he fell down. Or maybe a tooth has loosened. He used his tongue to feel his teeth and the insides of his mouth and realized that he had hurt the inside of his lips. It would have been awful had he lost any of his front teeth; not at his age he reflected.

"You do that once again, and I will kill you personally," glowered 'Muscles', still fuming and upset over his near tumble.

"If he does it again, it will be my pleasure to slice his throat from ear to ear." 'Dead glassy eyed' growled menacingly at Thrang, touching the point of his knife to Thrang's Adam's apple. Thrang rued the fact that he was bound; this was one fight he would thoroughly relish, giving vent to all the frustrations and anger that had been building within him. With his lips taped, Thrang had to silently endure the obscenities and threats directed at him. His heart was pounding with the pain and exertion and he was breathing heavily. He tried to control his breathing and to calm himself; he cannot afford to be worked up in the present circumstances. As he slowly followed in the footsteps of 'Muscles', he felt the desperate rage of a helpless prisoner, simmering in the innards of his soul.

Thrang fretted irritatingly at the brazenness and boldness of these die-hard goondas; how they can carry out their heinous crime with impunity in a country they don't even belong to. Thrang was sure that these hardened criminals were from the other side of the international border who had been lured by the rich coal mines of Jaintia Hills, where there were rich and easy pickings, especially for men of their profession who had no scruples. Thrang was pained to see the daily crimes being perpetrated on innocent folks because of obstruction, land-grabbing or plain jealousy; how kidnappings for ransom, unheard of till recently, had become the order of the day. These illegal immigrant 'labourers' enjoying the patronage of their coal baron bosses, have degenerated and degraded not just the pristine landscape but the very social and moral fabric of the local community. And no one could keep a tab on the comings and goings of these despicable and undesirable elements. Thrang swore in his heart, furiously irritated at the horrific and unimaginable menace that is spreading throughout the state. His anger bounded on the sad reality that he was totally helpless in stopping the immigrant riff-raffs and outcasts from the neighbouring country riding rough-shod over the poor rustic life of the simple people. He himself was now a victim of such brutality; knowing very well he would have been dead by now, had they not planned a more sinister end for him and to consign his body to the dark void beneath the surface of the earth.

The mind is a marvelous thinking machine; even when confronted with the greatest of danger it oftentimes find ways to cool down the frenzied activities of its grey cells by leading away to paths more soothing – stabilizing the screaming and hyper-active threats of insane wanderings. In spite of the imminent sealed doom he was heading for, a gentle crease appeared on his dirt and blood smeared face as out of nowhere the lines of Homer flashed through his mind and in a firm and reassuring voice murmured:

High at the head a branching olive grows
And crowns the pointed cliffs with shady boughs.
A cavern pleasant, though involved in night,
Beneath it lies, the Naiades delight:
Where bowls and urns of workmanship divine
And massy beams in native marble shine;
On which the Nymphs amazing webs display,
Of purple hue and exquisite array,
The busy bees within the urns secure
Honey delicious, and like nectar pure.
Perpetual waters through the grotto glide,
A lofty gate unfolds on either side;
That to the north is pervious to mankind:
The sacred south t'immortals is consign'd."

"Kya aap ki bare mae bakbakh rahe he? What are you murmuring about?" 'Muscles' asked him, turning back and looking at him suspiciously in the dark and silent night.

"Mein prarthna kar raha tha. I am just saying my prayers," Thrang replied back, which seemed to pacify 'Muscles' as he turned around and continued his laboured climb.

Surprisingly the poem did wonders to uplift the sagging morale of his spirit. His muscles and the conflicting emotions that were tearing inside him began to relax as his mind accepted the nightmarish and inevitable looming curtains that were closing in on him. His mind cleared of anguish he accepted the reality of his present position though he still had a chance – a very slim one maybe, but still a chance; and when that window opens he would fight, to survive or die he knew not which. At least if he were to die he would do so in a befitting way; he would take some of them if not all. At that moment the clarity of his thoughts sharpened, as cleared of doubts and apprehensions, he regained calmness of composure allowing him to focus all his inner energy into that one burst of surprise – that could be his freedom.

"Ai giya," He heard the driver say in a hushed and subdued voice. Thrang knew the driver was spooked, as well as the third man. In no way did they look comfortable as they cast nervous and anxious glances at 'Muscles'.

They had reached the clearing, which Thrang remembered so well. It was not so dark in the clearing, and Thrang could easily make out the hungry mouth of the cave. It looked ominous in the silent dark of the night, as he felt the cool draught rising from its belly. *Fancy that my body would probably lie on the same spot where the Daloi's body was found; such a long time ago it was, he felt. And now it has come full circle; this magnificent cave which had been his dream will now be about to claim him – its dark bowels will be a repository for his gleaming bones which would eventually be calcified for eternity. Or will it? He asked himself; for he was not yet ready to accept his fate, which lay grim and stark before him.*

He looked up at the moonless sky as if seeking for a falling star; a falling star which would answer his prayers and save him from the jaws of death, even at the last moment. But the night was still and the sky stiller. The stars that hung in the heavens seemed to be staring down at him, staring at him helplessly; as mute and silent witnesses to his ignoble and treacherous end. Orion too watched in humble submission – Orion his constellation friend who was to lead him to his love. *What Orion, can't you save me for my love? Will all your silent promises end up as hollow and void as this deep, dark hole before me? Will you just watch me disappear from your sight forever? Will I not ever know love? I cannot believe it will be the last time I will ever stare at you again, beautiful as you are up in the deep solar night sky.* A pine needle fell and brushed against his cheek startling him and bringing him back to the nightmare at hand.

'Muscles' who had been panting after the climb, had regained his breath, and had had a brief, hushed conversation with 'Dead glassy eyed'. Why talk in such hushed tones, wondered Thrang; there is no one here to hear them except the dark and gloomy forest. And he was as good as dead to them anyway, so why bother? Maybe the bravado they present was just a front to hide the fear and spookiness they have of the famed evil place. Hardened criminals they may be, but still fearful and wary of the unknown. A night bird suddenly called out in the dead night, spurring the abductors to get on and over with their murderous intent. Thrang tensed, as they menacingly turned towards him. *This is it!* He thought. His body quivered with anticipation of what was to follow.

'Muscles' was undoing the rope around his own waist. *It is now or never,* he thought, the moment the other end of the rope was loosened and dropped to the ground from 'Muscles' waist. The face of Ri flashed through his mind as he prayed, "God, help me please."

In that fraction of a second, when his heart was pounding with adrenaline and his limbs tensed for the break, and the sudden cry of the night bird piercing through that murderous night, he heard the crack of a rifle and 'Muscles' slumped to the ground with a half choked grunt. A voice shouted, telling him to drop down to the ground. Everything happened in a flash and even as he dived, he heard another shot; then everything went blank as his head hit the limestone rock jutting out of the rocky ground.

When he regained consciousness he felt his face wet and cold and his head ached with pain. The pain was sharp and sore, as he tried to make sense in his muddled mind, as to what had happened to him. He felt someone cut through the rope that tightly bound his hands and slowly loosening it from his aching and bruised wrists. It was great relief to feel the blood circulating freely into his hands again and ease the pain on his shoulder joints. He knew he was lying flat on his face as he felt hands under him, lifting and moving him into a supine position. His whole body ached as if he had passed through a grinder, and he gave in to the gentle ministrations with a sense of trust and security overcoming him.

"Bah? Khei! Peit mat noh." He heard the words, as if from afar, and felt his body being shaken. Gathering his wits around him, he gradually opened his eyes to look straight upon the face of Rodik, the guide who had first shown him Krem Khung.

Rodik grinned showing his red stained teeth and mouth.

"Bah Thrang? Ym lei lei shuh. Nga lah siat ia uwei. It is alright now; you are safe; I shot one of them." He said, pointing to the prone figure a few feet away from him.

It all came back to him then; the rifle shot and him leaping to the ground. He was sure he heard another shot before he passed out. He realized that his mangled body could have been lying at the bottom of the shaft at that very moment. He got up slowly with the help of Rodik and the young teen-age boy. Once on his feet, Thrang hugged Rodik and in a voice shaking with emotion and gratitude thanked him: "Bah Rodik, Thank you; I will always be indebted to you, for you have saved my life."

"Bah Thrang,' Rodik said, grinning at him, showing his red stained teeth and mouth, 'I only did what anyone would have done in the circumstances. God was with you; for it was just by chance that I was hunting in these woods tonight. We were supposed to go hunting elsewhere, but my friend didn't turn up."

He paused awhile, and continued. "When my friend didn't come, I invited my nephew, this young boy, to accompany me here. Well not exactly here, but a kilometre away; however after stalking a deer we somehow landed right at the mouth of this cavernous black hole, where we have been lingering ever since, because of the cool breath it is emitting. We were about to leave for home an hour back, but something compelled me to stay on a while longer. And when I have such feelings, I know something always happens – an animal would somehow or other present itself before my sights. Today however was different; I did not take the life of any wild animal but saved the life of a friend; a great day for me indeed!"

"Lucky for me, you did,' Thrang interrupted, 'otherwise I would have been lying at the bottom of this shaft."

"Yes, you could have ended up like the Daloi; but God had protected you," Rodik agreed. "For it was getting very late and cold and I had given up. We were about to leave, when my nephew saw a faint light through the bushes; we then heard a voice. We stopped and hid behind some trees. I strained my eyes to see who they were. When they emerged into the clearing, I saw five men, one of whom appeared to be a prisoner. I was shocked, tensed and afraid as I knew we were about to witness an ugly scene. The boy was frightened; and I whispered to him not to look but to lie flat on the ground. I saw the fat man untie the rope around his waist and realized he was not a local but a *dkhar*. When the rope was untied and the fat man was coming towards you, the light of the torch fell on your face. I was shocked and horrified to recognize it was you. I realised immediately that they were going to kill you and then throw your body down that black hole. There was no time to be lost; I aimed my rifle at the fat man and fired. I then shouted to you to get out of my line of fire and fired another shot at the fleeing figures. I don't know if I hit any one of them as they disappeared into the jungle. And I couldn't go after them leaving you here."

Rodik took out a much used home-made pipe from his pocket, filled it with tobacco, struck a match and putting the flame to the bowl of tobacco, dragged long and hard. Thrang managed to get his nostrils out of the range of the tobacco smoke, trying his best not to offend someone who had just saved his life.

"Bah Rodik, I would have been dead but for you," Thrang acknowledged.

"The fat man is dead; the other three have escaped. But thank God, you are safe," Rodik said, beaming with pleasure.

"Let us go and get help. You have an ugly gash on your head which needs attention. You can tell me your part of the story later," Rodik ended, guiding him out of the eerie and foreboding surroundings.

6

The Police did not take long in coming. The headman of the nearest village they had gone to had immediately telephoned the Khliehriat Police Station. Thrang's face lit up when he saw the inspector, Harlin Passi.

"So here you are, and we have been looking out for you all over the place," the inspector said, grinning.

Thrang grinned back at him, rather sheepishly.

"Come, I have to take you back to Jowai immediately," he said and directed his assistant, a sub-inspector to take the three constables with him and go to the incident site, accompanied by Bah Rodik, and retrieve the dead body of 'Muscles'.

"And check if the dead man has any identification or any papers with him," he barked after them.

On their way to Jowai, Thrang briefly told him of his near fatal ordeal. He also gave a description of 'dead glassy eyed' and the other two men who had escaped. When he had finished, the inspector paused and looked sideways at him.

"You were very lucky otherwise you would have met with a terrible fate – an end more horrible than that of the Daloi. As for those criminals I will send an alert throughout the state; though I doubt if we could apprehend them. They would escape by mingling with the thousands of the immigrant labourers and then slip through the very porous border. It is really a nightmare for the police working in these areas. Their coming in and going out of the state is nobody's business."

The inspector gave a sigh, his face furrowed with despair at the existence of thousands of unregistered labourers most of whom with dubious and criminal antecedents. He knew it will be like searching for a needle in a haystack and he felt himself impotent in the face of such unknown and unseen adversaries.

"Do you know that on the night you were abducted, the Supreme Court had earlier in the day, passed an order banning all mining activities in the state of Meghalaya, till such time the state government adopts a mining policy and identifies areas which have no significant cave systems, for such mining?"

Thrang was taken aback. "No, I have no knowledge of it," he said, feeling pleased at what he had just heard.

"Yes, and we have been alerted about your safety, but it was too late," the inspector admitted, regretfully.

When they reached Jowai, he was first taken to the Civil Hospital where his wound was cleaned, a couple of stitches put in, some ointment applied and the head neatly dressed. His bruised legs and wrists were also disinfected and antiseptic cream applied; he was then taken to the Office of the Superintendent of Police. The SP, a smart and intelligent looking man in his late thirties, introduced himself as Hehbok Phanwar.

Thrang was surprised. He had expected to see Mr. Snowell Pala; *must have been transferred out*, Thrang presumed.

"I have been informed of your adventures. I must say you have had a charmed life, but you've got to be careful for you have raised a hornet's nest – in these parts atleast. These mining mafias are a dangerous lot; killing a person is like wringing the neck of a chicken. They would go to any length just to protect their own interests. Anyway let us go, I will take you back to Shillong." The SP Mr. Phanwar said.

"Thank you," Thrang replied, simply.

Thrang was too tired and sleepy to answer most of the SP's questions, who on realizing this, held his silence. Except for the murderous coal trucks which never seemed to sleep, the road was more or less free. Thrang tried to keep himself awake but must have dozed off in snatches. He was tired, as tired as he could ever be. When he tried to keep awake and was watching the road ahead, he could see or register nothing; as though he was looking with unseeing eyes or eyes that could not focus. His eyelids were so heavy that everything he looked at was a blur. The events of the last many days, was catching up on his body, dulling his mind into a stupor of 'nothing matters anymore' as his body gave in to a complete and blissful surrender.

Dawn had broken through the dark stillness of the night when the police vehicle reached the front of Thrang's house with a resounding screech. He woke up with a jolt, unsure where he was.

"Thrang, you are home," he heard the SP's voice break through his muddled mind. It took some time for him to realize that he was really in front of his house.

As they got out of the vehicle, Thrang's mother opened the door of the house. Worried to death as she was, she had not had much sleep. Frankie had informed her very late that night or very early that morning; that Thrang was safe and sound and was on his way home. She couldn't sleep after that; waiting for her son to arrive home.

She came out into the front porch and hugged her son.

"Thank God, you are alright. I was worried sick and Ri, who was here with me the whole day yesterday, was distraught," she said happily, looking at the SP in appreciation.

"Why don't you come in and have a cup of tea?" she invited him, covering a yawn discreetly with her hand.

"No thank you, ma'am; some other time, perhaps; Thrang needs rest; and you too I believe, have been up the whole night. You are all tired and need some sleep, so I think I had better go," he apologized.

"By the way,' he said turning around, 'I have posted some police personnel around your area."

"Don't worry ma'am, they will be as discretely invisible as can be," he added on seeing her bewildered and concerned look.

It's so good to be back home, thought Thrang, as his mother handed him a cup of black tea. He had refused any food; he was very tired and just wanted to sleep, which he did immediately he finished his tea, and after telling his mother to do the same.

But tired as he was, sleep did not come. He tossed and turned, realizing that he could have been dead and his body lying where no one would have been the wiser. His body shook uncontrollably and he wept in gratitude at having another lease of life; a life that is so precious and meaningful. *Ri, I will not fail you, ever*, he murmured, a smile crinkling the corners of his lips as slumber eventually overcame him.

He slept as one dead to the world; contented and fully surrendering himself to the warm and familiar comfort of his bed. It was a blissful luxury to be able to surrender one's tiredness of body and mind in total freedom. When he awoke, he thought he heard the lock of his bed-room door click. He listened, but all was quiet; *probably his mother looking in, to see if he was awake.* He slept on, luxuriating in the security of his home. Then the events of the night returned to shake him back to reality.

He got up, stretched himself and felt the soreness in his whole body. He felt dirty and very untidy, with the stubble of a couple of day's growth of beard. *A shave and a hot water bath, and I will be good again. He realized that the two years of strain, tension and the many attempts on his life, had matured and molded his character to a more pleasing, tolerant and understanding personality. He had outgrown the limited confines of his own understanding and the subtle meaning of life.*

He opened the window of his room and looked out into the backyard, and was surprised to see that the sun was just dipping behind the horizon; lighting up one quarter of the sky with a deep orangey- pink that would have delighted a Van Gogh. He himself was so pleased and happy at the beautiful sight that presented before him. *I must have slept for more than thirteen hours,* he mused, surprised at himself.

The garden was overgrown with weeds and knee-deep grasses and looked totally unkempt and uncared. He must do something about it, immediately; maybe get a daily-wage labourer to clean and trim the garden back to shape. He would love to do it himself, but he realized he would not have the time, being so caught up with so many other things. The lagerstroemia tree in one corner of the backyard, which was bare just a week ago, had now burst out in thick and glossy foliage and in another two months it would bloom. It was the season of growth, activity and life and he was thrilled with all the greenery he saw around him. He was romancing himself on a pair of red-vented bulbuls, twittering about on the branches of the tree, trying to soak the last rays of the dying sun before they roost for the night, when he sensed the door open ever so softly. He heard the footsteps treading lightly towards him. He turned around when the soft and subtle fragrance of her aroma was upon him.

For a millisecond they stopped and faced each other; the next they were in each others arms, tight as if the other would escape.

"Oh Thrang, my darling," she whispered, her body trembling with long pent-up emotions. She looked up into his eyes, unmindful of the tears coursing down her cheeks, and in a clear resonant voice said, "I love you."

"My Princess, I love you with all my heart and soul," Thrang said, revelling in the excitement of holding her warm body tight to his.

As their lips met, in a crashing bliss of heavenly sensations, Thrang could taste the salt of her tears which had blended with his own.

EPILOGUE

When the Supreme Court finally gave its verdict, it set about a ripple of dismay, anger, relief and jubilation, as the case may be, to the different sections of the people of the state and in the corridors of state politics. The Supreme Court had ordered an immediate ban on the mining of coal and limestone, till such time, proper mining regulations and proper demarcation of valuable karst areas for protection, are put into force by the state government.

The state government which had been dragging its feet on the finalization of its mining policy woke up from its blissful lethargy. It acted swiftly, fearing huge revenue loss by the day. The Mining Policy was soon adopted and implemented in record time.

The state government, guided by the orders of the Supreme Court and with the help of the members of the Meghalaya Speleological Group, demarcated and notified certain caving areas as heritage sites for conservation. To show its interest and unstinted commitment to the conservation of the environment, the state government proclaimed the Shnongrim Ridge as an adventure-park, which was heralded and received very well by the people of the region. Being given the status of an eco-park, the long term benefits of tourism that would be generated would be a great boon to the local villages of the region.

The miners were soon resigned to the strict regulations which required proper scientific ways of mining as also the creation of a fund for the development and restoration of the mined site once it is worked over. Further, should a cave be discovered in the course of limestone extraction, the mining company or owner should report it to the Meghalaya Speleological Group, which will map the cave and assess it for consideration of any protection or otherwise.

The verdict of the Court was a triumph for environmentalists; more so for the down-trodden villagers, who had over the years borne the brunt and spoils created by the rich, powerful and unscrupulous. The verdict had given them a voice and they became assertive of their rights; rights to protect their water bodies, their paddy fields and their simple way of life; rights to electricity, health care, faster communication and all other modern amenities to live a more healthy and comfortable life, without any undue intrusion or outside influence.

For years they had been at the receiving end, with the degradation of their lands and the ecological imbalance being perpetrated by the mining lobby - when their subsistence was taken away from them and they had to rely on menial work like breaking rocks into stone chips; when a small pan of water was all they had to bathe four or five of their children, till the colour of the water took a dark and angry corroded earth spent off all its vitality; when the water they drank was deemed to be totally unsafe; when the air they breathed was certain to infect and disease their lungs; when the morals of the people took a drastic nose-dive to depravity; when their school-going children joined the ranks of the army of school drop-outs; when the youth succumbed to drug abuse and the pleasures of lust and when the very social fabric of their community was all but split asunder by the aggressive and uncouth behavior of the unkempt and unwanted immigrants who had invaded their very hearth and homes - their only solace was in their silent prayers to their Gods, and in the joyful exultation of their Creator in the beautiful and splendid churches that had sprung up from the ill-gotten wealth of those coal barons who were trying to soothe their own conscience. God who had been silent for so long had finally answered their prayers.

Printed in Great Britain
by Amazon

40973986R00128